DIRTY PINK

Dirty Pink - Copyright 2020 © Gayle Young in partnership with Bluewater Publications

First Edition
ISBN 978-1-949711-34-9 Paperback
ISBN 978-1-949711-41-7 Ebook

Library of Congress Control Number: 2020902968

Bluewater Publications
Bwpublications.com
Printed in the United States

This work is based on the author's personal perspective and imagination.

Editor – Sierra Tabor
Interior Design – Rachel Davis
Cover Design - Maria Yasaka Beck
Managing Editor – Angela Broyles

Dedicated with love to Donna Rae Estill,
my cowriter and coconspirator.

With special thanks to my editor, Sierra Tabor.

1

Normal can mean many different things. As a history professor at a community college, normal means having students from all walks of life, from teenagers to senior citizens. And, perhaps, normal can also mean having a student bring along her nine-year-old child to my 8:00 am class, because he was suspended from school and she didn't have a babysitter. It's also not that unheard of for a kid to have a small, furry animal as a pet. Therefore, a normal workday can consist of me kneeling on my desk and screaming as a ferret runs freely around my classroom.

On the morning before it all started, my lecture on the Cold War came to a screeching halt as the rodent-like creature escaped a backpack the deviant child had used to sneak it in. The screams and laughter from my students took several minutes to die down as the kid caught and restowed his pet. Inquiries from curious passersby in the hall, apologies, and explanations took longer still, but eventually, the event was over. Stressful, but still not out of the realm of possible occurrences on a normal day. Although, maybe I should have seen that small, insignificant dose of chaos for what it really was—an omen.

The rest of the day went by with office hours, another class in the afternoon, grading papers, and answering emails. Most of the emails were from students asking for ways they could improve their grades, which is very usual towards the end of the semester. As I drove home on that pleasantly warm spring evening, I blessed the mildly-congested traffic while trying to decide whether to stop for fried chicken or just have a sandwich for dinner.

When I entered the kitchen, I threw my books, briefcase full of ungraded papers, and purse on the table and perused the refrigerator. It was, of course, full of various leftovers collected over the last few weeks. After checking the dates on the bread, ham, and cheese, I made myself a sandwich. Normal. Before eating, I changed into an oversized, faded, pink t-shirt and jeans. Normal still. With my Coke Zero beside me on the end table and remote in hand, I took a bite of sandwich and was still chewing and channel surfing when all normalcy came to an end.

I've never believed in astrology or stuff like that, but I can't come up with any other explanation as to how in one instant my life turned upside down. That very minute must've been when Jupiter and Mars collided or whatever astrological event is supposed to signify approaching doom.

Jason walked calmly into the den and said the phrase that has inspired fear in every relationship ever: "We need to talk."

Not normal. I stared at him, waiting for him to say that something awful had happened, that someone I loved had been injured. Maybe my fifteen-year-old son, Danny, had been in a car accident or wrote on the classroom wall again. What he said instead, I didn't expect. Well, actually, I had expected it, but not this soon.

"It's time," he said, stuffing his hands in his jeans' pockets and looking down at the fake-oak, laminate floors streaked with black dog hair. "I can't go on like this."

"Huh?" I said, my mouth still full of food. What couldn't he go on with? Our relationship? Of course not. We'd talked about that. The end was somewhere in the future, at a mutually-accepted, convenient time.

He looked up, and I saw the expression on his face, the one I recognized and dreaded. His deep blue eyes were as hard and cold as a frozen marble; his tall, lean body was rigid like it was made of steel. He was in one of his moods. I knew better than to try to argue with him. He'd yell and scream for a few minutes, then he would turn to ice and retreat to the backyard where he'd pull weeds or chop down one of the trees in the woods that surrounded the house.

"You heard what I said." He slid his right hand from his pocket and rubbed it through his hair, the beautiful, sun-streaked, sandy-blond hair that always smelled of freshly-cut wood and musky shampoo. The way he always did when he was anxious or confused.

My throat was dry and tight, and I didn't know what to say. My mouth still full, I managed to growl, "Not now; I'm busy," and kept chomping.

"Now." He snatched the sandwich out of my hand. "You don't love me, and I don't love you. I can't stand the charade anymore."

I tried to soothe the rising tempest in my head. Okay, Samantha, remain calm. Speak slowly. Deliberately. But the fighting instinct in me took over. I jerked at my sandwich. He let go. Bread, ham, cheese, and tomato slices dropped onto the floor.

"I'll help you find a place tomorrow." He calmly turned and walked out the back door.

"You can't stand me for another three weeks?" I screamed after him. "After five years, you can't wait just a few weeks?" The words reverberated in my head as if someone else was in there shrieking. "I'll go when school's out. Not before." I wanted to hit him with a skillet and watch him bleed; I longed to throw my arms around him and cry.

He was wrong. I did love him. I couldn't leave now. No, not now. It wasn't supposed to happen like this anyway. On our last night together, we were going to sit at the kitchen table across from each other and promise we'd always be friends and love each other in a platonic sort of way and keep in touch. That sort of thing. Why didn't he love me? What was wrong with me?

He did love me; I knew it in my heart. If we could hold on just a little while longer, he'd realize he loved me. We'd talk things over, and after a while, we'd laugh and make up. I felt so sure that he was just being dramatic. How could I have known then that that was the last time I'd see him as a part of "us?"

The house suddenly became as quiet as a tomb. The TV was on mute, the dog was in the backyard, and Danny had gone to a friend's house after school. My mind tried to pull up a solution. I sat still, afraid to move. Afraid of what, I didn't know. Maybe the silent emptiness of the house, my mind, and my emotions. Or maybe I was scared of having to start all over. Again. The refrigerator clicked on and hummed.

I unmuted the TV and tried to watch, but I couldn't concentrate on the bright colors flashing across the screen or the drone of the anchor's voice. I hit mute, picked up a People magazine, and flipped through its pages before tossing it back on the coffee table in a huff. I pushed myself up from the couch and started pacing. From den to the dining room, kitchen, living room, and back to the den. Everywhere I turned there were reminders of our relationship. At a yard sale, we'd picked out a huge landscape that had reminded me of those Hudson River paintings. Together. We'd hung it on the living room wall. Together. Put down the laminate flooring ourselves. Together. Had started laying tile in the bathroom. Together. This was my home and had been for five years. But it wasn't. It was his. Only his name was on the deed.

Several times I picked up my phone to call him but couldn't, wouldn't. When Danny came home from his friend's house and asked what was wrong, I told him I was sick. I went into the bedroom I'd helped paint, and laid down on the geometrically-designed comforter I'd picked out. While Danny rattled around in the kitchen, clanging dishes and silverware, and the TV blared out crashing noises and loud voices, I closed my eyes. Who was I kidding? I couldn't sleep. I sat up and touched the dirty socks, white t-shirt, and brown belt Jason had left on the bed, then I grabbed them and flung them as hard as I could. I wanted to throw the flashlight he kept on his bedside table and smash the dresser mirror, but even in my anger and despair, I couldn't bring myself to damage anything. The scent of the Irish Spring soap he kept stacked in a pyramid on the counter floated in from the bathroom. I collapsed back onto the bed in a fetal position and cried. And then I waited.

Finally, sometime after midnight, I gave up. He wasn't coming home, and I knew exactly where he was. At her house. The woman he talked to on the phone sometimes when he was upset. The one he'd known for years but who was "just a friend." The one who'd been on the periphery of our relationship the whole time. Carrie.

She and I had never met face-to-face. She must be a lot prettier than me. Maybe he didn't like my hair. It did frizz when it was humid outside and it seemed like it was always humid in Parkville, Alabama. Except during last summer's drought. It looked pretty good then. Or maybe I should lose a few pounds or wear high heels. He was always looking at women in high heels. But they made my feet hurt, and I waddled when I walked in them. I disregarded these thoughts as the result of stress and of not wanting to delve into why he really wanted to leave me.

The phone rang. Without looking to see who it was, I grabbed it. It wasn't Jason.

"Samantha Grace, how are you?" the familiar voice asked, an echo of a long-ago time filled with both my greatest joy and misery.

"Greg?"

"Yeah. I was just thinking about you."

The blubbery tears, moans, and sobs erupted from somewhere inside me, and I couldn't stop. I didn't want Greg to hear but didn't hang up. For a moment, he said nothing. Finally, my outburst subsided.

"I'm sorry," I said. "You called at a bad time."

"What happened? Want to talk about it?"

His voice and kindness made the rain inside me start again. "I can't talk right now. I'll call you back later."

"Love you," he said, "If you need to talk, you know I'm a good listener."

Yes, I remembered that about him. "Love you too," I said and hung up.

At one time, when I had lived in Valparaiso, Indiana, Greg and his wife, Anna, had been friends with me and my first love, Daniel. Until I became pregnant. Daniel Sr. had screamed and blamed me like I'd done it just to punish him. A few days later, he had thrown a hundred-dollar bill on the dresser, told me to get an abortion, and stormed out of the house. He never came back. If he had, I think I would've strangled him with my bare hands.

Greg and Anna had consoled me. She had gone with me to my doctor visits, and they had invited me over for dinner almost every night, let me tag along when they went to the movies or plays in downtown Chicago, and listened to my tales of woe. Then, all of a sudden, Anna left Greg and took their children with her. Greg and I had clung to each other while we complained and talked endlessly about our lost loves and how they had ruined our lives forever. We were platonic soulmates. I'd often thought if we'd met in another time that maybe we could've been more. Eventually, I moved back to my home state of Alabama, and he and I had stayed in touch. But ever since I had moved in with Jason, I had been hearing from him less and less.

Why had Greg called? That morning, no it was yesterday morning, whenever it was, it had started out as a typical day. What in the world happened?

Suddenly, I wasn't thinking about Jason anymore, but my son's father. We never even got married, but he'd left me with a gift. My beautiful baby boy. I might never have Daniel Caldwell's name, but his son would. I named him Daniel Caldwell McKenzie. He had the same dark brown hair and perfect white teeth as his father, and he was growing taller every day and beginning to fill out some.

I pulled myself together and called Greg back. If I didn't do it now, I may not have a chance to later.

"Feel better?" Greg asked as he answered.

"I'm sorry," I said. "Jason and I broke up tonight."

"Are you okay?"

"Oh, Greg, I wish you were here." And I meant it. I needed a friend I could talk to.

"Why don't you come see me? We'll drive up to Chicago, go to the art museum, walk the shores of Lake Michigan, get your mind off your troubles."

"I have a son, remember?"

"He can stay with your mom, can't he?"

"Well, sure, but . . ."

"Think about it and let me know."

"I will."

We hung up again, and I tried to go to sleep even though I knew it would be nearly impossible. I spent the next few hours tossing and turning. I had been just fine on the old path; I didn't like this new one at all. While I was trying to figure this out, the phone rang again, and I just about fell out of bed trying to reach it quickly. It wasn't Jason. I didn't recognize the voice, but apparently, he knew me.

"Ms. McKenzie," a calm masculine voice said. "Your light is dim."

"Excuse me?" The Jupiter-Mars crash was worse than I thought.

"Your light is dim. I'm coming to help you."

"My light?"

"Do you still live in Parkville? I'll be there soon."

"Who is this?"

"You do remember me, don't you? Michael."

"The archangel?"

"Michael Larsen. From your history class."

"Oh." I shook my head, trying to unscramble my brains, and stared at the phone like it might give me some clue about this guy and why he was calling at 3:00 a.m. "You're in my history class?"

"Not anymore. I was one of your students your first year as a teacher."

My mind raced back through time and stopped on a weird but likeable Michael. It seems like he'd been a nursing student and, yes, he'd told me back then that I had a glowing aura around me. I had figured he was saying it so I'd give him a better grade, except he was actually a good student. A little slow at first, but he'd worked hard and improved his grade.

"You were one of my favorite teachers, and now that your aura is dark, I want to help you get it back. Where are you?"

"What? It's three in the morning."

"I'm coming to see you. I'll call when I get to Parkville."

I got up and walked over to look out the window. Nothing. Overcast. Not one visible star. No moon. No weird crossed planetary orbits. Yet I was sure I wasn't still on Earth. Or Earth had left its orbit. Everything was upside down and out of place. My life was spinning out of control, and I wanted the sameness of my old life back.

I got back into bed and pulled the covers up to my neck. Images of Jason fluttered through my brain. He was standing in front of the grill, sweating and flipping burgers. He was climbing a tree to saw off a limb he didn't like. Feeding the cardinals that lived on the hillside. I saw, as vividly as I saw the ceiling fan turning in circles, his mischievous smile and the crinkles around his eyes when he was up to something. Where was he? Slowly, I managed to calm a little; sleep seemed close, so close.

The jingling, vibrating traitor of a phone woke me up. My hand automatically searched for the noisy intruder, but my mind refused to engage. It was still dark outside. Terror struck. What was wrong? Who died? Where was the damn phone? Finally, it quit. I sank into the pillow. *Think, Samantha. Think. Who would be trying to call?* Danny was in his room. Wasn't he? But where was Jason? The memory of him leaving the house yesterday slapped me awake. The phone rang again. This time I located it.

Before I could say anything, Michael said, "Ms. McKenzie, I know you're confused; your aura's fading. You need peace of mind. I can help. I found this lovely little cemetery not far from you. Right now, I'm lying in the grass by a huge tombstone, and there's a carving of an angel looking up at the stars and moon. It's so peaceful. Why don't you join me?" His words were soft, like a lullaby meant to assuage a disturbed child.

Now I was freaked out. I held the phone at arm's length and stared at it, unable to come up with words. After a moment, I brought it back to my head to screech "Are you crazy?"

"You're not ready yet, are you?"

"Ready? For what?"

"I'll call you."

As the line disconnected, I stuffed the phone under Jason's pillow, praying, "God, please, *please* let this night end. Wake me up if this is all a bad dream."

The next time my eyes opened, light shone through the slats of the blinds. It was morning, and I was still alive. Tired, but alive. When I sat up, my head hurt as if it had been caught in a vise and twisted. My stomach quivered. At least I was able to get out of bed and walk. Slowly. The air was as dense as water and pressed against my skin.

The first thing I did was check on Danny. He was splayed out in four different directions on the bed, his chest rising and falling to the rhythm of his breathing. His hair was spread out around his head and pillow like a halo. Even asleep, his presence had a calming effect on my nerves. This was reality. Last night had been a bad dream. Today would return to normal.

Except . . . Where was Jason?

Before my son and I began our frenzied early morning routine of getting ready for work and school, running late, and flying out the door to our separate worlds, I sat on the back porch and inhaled the morning air. Jason was still gone. But Greg and

Michael, two men out of my past, had suddenly come back. Greg was my friend, and even though we hadn't spoken in a while, it wasn't entirely out of the blue for him to call me. But Michael? I hadn't thought of him in years. Had never expected to see or hear from him again. Maybe I had dreamed it.

I circled back to Jason and his declaration that he couldn't stand the charade anymore. We'd talked about separating many times. The arguments had been getting intense and more frequent, but somewhere in the back of my mind, I had harbored an image of us smiling adoringly into each other's eyes as we said our wedding vows without one disagreeable word. We could've made it work.

As I tried to make sense of all the confusion from the past night, I had no comprehension of the magnitude it held in my life. It was a gamechanger. Even as I tried to convince myself it would all blow over soon, it was forever cemented as one of those events that I would come to measure time by.

2

That Thursday was definitely not normal. I was tired, weepy, and discombobulated. As I was walking from my car to my office, Sue, an irritatingly ever-cheerful English teacher, walked up beside me and chirped her Mary Poppins "Good morning." I looked around for her umbrella to stuff it . . . somewhere . . . and burst into tears.

When I got to my office, I locked my door, laid my head on my desk, and cried some more. My heart actually physically hurt, and my stomach was tied in knots. Never again would I love any man. And my work? What had possessed me to go into something that required so much and paid so little? My office was a small, rectangular, beige room with an old, scratched, wooden desk that probably started its life in the 1950s and a similarly old bookcase. I'd placed a five by seven brown rug with splashes of bright yellow on the floor and pictures of Danny, Mom, and

Dad, alongside prints of Monet's haystack series on the wall. A picture of Jason and me, both of us smiling, sat on my desk, mocking me, reminding me of the good times. But I didn't want to remember the good times. I wanted to hate him.

When I tried to grade papers, my mind kept going over and over the scene with Jason from the night before. His face had been hard and his jaw set, no sign of love or caring in it. How could he be that way? How could I still love him? Then my thoughts drifted to the way his face always lit up when his 20-year-old daughter came to visit or when his black lab jumped into his lap. I saw him flipping pancakes into the air and catching them with his skillet and grilling steaks and hamburgers in the backyard for his family, smiling, laughing, and having fun.

I loved that gentle side of him, but he also had a darker side. There were the times when he would lay in his hammock for hours and stare into the sky, even in winter. Especially in winter. For him, November through February were long, depressing months to be endured in order to get to spring, outdoors, and gardening. I called it his grumpy season. Nothing was ever right. He drank too much, complained too much. A misplaced tool or a glass left on a table was cause for an outburst. Still, I loved him.

But it was late April. Grumpy season was over. We'd already planted begonias and periwinkles, tomatoes and peppers, had gotten new bird feeders, and started a rock garden on the hill. Our Saturdays were spent at Lowe's. Together. How could he end it now? During our happy season? Damn him, anyway. My tears dried up as anger set in.

During my office hours, my mood continued to worsen. When I talked to an over-protective mother about her daughter's failing history grade, it took every ounce of diplomacy I possessed not to have a temper tantrum. I wanted to. Visions of my meager paycheck stopped me.

"But she's tried so hard. This class is ridiculously difficult. No one could do the amount of work you're asking," Mrs. Helicopter Mother whined, looking pitifully at her daughter, Chopin.

I looked pitifully at Chopin, too. Why would any mother give a baby she claimed to love a name like that? Then I turned back to the mother. I wanted to inform her that most of the students were, in fact, passing. But instead I said, "I understand. However, she has four unexcused absences and has failed several exams."

"You *don't* understand. She's been very busy and has done the best she can. She has a lot on her plate, and the stress you're causing her is making her sick, which means she misses more classes. What can she do to get the grade she deserves?"

My greatest desire was to reach across the desk and strangle this uppity woman. She wore a beautiful, Ralph Lauren, silk top and pants and carried a Coach bag; my clothes came from Target, and Chopin's looked like they came from the Salvation Army store. "I did give her the grade she deserves."

"Well," she said. "I demand to see your supervisor."

"Thank God," I said to the mother. Then, to Chopin, "You can do better; you're a smart girl, and with a little effort, you'll pass next time."

Chopin's mother looked at me with a superior stare, certain that she would win this one. I knew our vice president, however, and at least this battle I would win.

I had one more thing I wanted to say, and I allowed myself to say it: "You'll help your daughter more if you make her go to class and study. Do you expect to go with her on job interviews?"

The door slammed behind them. Sighing, I called the vice president to warn her.

During my 9:30 class, I simply couldn't stand in front of the class and talk and ask questions for seventy-five minutes, so I had my students divide into small groups and gave each a question about the assassination of John F. Kennedy and the theories surrounding his death. I walked around to make sure everyone was on task, but I couldn't talk to them and have fun as I usually might.

It was one of the worst and longest days of my life. The only thing that helped me survive? Six cups of coffee from my faithful Keurig—better than any man in my life. However, even that failed when my phone rang at 4:45. I jerked it up, hoping, praying it was Jason. It wasn't.

"Ms. McKenzie, Samantha, I'm at the Parkville Public Library. Please stop by on your way home. I'd like to talk to you. Your aura's almost gone. I can help."

"Michael?" As if I had to ask.

"Please come." He hung up.

Again, tears and anger threatened to leak out. I shuddered, coughed, swallowed, and breathed in as deeply as I could and stuffed them down. What if a student knocked on my door and heard me crying or cursing and throwing paper clips at the picture of Jason and me? What if the dean walked in? But I'd so wanted to hear from Jason, even if he fussed and asked why I was still at his house. At least I'd know he was okay.

To this day, I haven't the foggiest notion why I did it. Curiosity, maybe. I often wondered how my former students had turned out. Whatever the reason, I called Danny and told him I'd be home late and then drove to the library. As soon as I pulled into the parking lot, I saw him leaning against the rock building, his eyes closed. At least I thought that was him.

The Michael I vaguely remembered had been an average guy with medium build and a clean-cut appearance. The man who jumped up and ran towards me was skinny with long, shaggy hair that looked like it hadn't been washed in weeks. His baggy t-shirt and jeans were also dirty, and his shoes were so scuffed and dusty I couldn't tell if they were brown or black. He had an equally unkempt beard.

I stepped out of the car but hung onto the door in case I needed to make a quick get-away. He hugged me with way too much enthusiasm. My eyes darted around in all directions to make sure there were other people in the vicinity. What had I gotten myself into this time? And why?

"Michael?" I said, pushing him away. "I almost didn't recognize you."

"You look great! You haven't changed a bit. Still beautiful as ever."

Beautiful may have been an overstatement. I didn't think I was ugly, but I was about fifteen pounds overweight, and, of course, there was my shoulder-length auburn hair that frizzed.

When I was kid, I'd ironed it, literally, with my mom's iron. That morning, however, it was all I could do to get some clothes on and nag Danny until he got ready for school. No time and no interest to fuss with my hair or makeup. I'd avoided mirrors all day, but I was sure my hair had fuzzed into a ball surrounding my face, and my eyes were puffy and red, which matched my naturally ruddy complexion. When I didn't wear makeup, I looked permanently embarrassed. And I had a big pimple beside my nose. I blamed it on allergies.

"So, would you like to get something to eat?" He motioned to the Jack's across the street.

"Sure," I said. I'd like to not be alone with him, but I didn't want any of my friends to see me with him either, and it was awkward standing in a parking lot with a man who looked like he'd been stranded in the desert for nine years with no change of clothes. He didn't smell dirty, though. Besides, the sun was disappearing and cool darkness was closing in. He was probably harmless. Yeah right. Ted Bundy had appeared harmless, too.

As we dodged cars and managed to run across four lanes of traffic, the sky turned shades of gold and peach that, if not for the clutter of humans, traffic, and storefronts, would have given the world around us an atmosphere of beauty, peace, and serenity. In the midst of threats of bodily harm and sudden death from the drivers, in my mind, for a few seconds, I was on the beach, watching and listening to the waves and seagulls and gazing at the sunset. Unfortunately, when I returned to reality, I was still in Parkville. We walked inside the Jack's, and I ordered my hamburger, fries, and Coke and stood aside while he ordered his. The girl rang it up. I waited for him to pay. He waited for me. The girl waited, rather impatiently, for one of us to pay, so I pulled out a twenty and gave it to her.

"I've been out of work for a while," he explained when we sat down in a corner booth.

Who would've guessed? "What kind of work do you usually do?" I asked. I was pretty sure he was the Michael I remembered, but his answer confirmed it.

"I used to be a nurse." He took a huge bite of his burger and wiped his mouth with a napkin.

"Used to be?"

"It was satisfying for a while, helping those who couldn't help themselves, but I got a higher calling."

What could I say to that? His voice had no inflections, just flat and monotonous, like those priests on TV who sit in a little box and listen to some man on the other side confess to murdering his girlfriend. So I just looked at him, waiting for him to explain.

"I'm Jesus, Samantha." He smiled and touched my hand. "I go from place to place helping people, doing what I'm supposed to be doing. When I need food or shelter, God provides."

No words could form in my head, much less find their way out of my mouth. But my hand, on its own volition, pulled away and dived into the fries while I surveyed the room. There were a couple of men in some kind of dark-green uniforms who would surely help me if I screamed, and we weren't far from the exit doors if I had to run. But Michael was no threat to me or anyone else. He appeared to be a gentle person, thoughtful, and he hadn't said or done anything the least bit threatening to me. He just wanted to help. It's just that he said the creepiest things. Did he really believe he was Jesus?

"I'm here to help you." His voice was just above a whisper, still no intonation. "Your heart's shattered, and your aura's fading."

I glared at him, trying to figure him out, and while I was at it, figure out what I was doing here. Maybe Jason was home at that very minute while I was sitting at Jack's talking to a nutcase.

"No, Jason isn't at home," Michael said. "He has some complicated problems he has to work out. You need to let him go. Let him deal with what he has to deal with. You have to take care of yourself."

"Huh?" How did he know what I was thinking?

"By this time next year, you'll be in a much happier place. But to get there, you have to let go of your life here and go home."

Did Jason pay this guy to come here and say this stuff? I wanted to run, fast and hard, and get away from Michael. He was just too odd, but, for reasons unknown to me, I chose to stay.

"Try to understand. You and Jason were never meant to be together."

"So, when you say you're Jesus, do you mean you are Jesus or that you're trying your best to be as much like Him as possible?" I asked the question calmly as if I were just curious, not ready to call a mental hospital to put him in a padded cell.

He smiled and kept on talking. "This is a difficult time for you. The hurt you're feeling now will soon turn to anger and revenge. You must control it. Lead with love and forgiveness. Your son will need you to be strong."

"My son?" Now, he'd gone too far. If anything happened to Danny, I'd hunt Michael down and run over him with my car. Ten times.

"Your son likes living with Jason. He's like a father to him, and he likes his school and friends. Leaving will be very hard for him. You need to be there for him."

"How . . . how do you know all this?" To say I was skeptical and creeped-out would be an understatement, like saying teenagers are difficult. But I felt unwillingly drawn to him, his soothing voice, all-comprehending eyes, his calm assessment that things would get better, and the implicit understanding that I was strong enough to be what Danny needed.

"Always lead with love, Samantha," he said as he stood up, leaned over, and kissed me on the cheek. "Thank you for the dinner. I must go now, but I'll check on you tomorrow."

He picked up his mess, threw it in the trash, and left. I waited, dumbfounded, to watch him walk past the window and into the traffic, but he never did. I was afraid to move.

3

I couldn't sleep that night, although I was beyond exhausted from my previous sleepless night. It wasn't like Jason to just leave his house and Pepper, his black lab. He'd told me to leave, so he had some nerve assuming I'd take care of his damn dog. But what if something was wrong? Did his daughter, Hayley, know where he was? Or his mother? Should I call them? No, not yet. He could have at least shown me the decency to call and let me know he was okay, even if he didn't love me. I couldn't help it; I called his cellphone. Voicemail.

It was already getting light outside, about the time I normally wake up, when I finally dozed off. It was also when Pepper jumped on the bed, licked me in the face, scratched on the comforter, and then turned around and around until she found the perfect spot—right next to me. Usually, I petted her and thanked her for waking me up so I wouldn't be late for work.

That morning, I shoved her away, screeched at her, and told her to leave me alone. I turned over and tried to go back to sleep. No such luck.

I pushed myself into an upright position with my feet on the floor, stood up, and ambled into the bathroom. While I was still in the shower with warm water washing over me and shampoo trickling into my eyes, the phone rang. I finished rinsing my hair as quickly as I could and ran to grab it off the dresser, still dripping wet and wrapped in a towel.

"Hi, Sam," Greg said. "Just called to see how you are. Feeling better?"

Disappointment swept through me and my stomach tightened. "It's six in the morning," I snapped.

"Sorry," he said, his voice conveying a bit of irritation. "You're usually up."

"I have to go now." I hung up the phone.

Rude. I wasn't usually rude, and he seemed to care about me, which was a lot more than I could say about Jason. Greg only wanted to help. I called back and apologized, explaining that I was in a bad mood and would call him later.

After two cups of coffee, I went into Danny's room. That's when the rest of my world erupted. The first thing I noticed was the smell: stale beer and grease. The second thing I noticed was the mess: beer cans surrounded by hamburger wrappers, left-over fries, books, assorted magazines, and several days of dirty clothes. The anger and grief of the last few days exploded volcanically.

"Get up!" I yelled. "Right now!"

He moaned, stuck his pillow over his head, and turned over. I jerked the pillow away and shook him as hard as I could. He turned over and opened his eyes—almost.

"Get up right now, or I'll ground you till you're thirty. Did you hear me?"

"The governor of Wisconsin heard you," he mumbled. His eyelids blinked a few times, so I knew he was still alive and awake.

"And why were you drinking beer last night? And where did you get it, and who was with you? Well? Answer me." All my words were loud and strung together into one long word.

"Jeez, Mom. Give me a break here." His hands moved to his head and rubbed his temples. "My head hurts." He used a couple of colorful adjectives to describe his headache, which made me jerk the bag with the golden arches and hit him over and over with it. Fries and breadcrumbs fell on him.

"I'll bet it does!" I yelled. "Get out of bed this instant and get ready for school. NOW."

I left his room and stomped around the house, listening for sounds of life in Danny's room. I wanted him to hear me, to know how angry I was and how much I didn't need this right now. He'd been such a good kid. Why did he have to turn into a teenager? His room remained silent.

I filled the pitcher with water and ice and walked from the kitchen to his bedroom, water sloshing out and leaving a trail all the way. Alcoholism ran in our family. Did he want to be a drunk like Uncle Willie and die of cirrhosis of the liver when he was forty-seven? Like Grandpa, who was an alcoholic, too, even if he wasn't as bad as Uncle Willie?

I flung his door open, marched over to the bed, and poured the water in his face. He'd managed to sleep through my tirade, but that woke him up. He jumped out of bed, shouting, "Damn it, Mom! You lose your freakin' mind?" He went into the bathroom and slammed the door.

For a few minutes, I banged on the door. "You'll be a grandfather before I let you drive my car again, and you can just forget about taking your driver's test!"

Finally, I slid down the wall and sat on the floor beside the bathroom. Mom always knew what to do and what was best for me and everyone else. Why didn't I? I had no clue how to raise a teenaged boy. I didn't want Danny to drink at all, but I knew he'd try it. All teenagers did, but I couldn't let him turn out like Uncle Willie.

When I was a little girl, Uncle Willie often came to visit us, and he was always lots of fun. He played ball with my older brother, Buddy, and me. At night we'd eat popcorn and play Monopoly or watch television while Buddy and I drank Coke and Uncle Willie drank beer. As I grew up, I watched him go from being a fun uncle to a sloppy drunk, from playing with us to cursing everything from the state of the nation and politicians to my father, who, according to him, never did anything right and was never good enough for his sister. By the time I was a teenager, he'd been banished from our house and then died soon after. Forever after, every time I'd been tempted to drink, I remembered Uncle Willie and swore never to let that happen to me. Not that I didn't sometimes have a beer at a party, but it made me anxious, uneasy, and afraid I'd turn out to be a drunk.

By the time Danny came out of the bathroom, I'd calmed a little. "I'm sorry," I said as I stood up. "I didn't mean to scream, but I won't stand for you drinking beer. You know that."

"Yeah, I know," he said. "Uncle Willie and all. I've heard it before. About a thousand times." He walked around me, went into his room, and for the second time that morning, slammed the door.

He'd never met his father, but since the teenage mind and an ever-deepening voice had overtaken him, Danny had acquired that same patronizing tone that implied "I'm smarter than you so leave me alone." And his defiant walk and the way his right hand came up, almost pointing a finger in my face, all reminded me of Daniel Sr. Not to mention that he had the same thick, dark-brown hair that spilled over his forehead, and he was growing taller and the baby fat of his preteen years had totally disappeared. His father hadn't really left me. He was there with me every day, reminding me that I hadn't been good enough for him. Thankfully, Danny at least loved me, or he had before he turned thirteen.

While I sat, sipping coffee at the kitchen table and gazing out the window, remembering his soft, warm arms around my neck, his slobbery kisses on my cheek, and hearing his "I wuv you, Mummy," he came into the kitchen, dressed, with his books in his hands. "You don't need to take me to school. I'll take the bus."

"Seeing the beer cans was a shock to me." I figured it wouldn't hurt to try to reason with him. I was wrong.

"A shock?"

"Yes. You're my son, and I love you and want what's best for you."

"Yeah? Where were you last night? I sat right there in the den drinking beer and watching television. Where were you?"

"Here. Home."

"You were in your room, crying about Jason. You didn't even know I existed."

"But . . ." He was right. I couldn't think of a defense.

"You're pathetic. He loves Carrie. Doesn't give a shit about you or me. If you had any sense, we'd be out of here."

Until that minute, I didn't realize how hurt Danny was. I wanted to take him in my arms and hug and soothe him like I had when he was little and tell him everything would be fine. Instead, I watched him walk away and slam yet another door behind him.

Danny 3; Mom 0.

By the time I got to the college, I felt like I'd been working in the fields for eight hours straight, without food or water. I was hungry but couldn't eat anything, not even the cheese crackers I'd tried to eat for breakfast, and my cup, when I tried to get it from my desk to my mouth, wobbled and splashed coffee on my white blouse. I tried to get the stain out with a paper towel, which made it worse, so I put my black blazer on, buttoned it, and started gathering my stuff for class. *Okay, Sam, where're your notes?* I shoved aside and looked under and around books, Post-it notes, newspapers, huge stacks of un-graded papers, an incomplete syllabus I'd started working on for the next semester, and a paper plate with the remnants of yesterday's peanut butter sandwich I'd tried to eat. Where in the world was the Vietnam War? Not there. Almost class time. I placed my elbows on my desk and my hands on my temples and tried to think, but my mind wouldn't cooperate. It hovered between Danny and Jason. What was the best way to mend things between my son and me? How could I help him get through the move from Jason's house, a place he'd grown to love?

How dare Jason treat us this way? I thought he at least loved Danny. Who did he think he was? I'd show him. I called a moving company, but they couldn't move my stuff until the next Thursday. Good. Because I didn't have a place to go. I had to find a house to rent; an apartment wouldn't do. If I got one in Parkville, my son wouldn't have to change schools. I texted Jason and told him I'd leave in about a week.

He didn't answer. *Damn. Damn. Damn.*

Finally, the notes I needed for class showed up, hiding in my briefcase. Thank goodness it was Friday and I had only one class. If I didn't have to be on the search committee with five interviews set for that afternoon, I could've spent a few hours grading papers. As it was, I'd have to spend most of Saturday trying to catch up. Plus, I still had to finish preparing for the next week. Of course, the English teacher position was important. I'd have to concentrate and listen to the applicants and not let my mind wander to other times and places and what I should have or should not have done, and I definitely could not fall asleep. But how could I try to assess candidates when all I could think about was Danny and Jason?

Before going to my class, I broke down and called my dad. He and Jason were friends. Jason worked for Dad, and they both dreamed of the day they could retire and make real wooden furniture—high-end pieces. They'd decided to become partners and start the business as soon as they'd saved enough money. That's how I'd met Jason.

"Dad, may I talk to Jason?" I tried to be polite and nonchalant, so he wouldn't think anything was wrong.

"I'd like to talk to him, too!" He described Jason in some colorful language and ended with, "If I don't hear from him soon, he can kiss his job goodbye."

"Thanks, Dad. I'll tell him to call you when he gets home." It was my feeble attempt to keep Dad from worrying.

If Jason hadn't gone in to work today, did that mean he hadn't gone in yesterday either? Where was he? Perky Sue, who was also on the search committee, came in to talk about an issue with the curriculum committee. I was trapped, and I had to keep mentally reminding myself how important this was so I could remain cordial and informed. If she'd just quit smiling and being so cheerful.

After she left and while I was finishing another cup of coffee and getting ready to go to class, the phone rang. It wasn't Jason. "Michael, I'm on my way to class right now."

"I know," he said in his priest-like voice. "Could we have dinner tonight?"

"No." I couldn't talk to him. I was in a hurry. I didn't want to hear about love and auras.

"Logan's in Trussville," he said. "At 5:30."

"Okay, alright, for Pete's sake." I'd have said anything to get him off the phone so I wouldn't be late for class. Maybe I'd throw my iced tea on him, the way the leading lady in old movies did to the guy she openly hated but secretly loved. Secretly loved? *Get a grip, Samantha.* Who could love that weirdo?

"I'm praying for you," he said and hung up.

While walking to class, I texted Mom and asked her to pick up Danny—he wasn't ever going home alone, ever again—and, with every thought in my brain fighting against me, I broke down and texted Jason's other girlfriend, Carrie. "Please tell Jason I need to talk to him."

Immediately, the answer lit up my phone. "I haven't seen him since Tuesday. You tell him not to bother calling me."

The rest of the day was a blur. I managed my class and the interviews without breaking down by sheer force of will. My eyes were scratchy with lack of sleep, and I felt almost sick with exhaustion.

When I got to the restaurant, I was ready to give up and smash my car into the light pole. With my luck, though, I'd probably damage the pole and my car, but I'd be fine and have to pay for everything. What I really wanted to do was go home, go to bed, and stay there all weekend. It wouldn't happen. I glanced in the mirror and immediately wished I hadn't. Red hair frizzed everywhere; I was pale, dark circles ringed my dark circles, and my blue eyes were blood-shot. I didn't even bother putting on lipstick since it clearly wouldn't help.

As I got out of the car, Michael came up to me and, without saying a word, put his arm around me. I almost broke down and cried. Again. But anguish turned to anger. Why was I here with a lunatic? Without speaking, we walked into the restaurant.

Thankfully, it wasn't crowded yet, we didn't see anyone I knew, and we were seated almost immediately, but the temperature felt like it was about sixty degrees. Good thing I'd worn my blazer. My fingers and nose were cold, and I whined and complained about it for a few minutes.

"It smells good in here though," he said.

"Yeah." I managed a smile. "Like steak."

"I've been thinking about you," he said. "Bad day at work?"

"No." It was the truth. It had been busy, but not bad. What was bad was my mood.

He reached across the table, took my hand, and covered it with his. "Jason's going to be okay."

"He's missing. Something's happened to him." It was the first time I said what I'd been worrying about for two nights and two days. "It's not like him to leave his house and dog and not come home, not even check on them."

"He cares about you too. You know that, don't you?"

"No." I wanted to talk about it, but I didn't want to talk about it. Not with Michael. Mostly, I just wanted to quit talking. All day I'd faced people and heard words and syllables and sentences that sounded like they were from outer space, and I'd tried to comprehend, but my mind wouldn't cooperate.

"I know you're hurting, Samantha, but it will get better. Everyone goes through hard times. It's how you handle it that either makes you stronger or beats you down. You're one of the strong ones. Remember to lead with love and understanding." He paused to see if I was listening. I was. "When you go home tonight, take a few deep breaths and sit quietly for a few minutes. Find something to be thankful for, even if it's something as mundane as running water."

I glared at him. What was wrong with this man? Jason was missing, and he was spouting clichés. "Yes, I am hurting, and yes, I will get over it, but will Jason? Something's happened to him. Don't you understand?"

He nodded. "I get it, but sitting around worrying isn't going to help you, Jason, or Danny. You need to take care of yourself so you can be there for them."

"Neither is having dinner with you." I reached into my purse and pulled out yet another twenty and threw it at him. "Enjoy your meal."

The waitress walked up at that minute and watched me as I walked out. I thought I heard her whisper, "Bitch."

When I got home, Carrie was there. She and Danny were sitting in lawn chairs in the backyard and appeared to be in deep conversation. Pepper sat beside her; Carrie's hand rested on her head like they were old friends. Damn traitor dog.

I'd talked to Carrie on the phone. I'd heard about her, sneaked and read a couple of text messages between her and Jason, and even looked her up on Facebook, but I'd never met her. I thought of her as a mean-spirited, home-wrecking, beautiful woman. She was forty-two, like Jason, and she was pretty, thinner than me but not svelte, and her hair was blonde with dark roots, pulled back into a ponytail. Her complexion was flawless, but she had tiny lines around her greenish eyes and her wide mouth and across her forehead. She wore jeans and an Alabama football shirt, and she didn't look too much older than Danny. I was immediately jealous.

She stood up and held out her hand. "I'm glad to finally meet you," she lied in a stiff, rehearsed sort of way.

"Glad?" Who was she kidding? She wasn't glad. I let my arms dangle beside me.

She laughed. "This is awkward, isn't it?"

I laughed, too. I didn't want to like her; I wouldn't like her. But she seemed like an okay person.

"We're going to look for him," Danny said. "The three of us."

I looked at him, then at her.

"I called Jason's mom and daughter. They don't know where he is. I didn't tell them he wasn't home or that you didn't know where he was. I'd like not to worry them."

"Right," I said, motioning for Danny to get up so I could sit in his chair, face-to-face with my nemesis. "Do you have any idea where he may have gone or what could've happened to him?"

She shook her head. "Wish I did."

"I called his job," I said. "They haven't heard from him, and he's in some serious trouble there."

"Think we should call the cops?" she asked.

I nodded and started to punch 911 on my phone, when my dad's bright red Dodge Ram pulled into the driveway.

Danny looked sheepish and admitted, "I called Grandpa."

Dad got out of the truck and walked toward me. He put his arms around me, and I laid my head on his shoulders. No tears flowed; no trembling anywhere in my body. His warmth and strength comforted me. Jason would be fine now. I knew it in my heart.

Dad had fought in Vietnam. He always said he'd seen the most vile and inhumane side of human nature and the worst the world had to throw at him. He'd watched his friend get shot and die in his arms; he'd killed men he didn't know, some of them probably no more than fifteen or sixteen years old, and he'd been shot at by teenagers. He'd been wounded and came home, not to a heroes' welcome as his dad had after World War II, but to jeers and scorn by young people his own age, who, like him, had been raised in comfortable, heated homes with plenty to eat, schools to go to, and decent clothes to wear, with no idea what the rest of the world was like. He'd wanted to tell them they were picking on the wrong person. He couldn't help going to war; his parents couldn't afford to send him to college or get him out of the draft, and he wouldn't flee to Canada, so he'd joined the Marines.

His experience during that time was what made me more interested in teaching the 1960s than any other period in history.

"We're going to find him, honey," Dad said. "I promise. I've already called the police, and your mom's at home right now calling her prayer group." We gave each other that knowing look. Mom's solution to everything, including world peace, was prayer, which in my mind was better than his response to difficulty. Before making any major decision, he always sat in his recliner, drank beer, and smoked weed—when he could get it.

Three other men got out of his truck, and then two cars pulled up and parked in front of the house. About a dozen people altogether came toward me, ready to help. In true Marine fashion, Dad barked orders at them, got them organized in groups, and in minutes they were searching the woods behind Jason's house.

"I'm going with them," Dad told me. "I want you and Danny and that young lady," he stopped and nodded toward Carrie, "to drive every inch of town and see if you can find Jason's truck."

We started by driving through all the streets in Jason's subdivision. It had been built in the early 1990s, all three-bedroom, two-bath houses with two-car garages. But instead of the developer going in and chopping down all the trees, he'd built the houses on one-half to one acre lots and left the surrounding woods and plenty of trees on each lot. It was one of my favorite neighborhoods anywhere.

For a while, we drove, slowly and silently, up the hills and around the lake, stopping at every other house so we could walk around in backyards and ask neighbors if they'd seen Jason. They hadn't. The sun set, and it was dark and cold, but we kept driving until about 10:00 p.m. when Dad called and said that some of his men had to go home. Then he suggested that we start again the next morning when we could all see better. Carrie and I didn't want to stop, but we decided maybe it would be better.

"Why don't you stay here tonight?" I asked her as we drove into Jason's driveway.

I ate a couple of cheese crackers and Carrie ate nothing, but Danny made up for it by eating two turkey and cheese sandwiches, a bag of potato chips, and half a bag of Oreos. For a long time, Carrie didn't say anything, and I didn't either. The air between us was so frigid and thick you couldn't stir it with a stick.

Finally, she said, "I'm sorry. I tried to stay away from him."

Was she kidding? "Obviously, you didn't try hard enough, did you?"

"We met in sixth grade. Went together through most of high school. We loved each other then and still do."

"That's why you both married other people?"

"Did you ever make a mistake, Sam?"

"No," I lied. "But you have, lots of them, and this one's hurting me and my son."

"If he loved you, I couldn't hurt you."

That one smarted. It was true; I just couldn't admit it, even to myself. "He chose me."

"He admired you. You went to college, have a good job. I'm a cashier. He respects your education and work; he loves me."

I stood up and was about to grab her hair, but Danny caught my arms mid-air.

"Mom, go to your room," he said. "Now."

I did. *Oh, Samantha, how far thou hast descended.* I sank into the bed and prayed, *Dear God, help me, please, and help Jason and Danny, and, if you must, help that other woman in there.*

Right on cue, my phone rang. Which one was it? Michael? Greg? Neither. I didn't recognize the number and didn't answer, but I did listen to the voicemail.

"Hi, Sam. I guess you never expected to hear from me. It's Daniel. Just thinking about you."

That was it. It was no longer just Jupiter and Mars. Pluto, that non-planet, was in there slugging it out with them too. Which one would succeed in ruining my life? After sixteen years, he was just thinking about me? He'd heard about his son and now, after all this time, he probably wanted to claim him. But he couldn't have heard. No one knew who Danny's father was, except Mom, Dad, Greg, and my friend Brianna.

I hit delete, hoping that would delete both the message and him.

Since Tuesday night, three men from my past had contacted me. The one man I loved, however, was missing.

I decided to try Michael's suggestion. I sat propped up on pillows in bed, closed my eyes, took a few deep breaths, and tried to think of something to be thankful for. I thought of three things. Well, three people, really. Mom, Dad, and Danny. I fell asleep with a vision of my mom in my head. She was calling her prayer ladies and ordering them to start praying for me. Again.

4

I startled awake to the sound of muffled voices and a door opening and closing. A gray haze filled the room, the sky outside my window, and my brain. Why was Jason up so early? Or did he leave the television on all night? The weatherman had said it'd be cool, overcast, and drizzly today. I'd have to wear a raincoat to search for . . . for Jason. Suddenly, totally awake, I sprinted out of my bedroom and confronted Danny and a large group of people at the bottom of the stairs.

With my hands on my hips and mayhem in my eyes, I asked "What—?"

Danny interrupted me, "Jeez, Mom. You forget something?" He squinted his eyes and backed away from me the way he did when I tried to hug him in front of his friends.

That's when it dawned on me; I was wearing nothing but an oversized t-shirt that thankfully hung to my knees. I touched my hair. Yep. Frizzing out in all directions. I started slowly backing up the stairs, pushing my shirt down. "Who—?"

"Volunteers," Danny said.

The strange people in my house immediately started milling around and talking, bowing their heads or gazing at the phones in their hands.

"Where'd they come from?"

He shrugged his shoulders.

Dad walked toward me with a frown and snapped, "Get some damned clothes on." Then he turned to the crowd and called out, "The police called. They've found Jason's truck at Turkey Creek. The search is moving there."

I dashed up the stairs, dressed, did my thing in the bathroom, pulled my hair into a ponytail, and was back downstairs in five minutes flat. Dad drove Carrie, Danny, and me to the search sight.

As soon as we got there, I finally understood how all these people knew about the search. Mom and seven of her friends from church, each armed with a huge carafe of coffee, were already there and pouring the steaming liquid into paper cups. Was there anything ever as enticing as the aroma of fresh-brewed coffee combined with the sugary scent of doughnuts? Especially on one of those wet spring mornings? Normally, I would have enjoyed it in a purely sensual way, but I doubted I'd be enjoying anything today. Mom had pulled together about twenty people to get up at dawn, walk around in a cold, drizzling rain, and search for a man they didn't know, and seven others to serve them coffee. That was my mom.

While walking toward her, I knew I was looking at myself in twenty-three years. People who saw us together frequently

said, "Y'all look like sisters." We were the same height, 5'5,"
same blue eyes and auburn hair. If it weren't for boxed hair col-
or, hers would've been streaked with gray. Like me, she was also
about fifteen pounds overweight.

The big difference in us was that she was an extrovert and
I was an introvert. She thrived on being around other people. She could walk into a room of strangers and any observer
would think she'd known them all her life. I, however, needed a
lot of alone time. At large parties or gatherings, Mom flittered
through the room talking and laughing with everyone, making
them all think they were special to her. I stayed with those I
already knew or at the back of the room, out of sight, the proverbial wallflower.

I've often wondered why I chose a profession that required
me to be around people so much. I think it was originally the
path of least resistance. Mom taught high school English and,
as far back as I can remember, had immersed me in learning.
Every PBS special, vacation, movie, and even the occasional
cartoon, was a lesson.

When she saw me, Mom walked around the card table and
handed me a cup of coffee with cream and sugar, the way I liked
it. "Don't you worry, honey," she said. "They'll find him today.
I feel it in my heart."

I honestly didn't mean to do it; I was only trying to show
her I appreciated all the things she had done for me. No matter
how mad I got at her, I would never pour hot liquid on my own
mother. In that moment, I was the opposite of angry. I was grateful and was about to hug her and tell her so, but at the same time
that I reached out to grasp the cup, my other arm went around

her, and hot, sloshing coffee spilled onto my hand.

Good thing Mom had quick reflexes and jumped backwards, except her butt hit the table and, of course, hot coffee splashed all over her trouser legs and shoes. The crowd roared and moaned. One cursing man grabbed the coffee pot, a skinny, young girl who was picking out a chocolate cream doughnut held onto the box as if it were a baby, and another guy managed to stop the table mid-fall and push it into its upright position. Several ladies picked up the little packets of creamer, sugar, artificial sweeteners, and those little stirrer sticks. When she regained her composure, Mom gave me her evil eye—the look reserved for when I'd done something exceptionally bad or stupid. Then she looked around at everyone staring at us, smiled, hugged me, and said, "You're welcome."

Grace in the midst of chaos. Yep. That was Mom. Too bad I didn't inherit some of her grace and charm genes or at least her ability to believe in God and the goodness of His creation. I longed to embrace her easy faith: believe in God and Jesus, do good and pray, and everything will turn out right. I wasn't so sure. Neither was Dad. He said he'd seen grown men cry and pray to God and for their mothers just before they were shot to death or blown to bits.

He came up to Mom and me, gave us both a brief hug, and started shouting orders. In a few minutes, he and the police officers had all of us organized into small groups, walking shoulder-width apart through the woods, down the narrow road, and beside the creek. Dad kept Carrie, Danny, and me together and instructed a tall, heavy-set man, a friend of Jason's, to be our leader. We obediently followed.

We were assigned the path beside the creek to the right of the main park area. We advanced slowly, pushing at bushes with long sticks, overturning piles of last winter's dead undergrowth. When I came to a tiny, debris-covered hill, I stepped over it, planting my foot down on the other side. My feet came out from under me and I landed painfully on my rear into a slimy pile of wet dead leaves. Carrie laughed. Our fearless leader grunted as if I'd done it on purpose. Only my sweet Danny asked if I was okay and helped me up.

When we finally stopped to take a break, I asked our guide, "So, what's your name?"

"J.W." he said.

I wanted to ask him what his name really was, but he said it in such a final way I was afraid to. He opened his thermos and gulped the hot coffee down like it was cold lemonade. For ten minutes no one spoke. Then J.W. stuck his thermos in his backpack and, without looking at us or saying anything, started marching through the vegetation again. We followed.

I wondered if Carrie, like me, was afraid we'd be the ones to find Jason and at the same time, afraid we wouldn't. I couldn't stand the thought of him all by himself, lying in the woods, helpless, hurt, and bleeding. If we did find him, I wouldn't scream or cry or break down. I'd have to be calm. I imagined the scene, playing with various scenarios to prepare myself.

It seemed like we'd been trudging through those woods for hours, but it was just barely nine o'clock when my cellphone rang. Before I could say anything, Dad shouted, "They got him! They got him!"

At the same time, we heard the wail of the ambulance and police cars growing closer and closer and started running as quickly as we could through the rock-studded, muddy path toward the parking area. Mom met us there and started running beside me as she pointed down the road toward a tower of rocks. "This way!"

An ambulance, a rescue truck, a firetruck, and several police cars, all with their lights ablaze and turning, met us around the corner. A much larger crowd than had been there earlier stood at the foot of the rocks, looking up and around while several police officers kept them back to the edge of the road. Carrie and I ran up to one of the officers and begged him to let us by; we had to get to Jason. Not a chance. I tried to sneak around to the other side of the formation but was met by two other cops. Damn them.

Finally, a swarm of people, including Dad and Jason's daughter, Hayley, came out of the rocks. Four paramedics surrounded the stretcher as they wound their way through the rock maze. The man ahead of the stretcher, clearing a path with his foot and a stick, pointing and calling out which way to turn and where to step . . . who was he? He looked familiar. No. It couldn't be. But it was. Michael. And he'd shaved and cut his hair shorter. It was its original shiny brown color, clean and neat, and he had on a blue polo shirt tucked into his clean jeans.

The old gray-haired lady next to me said, "That's him. He's the one that found him."

The scene in front of me wasn't real. It was a movie, a strange dream. How? I couldn't even come up with a question, just "How?" Without any forethought, I broke through the police line and started running toward Jason and Michael. The officer grabbed my arm and pulled me back. I kicked his shins. He squeezed tighter. That word, that word I never said, came rushing out of my mouth followed by "filthy pig." Now, I was going to hell.

And that's how I happened to land in the backseat of a patrol car and Carrie got to ride with Hayley as they raced behind the ambulance to the hospital. Danny rode with Mom and Dad while Michael rescued me.

As I sat in the back of the car that smelled like stale sweat, probably from some recent prisoner, I heard Michael's droning voice and the officer's adamantly protesting one, but not what they were saying. They occasionally glanced at me, nodding or pointing toward me or the spot where I had uttered the unfortunate series of offensive syllables. Then, they seemed to lapse into a friendly conversation, punctuated by occasional laughter.

I was growing more and more irritated by the minute. The red and blue lights were no longer twirling, and most of the patrol cars and searchers had left. The ambulance was probably already at the hospital, the paramedics rushing inside while a swarm of doctors and nurses in white surrounded the stretcher, the way I'd seen it so many times in TV shows. When the sun came out, the rain stopped, and it was getting hot in the car; they were still talking. I was still damp from the rain, and now sweat was beginning to dribble down my face and collect on my skin and under my arms. I could smell myself, as if I hadn't bothered to shower that morning. Oh yeah, I hadn't. What a mess I was.

What else could I do but settle back and try to be patient? I took several deep breaths and gazed at the water rushing over the small rock waterfall, willing myself to calm down. In my imagination, I saw two, ethereal children sliding down it into the small pool below. It was my brother, Buddy, and me, during one of our many family outings to Turkey Creek when I was young. We splashed and chased each other as we climbed the rock formation and slid down again. Mom sat beside the creek on a large, flowered tablecloth with a picnic basket. Dad lowered a huge watermelon into the flowing waters to let it cool. I longed to go there, back in time, and tell my brother I loved him and missed him. As I closed my eyes against the swirl of emotions, the car door opened, and the officer said I was free to go.

Michael offered to take me to the hospital. The drive seemed to last forever and all I wanted to talk about was Jason. What did he look like? Was he able to speak? Michael informed me that he had a concussion, some lacerations, and contusions.

"The thing to remember, though," he said, "is that he'll recover. It'll take a while, but he'll get well."

"How could you possibly know that? And how in the world did you find him?" Agitation reigned inside me.

"I'm a nurse, remember? And I woke up early this morning, before dawn, and had an urge to go to Turkey Creek to walk and meditate, so I borrowed Mother's car and drove there."

"And you just went straight to him?"

He glanced at me and smiled. "No, I joined the search party. I happened to be one of a small group that was able to climb the rocks."

"Of course, you just happened to be there at the right time and the right place? If you don't start giving me straight answers, you're going to be the one in the hospital."

Michael didn't take his eyes off the road when he said, "Yes."

Total exasperation. "Well, was he awake? Was he bleeding?"

"No and yes."

I imagined Jason lying in the grass and rocks, his body twisted, lying in a pool of blood, his eyes closed, his face pale.

As if reading my mind, Michael said, "Don't go there, Samantha. Picture him alive and well, laughing and talking. Or think of something else. Don't dwell on the negative."

If looks could kill, he'd have been dead with his head hanging over the wheel and his mother's car zigzagging across the highway.

He smiled and said, "Don't go there, either."

What was it with this guy? Why did I like being with him? Yes, I had to admit to myself that despite all the confusion, I liked him—as a friend. For a few minutes, I closed my eyes and tried not to worry about Jason. I willed myself to think of something pleasant and unhateful to say.

What came out of my mouth was, "You clean up nicely."

"You noticed? "

"Hard not to."

"I've had a different calling. Been at Mother's house for the last few days. That's where I was headed the night I saw your aura fading, which is almost gone now. Seeing her walk so slow and her hands shaking, I figured I'd like to help those whose time is limited. You know, people in nursing homes or too sick to get out of their houses, or maybe even those who're transitioning from this life to the next."

"Well, it'd certainly help me if Jesus was there in the flesh when I transition." An attempt at sarcasm.

"Finding Jason, being there for him, was a test for me. To see if I'm ready."

"What? You just got up this morning with a feeling that Jason was going to die and decided, 'Yeah, this'll be a good test for me. Let's see if that's what I want to do?' Is that it?" Who did he think he was? Oh, yeah. Jesus.

"He came very close, Samantha. I'm glad I was with him."

This was too much. "You don't even know the guy. Whether he lives or not has nothing to do with you. You understand that, don't you?"

"Anytime you're there for someone in need, it helps them and you. Do you understand?"

He was getting on my nerves. Again. "I understand you're crazy."

"I understand how you would think that."

If we didn't get to the hospital soon, I was going to grab the steering wheel, aim the car at a light pole, and kill us both.

He talked on and on about the best way to help others, how our thoughts determine the quality of our lives, and that we can be calm and serene in the middle of a storm. His voice began to blend in to the rhythm of the churning engine, tires speeding across asphalt, and the sound of Bruce Springsteen on the oldies station.

I'd almost calmed a bit when he said, "You're fulfilling your calling, Samantha. Your students need you, and you're doing a great job. You care about them."

"How could you know that? I might be the worst teacher on the planet." I knew I was being irrational. He had been my student. He knew.

Not a change of voice, no exasperation with me. "Are you?"

Any minute my insides were going to explode. Fortunately for him, he shut up. Finally, just Bruce and me and the engine noise as the storefronts, trees, a fire station, and a library flew by. My thoughts went from premeditated murder to a delicate state of peace. In my heart I knew Jason would recover, but I also knew he and I would never again be "us." Just because I knew it, though, didn't mean I accepted it. By the time we got to the hospital, I was almost like a normal person.

I shivered in the dreary and frigid waiting room in my still-damp raincoat. In the back corner of the room, Carrie sat on one side of Jason's mother and Hayley sat on the other. Their faces were somber, as if they were at a funeral; their eyes were red and swollen, and they sat, saying nothing, staring at the door. Jason's mother, Brenda, was rigid. Her hands clutched the armrests like a petrified passenger on an airplane rushing toward the ground. She had no one except Jason and Hayley. No brothers, sisters, or parents, and her husband had died of a heart attack when Jason was twelve.

In the facing chairs, Mom and Dad whispered to each other; Danny sat next to Mom playing games on his phone. I sat next to Dad with Michael on the other side of me.

"Have you heard anything?" I asked out loud, fearing the answer.

As if coming out of a trance, Brenda looked up and said, "He's hurt bad."

"I'm so sorry," I said, unable to think of anything that might make her feel better.

For a long time, we all sat there staring at the door. Waiting. Hoping. Praying. I decided to check my messages to pass the time. Greg wanted to know if I was coming to see him. Daniel Sr. wanted to talk to me. Why hadn't I answered his phone calls? I didn't answer either of them.

Finally, when the doctor came out, he told us Jason was still unconscious, had a concussion, bleeding in the brain, lacerations, contusions, and an infection. I glanced at Michael. He hadn't been totally correct in his diagnosis, but it was eerily close.

"He's in ICU right now." The doctor looked at his watch, looked straight at Hayley and Brenda, and told them, "You can go in to see him in about twelve minutes."

When the doctor left, Brenda said to us, "Y'all need to go home. Hayley and I will be here for Jason."

"You'll need to rest," Carrie said, "We can be here for him, too."

Mom, even more like a Marine sergeant than Dad, said, "Why don't we make up a schedule? That way, whenever we can see him, someone will be here for him."

Hayley said, "He doesn't know whether we're here or not right now. Gramma needs to see him, be with him. You all go home right now and let her do that. I'll call when we know something or if we need you." Her words were abrupt and final. She turned away from us, toward her grandmother, and both walked away.

I felt like I'd lost my last friend on earth. I'd lived with Jason for five years. Five years, and they threw me away like trash.

Hayley and I had been close. We'd planned birthday and Father's Day cookouts for Jason, shopped together for presents for him, and spent lots of weekends hanging out, playing Ping-Pong, and grilling. She'd dismissed me. Just like her dad had. I was nobody to them, probably never had been.

Mom gave me cheerleader talks. Jason would be fine, I would be fine, and everything has a way of working out for the best. I wanted to tell her she was just making it worse, but I couldn't speak. The weepy weariness was just under the surface of my skin, behind my eyes and in my heart. I had to get away, be alone.

Finally, I found a few words in my brain that managed to find their way out of my mouth, "Michael will drive me home. Can Danny stay with you tonight? I'll call you later."

As I climbed into Michael's car, all the pent-up anguish and tears broke loose. He turned toward me, took my hands in his, and listened as if taking it all in, but he said nothing. For no reason at all, through all the blubbering, I told him about Danny, Greg, and Daniel Sr. and how worried I was about Jason. "Why doesn't he love me?" I blubbered.

"I don't know," he answered as he started the car and pulled out of the parking lot.

"And Hayley? Why did she treat me like that?"

"I don't think she meant to hurt you. She's trying to take care of her grandmother and she's worried about her dad. And I believe things happen for a reason. There's always a lesson to learn or something to overcome that will make us stronger."

I wasn't sure about that.

When we reached Jason's house, Michael asked, "Are your mom and dad bringing Danny home?"

I shook my head. "He's spending the night with them."

"Do you want me to go in with you, so you won't be alone?"

"No, I need to be alone, but thanks."

"If you need me, Samantha, call. I'll be here for you."

5

The house that had been home to me for five years seemed like a foreign land. A place where I didn't know the language or where to go or how to get there. There were no sounds. It was too cool for the hum of the air conditioner, too warm for the heater, and the refrigerator also remained silent. It smelled faintly of dog and those little things we plugged into the sockets to overcome the odor. I walked from room to room, wanting desperately to keep everything the way it was, but knowing that when Jason came home, he'd want me to be gone.

I didn't know what to do. Did Jason and I even still have a chance? The little voice of reason in my head said no. The dominant voice of eternal optimism and hope—and stubbornness—said yes.

Hayley made the decision for me. While I was in the bathroom, inhaling the scent of Jason's Irish Spring soap pyramid, she came in through the backdoor and called my name. I met her in the den, approaching her uncertainly. To my relief, she hugged me.

"I'm sorry if I was rude today," she said. "I'm worried about Dad, and I didn't want you or Carrie upsetting him. Maybe he does know we're there and what we're saying. I don't know, but I do know I want him to be able to rest, and I want Gramma and me to be there with him when he wakes up. I hope you understand."

"No, I don't," I said. "Do you honestly think I'd do or say anything to hurt him?"

"Maybe not intentionally, but I need to tell you something. He confides in me a lot. I know how he feels about you. I know he respects and cares about you, but he doesn't love you the way he thinks you should be loved. He's wanted to break it off for a long time." It sounded like a speech she'd rehearsed several times.

"I know that," I said, "but if we just had a little more time . . ."

"Please, Samantha, find a place to stay now, before he gets out of the hospital. I want to be here when he comes home and stay with him until he gets well."

"What about Carrie?"

"What about her?"

"Is she going to be here too?"

"Is it any of your business?"

It wasn't. "May I see him?"

"Yes. When he's awake, out of danger, and in his room, I'll call you."

"I'll be out of here by the weekend," I said.

"I hope you understand," Hayley said. "I just want what's best for Dad. I still care about you."

I didn't understand, but nodded, anger quickly replacing self-pity. When she left, I went online and started looking at houses and apartments for rent in Parkville. Surely, hopefully, I could find something quickly. While I was doing this, Daniel Sr. called. I stared at the phone, at his name. Sixteen years ago, he'd abandoned me, without even a goodbye, no explanation, no forwarding address. And now he had the nerve to call, to keep calling. I answered.

"Hello," Daniel said. "This is—"

"I know who this is," I said, cutting him off. "Why are you calling?"

"I want to talk to you. Rehash old times."

I hung up. He called back.

"If you want to talk to me," I said, "just tell me what you really want."

"I was in Tuscaloosa not long ago and ran into a friend of yours. Remember Brianna?"

My body tightened; my hands froze. I couldn't speak. He knew. Brianna, that traitor, told him.

"I want to see my son," he said.

"It's a little late for that, isn't it?" I couldn't help it; I began shouting. "You left me alone, stranded, in a place that was as cold as the North Pole with no money and pregnant! And now you want to see your son? Go to hell!" I turned the phone off, wishing I still had a landline that I could slam down.

I didn't know what to do. I was so mad I thought I was going to burst wide open. I opened the back door and let Pepper in, snapped her leash on her, and ran with her through the neighborhood. My hair was disheveled, my eyes were red and swollen, and my face was still dirty from my trek through the woods at Turkey Creek, but I didn't care. All I wanted to do was get away from everything and everyone. When a neighbor waved at me, I waved back but kept running.

An hour later, when I returned home, no, when I got back to Jason's house, I was hot, sweaty, tired, and smelled like a farmer who'd been hauling manure in the sun on a 98-degree day. Even after both a shower and a leisurely bath, I was still angry. I couldn't eat or sleep or watch television, so I spent the evening looking online for a house for Danny and me. I found one not far from the high school that was ready to move in, filled in the application, and hit send.

I called Mom to tell her about Jason and me breaking up and how I'd have to move.

"You know you can always stay here," she said.

"Thanks, Mom, for always being there for me." And I meant it. But I couldn't move back home and become their little girl again. I'd done it once, when my son was born. Not again. Ever.

"I'll come get Danny," I said. "I need to talk to him."

There was a pause on the other end of the phone, then Mom said, "I thought he went home. He left here with his friend, what's his name, the one with the black hair that plays the guitar? He said he'd take Danny home."

"Thanks, Mom. I'll call his cellphone."

I hung up quickly and touched his name on the screen. Where was he now and what was he up to? He didn't answer. I left a voicemail telling him he'd better call now or he'd regret it. *Okay, Samantha, do something while you wait. Grade papers.* Yes, that was it. I took out my stack of essays on the 1960s, picked up the first one, and, with my red pen in hand, started reading.

What if his friend was driving drunk and they had a wreck and were lying in a ditch somewhere? *No, Samantha, back to the 60s.* What if he was out with some girl? What if she got pregnant? *Back to the 60s.* If I could finish one essay an hour and had thirty to do, I'd be finished sometime Monday morning. I barely knew the friend. What if he was one of those perverts? What if...? I punched Danny's name on my phone again. No answer.

I couldn't sit still any longer. Even though I'd just gotten back from a run a couple of hours ago, I needed to move my legs again. I went out the front door and breathed in the cool night air as I walked down the steps and toward the street. That's when I heard the muffled laughter and garbled, loud words, like a couple of drunks on a bender. *Oh no. Now what?* Images of sloppy men pointing a gun at my head flashed through my mind, and my body went into fight or flight mode.

One voice yelled, "Gimme one," and it sounded like it came from the backyard.

I turned and ran toward the house to get my gun and call 911, but stopped abruptly when I heard, "Shhhhh, she'll hear us." And I knew. Danny.

I changed course and marched, anger rising with every step, to the backyard. He and his greasy-haired friend were lying with their feet and legs under the trampoline, their heads and shoulders in the grass, surrounded by beer cans, dozens of wrappers of chips, cookies, and beef jerky, and the unmistakable smell of marijuana. They were simultaneously laughing and trying to talk, their words slurred and unrecognizable, though they seemed to understand each other perfectly and thought every word was funny. I didn't. I screamed at both of them and ordered them into the house and out of sight of prying neighbors.

Once inside, I told the friend he'd better call his mother or father to come get him, or I was going to haul him off to the police station and leave him on the front steps. A few minutes later, a car pulled into the driveway; the horn honked, and the friend whose name I couldn't remember tumbled out the door. Later, I felt guilty that I didn't go out and meet the mother or father and make sure the kid got home safely, but then all I could think about was my own son.

Danny hung onto me, barely able to stand, as I steered him up the stairs and into his room. I let go of him and he landed on the bed. I went straight to the kitchen, found some sleeping pills, took one, and went to bed.

6

Hayley called me the next morning to tell me there was no change in Jason's condition; he was still in the ICU. I tried to hold onto my anger at her but was grateful that she called, and I ended up telling her everything would be okay. Greg sent me another text to ask when I was coming to see him, and Daniel sent a text saying he was going to his lawyer on Monday if I didn't let him see his son. Michael didn't call or text.

It was a warm, sunny Sunday. I went out onto the back porch and watched the birds pecking at the seed in the feeder and on the ground. The trees and shrubs were alive with new green, including the irises that would soon fill the backyard with yellow, white, and purple blooms. I closed my eyes and breathed in the moist scent of spring. For some reason, I thought of Michael, and the tiniest bit of optimism crept into my brain. He'd said this time next year I'd be in a better place.

I decided to believe him. I'd get through this, and Danny and I would be fine. And so would Jason. We wouldn't be in the same vicinity or talk to each other, and he probably wouldn't think about me, but we would all be fine. I had to believe it. All I could do was what was in front of me. One thing at a time. I picked out the next essay and started grading. A little over an hour later, another one.

Sometime around noon, Danny, grumbling and moaning about how bad he felt, stumbled outside and slouched into the chair across from me.

"I'm hungry," he said. "And sick."

I kept my eyes down on the paper in my hands and pretended not to hear him.

"Can I have some crackers?"

"You know where they are."

"But, Mom . . ."

I started to get up and go get some saltines, to tell him to go back to bed, that Mommy would take care of him. Something stopped me, a voice from my past. It was Mom scolding me. *You have to learn to accept the consequences of what you do. That's how life is. Someday your dad and I won't be around to pick up the pieces.* I hadn't learned that lesson very well; I had to be sure that Danny did.

Torn between wanting to be there for my sick child and anger at him for getting drunk in the first place, I sat there weighing my options. After a few moments, I said, "Get your own crackers and go to bed. Sleep it off."

He had a look of genuine surprise on his face. "But, Mom. . ." He whimpered and groaned about his aching head and sick stomach, trying to look as pitiful as possible. He'd learned early how to push my guilt complex into full gear. This time it wouldn't work. He had to learn.

He walked, slower than an elderly turtle, into the house, and a few minutes later I heard the door to his room slam. Then came the music. Head-pounding, nerve-shattering noise, so loud it probably shook the house and irritated the neighbors. How could he stand that with a hangover? He didn't feel too bad, evidently.

Oh well, later. Back to the porch. The next paper was by a shy woman in her thirties, who made A's on tests but never volunteered anything in class. If I asked her a question, her face turned red and she stammered. In her essay, she said her grandfather had lost his arm in the Vietnam War, and when he came home, her grandmother left him with twin infant girls to raise and never came back. One of the twins was her mother. She wrote that she'd never met her grandmother, but when her grandfather died, they'd found a well-worn picture of a beautiful teenaged girl with long, dark hair and a yellow flower holding it back on one side. The name on the back was her grandmother's. He had held on to it all those years.

I didn't know what to do with the essay. I'd asked the class to tell me how they thought the 1960s had changed America and how the changes had impacted our lives today. Her story was sad, personal, and well-written, but did it answer the questions? I wanted to hug her, to tell her that she was good and lovely and nothing like her grandmother, but I didn't really know her. Maybe she was. Maybe her grandmother's actions had irrevocably changed her. Maybe I couldn't do anything to help her, anyway; I was a teacher, but my power to change things was limited.

It occurred to me then that whatever I did about my son's father, whether I allowed him to meet Danny or not, would change my son's life forever. It wasn't a matter of if; I'd have to let them meet. It was a matter of when and how. If I didn't, anger would fill my son's mind, and he might drink more and do drugs and start hanging out with guys who drove around all night and robbed liquor stores. He might resent me just knowing I'd never told his father about him or tried to contact him. I didn't want Danny to know his father. I didn't want to share him with an irresponsible, spoiled jerk. But what I wanted shouldn't matter.

I didn't know what to do about anything, so I put the paper aside and picked up the next one and graded until early afternoon, stopping then to make myself a peanut butter and honey sandwich. Danny came in and, without speaking to me, plopped into a chair at the kitchen table. His hair stood up on top and out at the sides as if he'd molded it in place with grease. His eyes were red with dark circles under them, and his arms moved with the grace of a sleepy elephant as he put them on the table and his head on top of them.

"Want a peanut butter sandwich?" I asked.

"Uh huh," he mumbled.

I gave him mine. Without moving his head, he took a bite. How did he do that without choking? I made another sandwich, laid my head on the table, and tried to take a bite. That very minute, Jupiter and Mars must've clashed again.

At the sound of my phone ringing, I waved my arm at Danny and uttered the life-changing sentence, "Will you hand me my phone, please?"

He sat up and grabbed my phone, but instead of handing it to me, he stared at the screen. "What the hell?" He was suddenly alert and wide-eyed.

I sat up. Panic took over my brain.

"Daniel Caldwell?" He stared at the screen; the phone kept chiming.

"Give it to me now," I said, as I reached out for it.

He held onto it as if in a trance. The chiming stopped; he scrolled through my recent missed calls and looked up at me with accusation in his eyes.

"My dad?" he asked. "You've been talking to my dad? The guy you said walked out on us, didn't want us, and never would?" His words could've cut frozen biscuits. "How long?"

"Since yesterday."

"Why didn't you tell me?"

"It's the first time I've heard from him in sixteen years, and we were all so worried about Jason, I couldn't even think about your dad."

"Maybe he wanted to talk to me!" he yelled. "Ever think about that?"

He threw the phone down and walked out the door while I was calling after him, begging him to stay so we could talk about his father. *Okay, Samantha, calm down.* He'd be back soon. How far could he get? Should I run after him, try to get him to come back? Or wait? I decided to wait and grade papers and try not to worry.

I picked up the next essay, this one from a woman who had to be at least seventy years old. She wrote that she'd been nursing her infant son while watching a soap opera when Walter Cronkite interrupted the show to say that the president had been shot. Then about half an hour later, Cronkite, looking distressed, took off his glasses and announced that President John F. Kennedy had died at a hospital in Dallas. She wrote that before the 1960s, America had seemed like a father who favored one son and gave him everything his heart desired: a mansion to live in, clothes, cars, and plenty to eat, but left his other children out in the cold. These other kids, black, brown, girls, gays, all knocked at the door and asked the favored one to share with them, but neither he nor the father listened. The children outside got angry, knocked louder, and cried out, but the father paid no attention as the favored one kept playing with his toys. One day, a fighting mad mob of America's children burst through the door of the mansion and demanded their share. The son said to the father, "I didn't know they were angry. Did you?"

Maybe Danny had been angry with his dad and me all these years and I hadn't known it, hadn't listened for it. I called my son to apologize and tell him to come home, that we'd talk about him seeing his father. Straight to voicemail. I left a message and called Hayley to see how Jason was. He was the same, still in the ICU, but there was no need for me to come. She and her grandmother could only see him at certain times and only one at a time.

Nothing to do but try to grade another paper. My mind kept wandering to Danny and Jason and back again. I plodded on, trying to be fair to my students and give each essay the attention it deserved. After a while, I noticed the sun glide closer to earth and disappear behind a hill and its trees, the sky slathered with hues of pink, purple, and gold. Danny had been gone for hours and still wouldn't answer my calls and texts. I called Mom and asked if he was there. No, they hadn't seen him, but she'd pray for us and Dad would drive around Parkville to see if he could find him. For the second time in one week, someone I loved had walked out on me. Literally. Jason, for reasons unknown to me, had gone to Turkey Creek; maybe Danny had, too, but it was too far to walk. Maybe a friend drove him.

The urge to find out trumped any compulsion to grade more papers. I leashed Pepper and loaded her into my car, not that she'd be much protection, unless she jumped on someone, knocked him down, and licked him to death. She was big, though, and scary looking. We arrived at Turkey Creek, and as I walked down the sloping, grassy hill toward the water, I told her to "find Danny" though she wasn't trained and we'd never asked her to find anyone before. She did sniff both sides of the trail, but we saw no one.

It was almost dark, and I knew he wasn't there and that I should leave. Instead, I sat on a rock and prayed, "Dear God, please bring my son back right now. I've got to see him, talk to him, know he's okay."

About that time, my phone chimed and lit up. I looked up at the half-moon and stars. "So, you couldn't give me my son, but you give me Michael instead?" If there was a deity, I was angry with Him.

"You're upset, Samantha. I can barely see your aura anymore." Michael said. "Where are you?"

I wasn't going to tell him, but an image of that old lady hollering "That's him. He's the one that found him" changed my mind. "I'm at Turkey Creek near the parking area by the waterfall."

The trees were dark shadows and the sky behind them had turned to dark navy blue while I sat there. I'd never been to the creek when it was dark. It was peaceful with sounds of treefrogs, crickets, and water rushing through the rocks. The moon and stars shone more brilliantly here, and the scent was of fresh, overturned earth mingling with new spring flowers. For a few minutes, I felt serene, my mind one with the forest, with the rocks, water, and small animals.

I looked around. It was so dark I could barely see my hand in front of my face. Which way was my car? Dear God, what had I done now? Why didn't I think to bring a flashlight? The headlines flashed across my mind: "Local History Teacher Found Dead at Turkey Creek." No, I couldn't get lost, so I sat paralyzed on my rock, waiting, while Pepper tugged at the leash and sniffed at the ground. My only hope now was that Michael would rescue me.

After what seemed like hours, but was probably only ten minutes, a round light came toward me. Pepper stood still, sniffed the air, and barked.

The light stopped. "Samantha?"

"Thank You, God!" I cried out. "Over here!"

When Michael reached me, before he had time to say anything, I hugged and held onto him while Pepper sniffed his crotch. He led us back to my car and followed me home. No, not home. To Jason's house.

While I poured wine for Michael and me in Jason's kitchen, which a week ago would've been an unthinkable circumstance, I called my son. Of course, he didn't answer, but as I set the glasses down in the living room, I received a text that said, "Mom, I'm okay. Don't worry."

I texted back, "Where are you?" No reply. I pressed the call button. No answer.

Michael sat at one end of the sofa and I at the other. For a few minutes there was an awkward silence, but it took only a few sips of wine before I was telling him everything. He listened as if he cared. This time he didn't give me any lectures but simply said, "I understand."

I poured more wine.

When I woke up, it was still dark outside, Michael was gone, and I was on the couch, still wearing yesterday's pink sweats and covered with a thin blanket. I tried to sit up. My head pounded, the world tilted, and I barely made it to the bathroom in time. For a long time, I lay on the cool, white bathroom tile, occasionally throwing up and constantly moaning and wishing I could go to sleep and not wake up until next week. I definitely felt a lot more sympathy for Danny and wished I'd been kinder to him.

Finally, I was able to sit up, and with my hands on the side of the tub, pushed myself into a standing position. With one hand on the wall for balance, I made my way to the kitchen, found a loaf of bread, and ate one slice. It felt like cotton in my mouth.

The offending wine bottle was on its side beside the sink, sniggering at me. As quickly as my aching body could move, I went to the sink, grabbed it up, and threw it in the trash. Michael must've drunk a lot last night. No, that wasn't right. Where was Michael? Oh, God, no. Not another disappearance. Bits and pieces of the night before began to take shape inside my head.

I'd sipped my wine, chattered incessantly, and complained about everything. For a while, Michael had been sympathetic and listened. Then he'd said, "Maybe you shouldn't have any more wine," and I'd said, "Go to hell," and started drinking from the bottle. That's when I got sick. And drunk. Now I was a failure. Again.

7

As the sky lightened and my sobriety returned, I came to
the realization that my teenage son had been gone all night.
I checked my phone to see I still only had that one text from
him. There were a few missed calls, but they were from Daniel.
I tried calling Danny again and still didn't get an answer. It was
Monday, but it was too early for school to start. I couldn't wait
to see if he would show up to get ready for school. I had to find
him now.

I began making phone calls to see if he was with any friends
or family, but no one answered. They must have all still been
asleep. I was beginning to panic. I couldn't wait any longer. It
was time to call the police. I was just about to dial 911, when
there was a knock on the door. I threw it open to see . . . not
Danny, but someone who looked very much like him.

"What do you want?" I snapped.

"Long time, no see," Daniel said, smiling that charming, utterly disarming smile. The same one that had taken me in so many years before. "Got a minute?" He was as handsome as the last time I saw him. His hair was shorter, but it was still thick and brown. "Danny's with me," he said, not waiting for me to answer him.

"What?" I demanded, looking past him at his car parked on the road.

"Not here. At my parents' old house in Mountain Brook. I'm staying there. I've been trying to call you, but you never called me back. I drove over here to tell you he's okay and he's safe."

Relief flooded through me, but I wouldn't be at ease until I saw Danny for myself. My voice shook as I asked, "Why didn't you just bring him home? I've been worried sick. Why didn't you make him call me back?" I rubbed my eyes, trying to keep in the tears. "He needs to come home. He has to be at school in less than two hours."

"He doesn't want to see you," he said gently. "He's really upset. We've been talking a lot—learning about each other."

"But—"

"I'll get him to school in time."

I huffed out a breath. My irritation was growing again. "How did you find him?"

"He called me last night and said he wanted to meet me. I picked him up at the gas station a few blocks from here," he said, pointing down the street.

I remembered Danny staring at the caller ID on my phone. He must have gotten Daniel's number then.

"He says you lied to him about me. That I'm not what he expected at all," he said, looking at me accusingly now. "At least he knew I existed though. Imagine how I felt, hearing my only son's voice for the first time on the phone. And he's practically a man now."

"He's still a child," I snapped defensively. "And he still doesn't know you like I do. I've been protecting him from you."

Anger flared in Daniel's eyes, but he kept his voice calm. "We need to talk more, but it'll have to be later. It's a bit of a drive to Mountain Brook, and I've gotta get Danny to school." He turned and stomped to his car.

"I'm calling the school at eight, and if he's not there, I'll call the police!" I shouted at his back.

I got ready for work, barely noticing what clothes I put on myself. Between all the unsettling emotions surrounding Danny and Daniel, still not knowing where I was going to live, and the pounding headache behind my eyes, I couldn't care less how I looked.

I got myself to work, called the high school, confirmed that Danny was in fact there, and pulled myself together for a day of teaching and office hours. At one point, I got a text from Daniel asking if we could meet during my lunchbreak. I agreed to meet him at a restaurant close to campus. I put the phone down on my desk, closing my eyes and trying to calm myself.

I'd been in college when I dated Daniel, old enough to know better. How could I have been so deluded by him? How could I have believed he loved me? We had met at a place called The Booth in Tuscaloosa. While my friend Brianna played pool with one of his buddies, he asked if he could buy me a drink. A few hours of flirtation led to him walking me back to my dorm. Even then, on that very first walk, I knew it would never work out.

He was a frat boy who liked to party, whose father was paying for his education, who'd never worked for anything. My dad, a carpenter, paid as much as he could, but I still had to work and save and scrimp to get my education degree. His family was old money; mine was blue collar. I had a dream—to become a history teacher. He dreamed about his next female conquest. For reasons unknown to me, I let wishes override common sense. I thought he loved me and that maybe I could change him into a responsible person. His parents had thought otherwise.

When I got to the restaurant, Daniel was already there and flirting with the blonde waitress.

"I see you haven't changed much," I said as I sat at the table.

"Nor have you," he said. "Would you like some wine?"

"Absolutely not," I said in a voice that was way louder than I intended. I looked around to see if any other people had heard me and were staring. They had, and they were.

He laughed. "Still too young to drink?"

We gave our orders to the waitress, and I was still stewing as she walked away. To make matters worse, Daniel gave me that same exasperating smile I always saw on Danny's face when he thought he was right and I was wrong. In a way, it was like Daniel Sr. had never left.

I decided to get straight to the point. "I didn't come here to drink or chit-chat about old times. I want to know where you and my son were last night and why you didn't bring him home where he belongs."

"I told you. He doesn't want to see you."

"I don't care what he wants. I'll pick him up from school today. By the way, did you bond with him in one night? Did you tell him what a jerk you are? That you wanted to kill him before he was born?" My words tumbled out in a flurry of anxiety.

Instead of answering any of my questions, he said, "I want Danny to spend the summer with me."

"No!" I shrieked so loud that the people at the table across from us stared and shook their heads.

"The three of us need to sit down and talk about it," he said, so logically it made me want to throw my ice water over his head. "I have an apartment in Chicago. It would be a great experience for him, and I promise I'll have him back before school starts. Here, this is where I live." He handed me a piece of paper with an address. "You can look it up. It's near a lot of your favorite museums. Just think of how much fun he'll have."

Was he nuts? "You're a stranger to him. Why? Why would you do this to your own son? To me?"

"Isn't that what you did to me? Take him from me? Couldn't you have called me or my parents, let us know you kept the baby?"

"You're crazy as a drunk bedbug." Now my voice had taken on squeal level. "First of all, you didn't want him. Second, they hate me. Of course, they might've paid me off and made life easier for Danny and me. In case you haven't heard from your lofty existence at the top of the food chain, teachers barely make enough money for one person to survive on, much less two. I haven't had a raise in eight years. Don't you think I wanted your help?" I knew I was being irrational. I heard the words and knew he couldn't have done anything for me since I didn't tell him. That didn't stop me.

"So why the hell didn't you call me? Let me know? I'd have helped you. You know that."

"How could I have known that? Remember all the nights you spent at bars, flirting with women and coming home drunk? You remember who worked and paid the rent and bought groceries? Or the night you left? Did you ever call me to see if I had the abortion? If I was okay? Not even once!"

He stared at me, cold and hard, like I was his worst enemy. I guess I was.

I calmed a little. "I did everything: worked, cooked, cleaned, and by the way, did it pleasantly, because I loved you and wanted to give you a chance to grow up, but you ran out on me. And you know what? I survived. I didn't need you then, and Danny and I don't need you now. And you sure as hell don't deserve to have a relationship with my son."

"I'll help you now," he said.

"Yeah, I've heard that before."

He had the grace to look abashed. "Look, I can't change the past, but I want to be a part of Danny's life now. I can make it up to you both, if you let me." His voice changed from irritated to sincere.

"Too late. I don't need your help." Actually, a little help with Danny's expenses would be great, but not from him. Never.

"I know about you and Jason breaking up. You don't a have place of your own yet, and Danny's feeling mixed up and lost.

He needs a father in his life, why not his actual father? Maybe I'm what's best for him. I can buy him some new clothes, a car, send him to a good college."

I hesitated and considered what he was offering. Maybe he really had grown up and would actually be a positive presence in Danny's life. Before I'd gotten pregnant, Daniel had shown a little spunk when we moved to Chicago together to get away from his parents' tirades against me. Of course, he later abandoned me there. Surely, he wouldn't do that to his own son. But then I thought again of how he'd wanted to terminate the pregnancy. How could I trust him?

"So, you think you can just come down here, get Danny, take him up north somewhere, and then leave him alone to fend for himself? Do you think your mother and father will accept my son any better than they accepted me? I can answer that. No. They'll look down on my child and make him feel worthless and not good enough to live in their world. Just like they did me."

"They're dead," he said quickly.

I was speechless.

"Mother died about four years ago. Breast cancer. Father died in a car accident a little over a year ago."

"I'm sorry," I said and meant it. I hadn't liked the old goat or his witchy wife, but I had never wished them dead.

He gazed at me, as if trying to figure out what to say next, or maybe he just didn't believe I was sincere.

"I really am sorry," I said. "How's your sister doing? And her children?"

"They're fine. They live in Atlanta now."

We were actually having a cordial conversation. "So are you going to sell the Mountain Brook house?"

He paused before carefully saying, "Probably. It's mine now. It depends on what agreement we make about custody."

"Agreement? You don't have any custody rights. You abandoned him." So much for cordial conversation.

"I couldn't have. I didn't know he was alive."

"You would have known!" I shouted. "If you'd bothered to call and check on me! If you'd cared enough!" Our conversation was starting to circle around.

"If we can't discuss this like rational people, I'll sue you for custody," he said, crossing his arms. "I doubt the court will look kindly on you even if you are the mother. You kept my son from me, for years. Not because I was a bad person or raped or hit you; because I was immature. What kind of mother does that?"

While he was still saying those words, my mind wandered to a courtroom where a middle-aged, male judge said, "Shameful, madam, what you did to this man. I sentence you to hard labor. You must wash and iron Mr. Caldwell's shirts, cook and clean up after him, and I award full custody of the minor child to said Mr. Caldwell, and you may see this child only at the discretion of his father."

"Samantha?"

"Huh?"

"Where were you?"

I stared at him. Could I trust him? Did I have a choice? The what ifs had started to take shape in my brain when Daniel touched my hand.

"Are you okay?" he said.

I startled back to the present, jerked my hand away, and stared at him.

"Samantha, I promise you, I would never hurt my own son, and I won't hurt you either. It's just I've had a hard time too, and when I found out about Danny, it was like a gift to me."

"I want to believe you," I said but didn't mean it. I wanted him to go away and never to hear from him again.

"My wife and I didn't have any children. Spent thousands of dollars and several years on invitro, but it didn't work. And then she found someone else."

"Payback's hell, isn't it?" As soon as the words were out of my mouth, I wish I hadn't said them. The hurt on his face seemed real.

"I didn't cheat on you," he said. "I may have played around a little, but I didn't leave you for anyone else, and I've never loved anyone else."

"No wonder your wife left you." When had I become so mean? And I wasn't sorry.

He took my hands in his. "Look, I'm sorry. Let me make it up to you and Danny."

He sounded so sincere; I remembered that about him. "Sounded" being the key word.

"Okay, you win. We'll talk about it later. Come by about 5:30, and the three of us can sit down and talk about it."

I left work early, drove to the high school, and waited in the car line while every kid at the school came out and got into cars or on a bus. No Danny. When I got to Jason's house, he wasn't there. I called his cellphone. No answer. I called Daniel. No answer. While pacing from room to room with anger and anxiety building inside me, I texted both and told them to call me. An internet search on Daniel Caldwell turned up hundreds of names. I narrowed the search to his age and Mountain Brook, Alabama and nailed him. I had to pay thirty-nine dollars for the information, but it seemed worth it to find out.

His last address was listed as Chicago. Recently divorced. Okay, he hadn't lied about either of those things. No occupation. Still wasn't working, though. Every ten minutes, I hit his name on my phone and left threatening texts and voicemails. I was going to call the sheriff's office and have him arrested for kidnapping. I'd get a restraining order, and he'd never see his son again. If I ever got my hands on him, I'd strangle him with my bare hands. I called Danny's closest friends, and they said some guy in a Mercedes had picked him up from school.

Okay, he's with his dad. He's fine. He would be home any time now. But I couldn't just sit there and do nothing, so I took a walk, inspecting every yard and around every corner for any sign of my son, though I knew he wasn't anywhere near that neighborhood.

When I got back, Michael was leaning against his car, his butt pressed against the door, his head bowed, staring at his phone. He looked up as I pulled into the driveway, stuck his phone in his pocket, and opened my door. "Bad day, huh?"

"Ya think?"

"He'll bring Danny back," Michael said.

I stared at him. Who was he? How did he know stuff? "Stop it!" I screamed. "You got me bugged or something?"

"Of course not." He wasn't upset. The man had no emotions.

"Then how do you always know what's going on with me?"

"I don't know," he said. "I sense things and say it."

"Then quit saying it."

"I have to say what I feel. I want to help you get your aura back."

"It's not working. It's spooky and annoying. Go home, Michael. Leave me alone." I was aware that my words were loud and shrill and my body trembled, but I was powerless to stop it.

As Michael put his arm around me, I realized I was having a breakdown. The realization only made my panic increase. I began to cry helplessly in Jason's driveway, muttering nonsense and flailing my arms at Michael's attempts to calm me. He was like a damn persistent fly. If that wasn't bad enough, Carrie suddenly drove up, jumped out of her car, and raced toward us.

"Let's get her inside," she said to Michael as if I was a child.

I was. While I shrieked and roared about Daniel and how I was going to tie him to a tree and set it on fire, they led me inside and into the living room, where I collapsed into a fetal position on the couch. Carrie got a pillow and placed it under my head and covered me with a blanket. It occurred to me, though I couldn't express it, that she knew her way around Jason's house.

When finally I got tired of shouting, my words slowed and quieted. Maybe, just maybe, if I pretended to be asleep, they'd go away. While I lay there and pictured Daniel tied a huge fire ant hill with me slowly pouring honey over him, I heard Michael and Carrie introduce themselves to each other and start talking as if they were old friends. It was weird, like I was in another world, listening through a mist.

I wanted to get up and tell them to go home, but when I tried to push myself up, my arms were too weak, and I fell back on the couch. My mind fogged and wouldn't pull up words for me. I heard her ask him questions I'd never thought to ask. Everything had been about me, my world, my problems. Not once had I wondered how he was or how he went from disheveled wanderer to well-dressed man. He told her he'd been staying at his mother's house, driving her car, and looking for a job as a nurse. He'd been homeless, wandering from place to place, working at odd jobs, but had decided to go home and make peace with his mother.

She told him how she and Jason had been boyfriend and girlfriend in the sixth grade through high school, but had gone their separate ways, married other people, and a few years ago, after they both divorced, found each other again.

Their voices grew faint and distant and the fog closed in on me. It was dark, and I was alone, trying to find my way home. "Mom," I called out. "Dad, where are you? Help me. I can't find Danny. Help me, please?"

Someone touched me on the shoulder and said, "Samantha, are you okay?"

The dark and fog disappeared, and Jason's living room appeared. "Huh?"

"You're talking in your sleep."

Michael helped me sit up. I looked around and my senses slowly returned. He and Carrie were standing over me, gazing at me like concerned parents attending their sick child.

"Would you like some water or something to eat?" Carrie asked.

I shook my head. "What time is it?"

"About midnight," Michael said.

"Oh my God. Where's Danny?"

I stood up, my head dizzy and my knees wobbly. "Where's my phone, dammit? Where's my phone?"

Carrie found it and handed it to me. No messages. What to do? *Okay, Samantha, you know he would never hurt his own son. Danny's okay. He's okay.* I lay on the couch again. This time I lectured myself. *Get a grip, Samantha. You can control yourself. Figure out what you must do and do it. It's the not knowing that's stressful.* I tried one more time to reach Daniel and Danny. No answer.

I had to call Dad. He'd been a Marine; he always knew what to do. Except he'd probably been drinking. In the morning. I'd call him in the morning. He'd take care of everything. I should've called the sheriff's office, but I couldn't do it. Not yet. Getting the police involved was a slippery slope. Daniel had said that Danny was upset with me. If I blew things out of proportion now, I risked my chance of ever healing our relationship. Gradually, my mind slowed down and darkness closed in.

When I woke up, I was still on the couch, my phone was ringing, and rays of sunshine hit me in the eyes. I jerked the phone from between the cushions. It was Hayley. She said Jason was awake, in a room, and feeling much better. He'd asked to see me. I told her I'd go to the hospital after work. She also asked when I was planning to move out. She wanted to get some of her clothes and things and move them to her dad's house. In my turmoil, I'd forgotten about moving.

As I traversed from living room to the bathroom, I looked for signs of Michael and Carrie, but they'd left. She'd even cleaned the kitchen and had left coffee brewing. I looked at the clock. 7:30. I had thirty minutes to get showered, dressed, and to work. I decided to stay firm on my determination to not call the police on Daniel yet, even though I would have been in my rights to do so. I had agreed to let them spend time together after all, and I was still sure that Daniel wouldn't let Danny come to any harm. If I forced Danny to come back now, what if all I accomplished was to push him further away from me? The best I could do right now, was to wait for him to come back to me on his own.

I made it to work just in time for a meeting of the search committee, but I had trouble concentrating. During the meeting, I texted Dad and briefly told him what had happened and asked him to drive to Daniel's house and see if Danny was there, and if not then to go make sure he was at school, where he was supposed to be. He said not to worry; he'd take care of everything.

After the meeting and before my next class, I went into the bathroom, checked to be sure no one else was in there, locked the door, splashed water on my face, and stared into my own eyes. Then, I gave myself the same lecture Dad would've given me if he had been there, "Okay, Samantha, you're still young, healthy, and strong, and you can do anything you make up your mind to do. You will get through this day with courage, strength, and determination and without falling apart. You will be perceived as normal and intelligent by your students and peers." And for good measure I added what Mom would've said, "God, please bring my son back to me today."

By sheer force of will, I muddled through another day.

8

After work, I went to see Jason at the hospital. He was propped up on a pillow, looking pale under the bandage wrapped around his head. He tried to smile, and there was a faint wrinkle across the part of his forehead that was visible, a large bruise on the side of his face, and his eyes were dull and surrounded by dark circles. His hair was standing on end and was oddly endearing. His entire face was taut and appeared to have aged ten years since I'd last seen him. The room smelled like disinfectant.

I didn't know what to say, so I smiled too and said, "Hi," as cheerfully as I could, dragging a chair up to his bedside.

"Hi, yourself," he said. His mouth seemed to be having trouble forming his words, which obviously hurt his lips as they rolled out.

"It sure is good to see you," I said. "We were all so worried."

"I know."

There were a few minutes of awkward silence, and I could tell that like me, he was trying to think of something to say. Finally, he said, "I'm sorry."

"Me, too."

"I didn't mean to hurt you." He stopped to catch his breath.

Some motherly instinct in me wanted to touch his face and kiss the cuts and bruises, but I was afraid to, so I placed my hand on his arm. "I understand. I met Carrie. She's a good person, and I wish you well. I'm still at your place, but I put in an application for a rental house. Do you know when you'll get to go home?" Even to me, my words sounded fake and insincere, but I was determined to be high-minded. I had practiced all the way to the hospital.

He shook his head.

I was on the verge of tears, yet again. I'd never seen him so frail and defeated. "You stayed with me as long as you did because of Dad, didn't you?"

He nodded. "I didn't want to lose his friendship. Or yours. Or Danny's."

"You won't."

He smiled. Another awkward silence. He coughed and squirmed, trying to change position, then grimaced and sunk back onto the pillows. His fingers tap danced over the edges of the white sheet and blanket that lay across him; his eyes darted from me to the open door. It was as if he didn't know me, hadn't slept in the same bed with me for five years, had never told me he loved me.

Our planets had passed each other one night five years ago, and now they had drifted in other directions toward other solar systems. As the minutes ticked by, I felt like I'd fallen into a black hole and was devoid of every thought except how to escape. The urge to jump up, run out the door, and slam it behind me was almost irresistible. The need to know what'd happened to him and to us triumphed.

When the anxiety and silence grew to explosive levels, I blurted out, "What on earth were you doing at Turkey Creek that night?"

"Thinking," he said.

"Thinking?" My voice got thinner and louder.

"About you and me and Carrie."

"And how did you happen to fall?"

He reached for the water glass on the bedside table, took a sip, cleared his throat, and said with some difficulty, "I was climbing the rocks. You know how I have to do something when I'm worried or upset. That's why my yard looks so great." For a second, he sounded like my old Jason.

I laughed a little and nodded.

"Something hit me in the head. I don't remember anything else. The police didn't find my wallet anywhere. It had some cash, my driver's license, a couple of credit cards, and pictures of Hayley, my mom . . . and you."

Okay, now I was going to cry, but I absolutely could not, would not. After considerable sniffling, swallowing, and coughing, I squeaked out, "Allergies."

"Funny thing is," he said. "When I left that night, I saw this old silver Honda, I think it was a Honda, parked across the street from my house. And when I got to the top of the rocks, there it was again, sitting by the side of the road out at Turkey Creek."

"That is strange," I said. "Did you tell the deputy that?"

He paused. "Not yet. It was just a coincidence."

We talked a few more minutes about how he was feeling, how his yard and Pepper were, and, hopefully, how he'd be able to go home soon. As casually as I could, I asked if Carrie was planning to move in with him. He just shrugged.

When I returned to Jason's house, I called Daniel to check how Danny was doing but got no answer. They were ignoring me. I sighed in resignation as I realized I would have to wait until Dad updated me to know what was going on.

I looked around the house that was no longer my home. It was time to get busy. I dug out my winter clothes from the back of the closet and began stuffing them into cardboard boxes. Thankfully, instead of getting rid of the boxes when I'd moved in, I'd collapsed them and stored them in the basement. Just in case. Maybe I had been more aware of the inevitable than I'd admitted to myself.

After a few minutes of packing, a message popped up on my phone. It was the rental management people saying my application had been declined. No rental history for the past five years and not enough income. I swallowed down a sob, once again refusing to let myself cry. Somewhere, there was a place for Danny and me to live. A nice house, in a nice neighborhood, at a reasonable cost.

"I'll make it happen," I said out loud.

Just then, another message. A text from Dad. He had seen no sign of anyone at Daniel's house. My stomach dropped. I should have known Daniel wasn't to be trusted. What kind of mother was I? Where had he taken my little boy?

And then my phone rang, and Danny's name was on the caller ID.

"Danny!" I cried as I answered.

"Hi, Mom." His voice was light, unbothered, with that touch of exasperation that I'd become so accustomed to hearing ever since he became a teenager.,

I was torn between giddy relief and anger at him for being gone so long. "Where are you? I need you to come home now."

"I'm in Chicago with Dad."

I couldn't believe it. I was numb with shock.

"He said I should call you and let you know. He's awesome." The speed of his words picked up as excitement crept into his tone. "We're staying at his apartment downtown. Tomorrow we're going to a science museum and a planetarium."

As he kept talking about how great his dad and Chicago were, my mind shut down. His words were drowned out by the beating of my heart and the fuzz in my mind.

"Mom? Are you still there?"

I couldn't answer. My throat tightened and clogged. My baby, the one person I lived for, was gone. What chance did I have of ever getting him back? He was old enough to choose who he wanted to live with. What teenager would choose poverty and Parkville over wealth and Chicago? What did it matter now where I lived or what I did?

"Mom? Mom?"

I mumbled something as I hung up the phone and let it fall from my hand. I walked into Danny's room and lay on the bed. My hands caressed his pillow and the red plaid blanket he'd had since he was four and picked up the hamburger wrappers and dirty clothes as if they were religious icons. I closed my eyes, remembering. He was an infant, cooing, drooling, and smiling; a toddler, pulling up on the coffee table and getting into everything within his reach. On his first day of kindergarten, Mom and I stood at the door and watched him sit shyly at the table while the other children ran and played. He and Dad tossed a basketball into the hoop in their driveway. He hugged me when I took him to get his learner's permit.

No, no, no. He couldn't be gone. How dare Daniel do this to me? But maybe this was best for Danny. He wouldn't have to worry about having enough lunch money, and as a man, Daniel could explain things that Danny felt awkward asking me. I couldn't keep holding on, like my mom, to the puppet strings. But would Daniel be good to him? How would I know? He might let Danny stay out late with abhorrent friends and take drugs and drink and not go to school or do his homework. And my son would love him for it. Until it was too late.

I lay there for the longest time, alternately feeling sorry for myself and trying to build myself up. Put myself down; pull myself up. I was young with a future; I was at the end of my life. How could I go on not knowing what was happening to my son? What did I have to live for?

9

I was awakened by a pounding on the front door. Was it morning? No, it was dark outside. With Danny's blanket pulled up under my chin, I inhaled the smell of the cheap cologne he used to impress girls, sat up in his bed, and looked around. Mom and Dad used to listen to a song by Frank Sinatra about being bothered and bewildered, or something like that, and that's how I felt. I couldn't get my bearings; sorrow and self-rejection resurfaced in my brain. I willed whoever it was to quit beating the door and go away and leave me alone. No such luck. I picked up one of my son's bats and tottered to the door like a scared old lady.

"Who is it?" I yelled.

"It's Dad. Open up."

When I opened the door, he rushed in and hugged me. "Are you okay?"

Yep, just like Ol' Blue Eyes, I was bewildered. "Why wouldn't I be?"

"Your mom and your son have been trying to call you. I can't believe you didn't answer. Worrying us both like that." He motioned toward the car. Mom slammed the passenger-side door and strode up the sidewalk toward me. It was her angry walk.

"I'm sorry," I said. "I guess I fell asleep and left my phone in the other room."

I was going to tell them to come in, but I didn't have to. Dad pushed me aside as they marched into the living room and sat down. Mom picked up my phone from the couch and handed it to me. "You really should keep this on you at all times," she said.

"Why're y'all here?" I mumbled, still clutching the blanket as I sat in the overstuffed chair opposite them.

"Danny called us. He was worried about you," Mom said.

My heart thawed slightly; he was worried about me. "Did he tell you where he is?" I asked.

"Yes, and that's no reason not to talk to him," Dad said abruptly. "He can't help it if Daniel carted him off to Chicago, of all places."

"I don't want to be rude, but will y'all go home if I promise to call him?"

"No," Dad answered. "We're taking you with us."

"Oh no, you're not." Hanging onto the blanket, I stood up and started pacing. "I need some alone time. To think."

"For Pete's sake," Mom said, "Get your clothes. You're going home with us."

"No." I almost shouted it. I'd done a lot of that this past week. "Now go home."

"Well," Mom huffed. "Of all the ungrateful . . . Come on, Craig, let's go home."

"Not without my daughter."

"I'm going to bed." I left them there, went into the bedroom, and lay down.

They followed me. "Go home," I repeated firmly.

At that minute, my phone rang. It was Michael. There was no God, no justice, no peace of mind anywhere in the world. I ignored my parents, who stood in the doorway of my bedroom, arms folded, waiting for me to obey them.

Lying on my back, wrapped in my son's cologne-laden blanket, I said, "Hello, Michael."

"Hang in there. Your aura's beginning to glow just a tiny bit."

"Are you crazy?" I snapped. "Oh, yes, I forgot. We've already established that." I waited for him to answer. He didn't.

"Is that all the advice you have for me tonight? I'm kind of busy right now."

A pause, as if Michael was trying to locate in his brain the right sermon, and then he said, "Just remember that everything is working out the way it's supposed to. You and Danny will be fine. Think loving and positive thoughts, even for those who provoke or anger you or treat you badly."

I hung up on him. "Wrong number," I said to my parents. They looked less than believing.

Before they could respond, the phone rang again. It was Greg.

"Haven't heard back from you yet," he said. "Did you decide if you're coming to see me or not?"

There was a God, He loved me, and He was giving me a ready-made plan. "Yes," I said. "This weekend. I'll let you know when to pick me up at O'Hare." Michael was right. Danny and I were going to be fine.

I turned the bedside lamp off and pulled the covers over my head as I began worrying about how I was going to pay for the trip. On my overcrowded credit card, of course. Visions of my new house were getting ever smaller and less extravagant.

My parents finally left, Mom mumbling and fussing as they walked out and Dad slamming the door. When I heard their car drive away, I got out of bed and changed into the "Hairy Otter" t-shirt I'd bought when Jason, Danny, Hayley, and I had gone to the aquarium in Atlanta. Before Jason and I knew it would never work, when we were all still friends. I looked out the front window to be sure Mom and Dad had really gone, and what I saw instead was an older-model, silver car parked across the street. Jason's description of the car at Turkey Creek flashed through my mind, though I had forgotten it in the chaos of finding out Danny was in Chicago. I couldn't tell if there was anyone in it or not.

I should've listened to Mom and Dad and gone with them, but of course, I was being silly. There were lots of old silver cars in the world. Or maybe I wasn't. Whoever owned it could've been looking for Jason. It was too late to call him now. It was just a car—an ordinary automobile parked on the street. What did it have to do with me? Nothing. So why was I scared? With

Danny's blanket around me and his baseball bat leaning against the headboard, I got into bed.

I didn't trust myself to keep it together on the phone, so instead of calling Danny, I sent him a text to tell him I was sorry for not answering before. I told him to be safe and that I loved him. I decided not to tell him or Daniel that I was coming to Chicago. In my mind, I planned out a surprise attack. Once I found them, I would call the police and have Daniel arrested on the spot.

The next afternoon, I went to see Jason. It had been a week since I'd sat on the couch in his living room, eating a ham sandwich and channel surfing, thinking everything was okay. My last few minutes of a peaceful, if troubled, existence. At that time, I couldn't have imagined that a week later I'd be in a hospital room, talking politely to Jason as if he were a distant cousin.

We dispensed with the pleasantries and lied about things being fine. Before I knew it, I was blurting out, "Daniel kidnapped Danny and took him to Chicago."

Jason jerked the covers back, slung one leg over the edge, and tried to start toward the door. "I'm gonna kill that son of a bitch!" Beeps and connected wires interrupted his process, aided by the alarmed nurses who came to the door and pushed him ungently back into the bed. He muttered and cursed, but nothing he did stopped them from prodding, poking, and checking his connections.

I couldn't believe how calm I was as I explained, "Danny's excited about it. He called me last night, and he's fine."

Jason growled and turned his stony-faced expression toward me and said, "You're okay with that?"

"Of course not," I said.

I had spent the morning researching parental kidnapping, and I was fairly certain Daniel had committed a felony by taking Danny out of state. It didn't matter that Danny went willingly. I was going to get my son back, and I was going to handle it myself.

"I'm handling it. We're going to be fine. You just need to worry about getting better." Once we were alone again and Jason had calmed down, I told him about seeing the old silver Honda parked near his house.

He rubbed a hand over his face. "Probably a coincidence," he said, grimacing and not meeting my eyes.

"Are you in some kind of trouble?"

"No." He was lying. His eyes darted around the room. One of the things I'd always loved about Jason was his dedication to the truth. He said what he thought, no matter who it hurt. Tactfulness wasn't his forte. Neither was lying.

"What's going on?" I asked. "And this time, don't lie to me."

He turned and looked me in the eyes with a carefully arranged expression. "I don't know." Another lie.

"What've you done? Are you sleeping with some guy's wife?" I put my hand to my mouth and gasped. "Carrie's married?"

"Of course not," he snapped.

"Then what in the world's going on with you?"

"Look, I can't talk about this now."

"You mean you *won't* talk about it? Have you told the police about the car?"

"Leave it alone, Samantha."

I could tell he was on the verge of shutting down. If he were at home, he'd be running out the backdoor and heading for the lawnmower.

My mind started searching for the right thing to say, something that would sound neutral but get him to tell me what I wanted to know. Nothing. So, I just asked, "So am I safe there? Is that why you're in such a hurry for me to move out?"

He avoided my eyes again. "Have you found a place yet?"

"No, but I promise I'll be out next week," I huffed angrily. "Stop trying to distract me. I want to know right now what you've gotten yourself into. Does my dad know about it?"

He had that look of guilt on his face, like a little boy who has his hand in the cookie jar but swears it's not in there. "No, he doesn't, and that's all I'm going to say about it."

He was exasperating; I couldn't talk to him anymore. I picked up my purse and walked out the door without saying goodbye.

Talk about burning bridges. In one week, I'd alienated myself from Mom and Dad, Jason was in some kind of trouble that I couldn't help him with, I'd lost my home, and, worst of all, Danny was staying with his dad. Almost audibly, I asked myself the question no one should ever ask. "What else could go wrong?"

10

When I walked out of the hospital, I noticed that the afternoon had turned from warm and sunny to gloomy with dark, ominous-looking clouds churning in the western sky. I remembered the line from *Young Frankenstein* that my friends and I had loved when we were young: "Could be worse; could be raining." Of course it was going to storm. I'd found a great parking space on the other side of the parking lot under one of those decorative trees, and the front half of my car had been in the shade, which meant I could've gotten into my car without suffocating or getting my butt burned. In the south that was the equivalent of winning the Kentucky Derby. But now I'd have to run for it to beat the rain.

I didn't make it. I was almost there when lightning and thunder struck at the same time. Without thought, my body jerked into a sprint and kept going until I reached my car. Just as I was about to grasp the door handle, the rain started—a few drops and then it came down on me like God had emptied a bucket of water right on my head. I stood beside my car, soaking wet and fumbling through my purse for my keys. *Why me, God? Why me?*

That was when I noticed the car parked next to mine. It was an old, silver Honda Civic with a man inside, and from what I could see through the driving rain, he was big. His head almost hit the roof and he filled up the driver's side of the car. He was looking down as if talking on a phone, so I couldn't see his face. I didn't hang around to make eye contact. My legs went rubbery, my heart pumped harder, and before I had a thought, I was in the car and driving out of the parking lot as fast as I could. A few seconds later, the Civic was about two car lengths behind me.

I turned left onto the road in front of the hospital. The Civic turned left and was right behind me. *Okay, Samantha, keep calm. Think.* I turned right at the main road. It turned right. What should I do? I couldn't go home, and I couldn't lead him to Mom and Dad's. I turned onto the highway. With its frenetic bumper-to-bumper traffic, I'd surely lose him. No such luck. My chest tightened, my head ached, and every nerve in my body seemed to twitch. I looked in my rearview and side mirrors. Where was he? All those car lights coming toward me lit the darkness, smudged together in the rain, and blurred my vision. I turned into a Target parking lot. There he was, right on my bumper. Now what? I'd have to go in. This time I chose a space close to the door. He found one across from me. A young, strong-looking guy and a woman were walking toward the store entrance, huddled together under a small black umbrella. What could I lose? I was already soaked. I jumped out of my car and started walking right beside them.

The woman looked around and said, "You okay, lady?"

Water oozed from my hair down my face, into my eyes, and into my mouth when I said, "I think there's a man following me." I realized immediately how ridiculous I sounded.

She picked up her pace and said, "Really?" She was humoring me. Clearly, she also thought it ridiculous.

I kept pace with them. We reached the entrance to Target, went in, and they scurried off in the opposite direction, not even stopping to get a basket. I stood beside a busy checkout, wiped at my face, unsuccessfully trying to stop the water dripping from my hair into my face.

I pulled my phone from my drenched purse and called Jason. "That damned Civic followed me. Now I'm standing in Target, soaking wet, and he's outside and I'm scared and next time I see you I'm going to strangle you with my bare hands."

I tried to keep my shaky voice from yelling or attracting attention. Too late. I was blocking the aisle. One old lady said, "Excuse me, please." Two teenaged girls pushed me as they went around me, and I moved to a cash register with no cashier.

"I'm fixing to hunt down a policeman right now, and I don't care how much trouble you get into." I took a few deep breaths then said, "I'm afraid to go home. I'm stuck here."

Finally, he said, "Listen, Samantha, and do exactly what I tell you. Go to the candy aisle and wait there."

"For what?"

Jason hung up. I wanted to go back to that hospital, jerk him out of his bed, and punch him in his swollen, bruised face. Okay, no. There was a perfectly logical explanation for the stupid Civic. Calm. I could remain calm. While I waited for who knew what, I walked to the candy aisle and started picking up various pieces of chocolate. Reese's, yes. Hershey's, yes. Godiva, of God yes. I had about six bags of chocolate in my hands and had opened one and was eating a Reese's Cup when Carrie found me.

"Put it all back," she said, jerking the candy out of my hands.

I managed to keep one clutched to my chest. "Not this one," I mumbled through the chocolate and peanut butter as I pointed to my mouth.

"We don't have time for the checkout."

"But I have to pay for it."

"Oh, all right. We can use it, anyway."

I grabbed all the candy back from the shelf and headed for the cash registers.

"This is what we're going to do," Carrie whispered as we walked. "I'm going to distract the guy in the Civic and you drive as fast as you can to my house. I'm going to text you my address. It's in Gardendale." Take the interstate. Do NOT get on the back roads. Understand?"

"Yes, but . . ."

"I'll explain later."

While I was paying for the much-needed chocolate, I noticed Carrie's clothes. I'd only ever seen her in jeans and a t-shirt, but right then she had on a short, tight black skirt and a white knit blouse with decorative pearl buttons down the front. Those buttons looked like they'd pop open if she breathed too hard, and her breasts would fly right out. When we walked outside, it was still raining. With an umbrella positioned over her head, she strutted toward the Civic. I followed, acting like I didn't know who she was. She stopped in front of the silver car and let one of the bags of candy spill on the ground. Then she backed up a bit, bent over, and started picking up scattered pieces of chocolate, her butt in the air and black panties showing.

I still couldn't see the details of the guy's face, but there was no doubt where his attention was directed at that moment. It was a shame I couldn't hang around to see what happened next, but self-preservation was high on my list of things to do. I jumped in my car, backed out, hit the gas pedal, and as fast as I could maneuver in the rain and crowded parking lot, I got out of there and headed for Gardendale.

Carrie's house was on a corner lot; a brick ranch with a two-car garage and a white vinyl fence around the backyard. I pulled into the driveway behind an old red Mustang and waited. Finally, headlights shone behind me. Carrie and I got out of our cars at the same time and ran for her front porch; she didn't offer to share her umbrella. She had her keys in hand, quickly opened the door, and we stepped inside. I stood there, dripping on the entrance rug, while she ran to get me a towel. It was a traditional 1970s house with a living room/dining room combination, decorated with mahogany furniture, cream-colored china, and several potted plants. It didn't fit my image of Carrie at all.

She came back wearing sweatpants and a t-shirt, and she handed me a towel and a fluffy, wine-colored housecoat. "You can change in there if you want to." She pointed to a door down the hall on the right.

It was definitely a boy's room, with solid, no-frills furniture. The boy was either grown, lived somewhere else, or was the most incredibly neat boy I'd ever heard of. In that bedroom, I felt safe, dry, warm, and almost giddy with momentary relief from fear.

Wearing the housecoat and carrying my wet clothes wrapped in the towel, I went in search of Carrie. On the hallway walls were portraits of an older couple, several children of various ages, and one of a younger Carrie. I walked into a lived-in looking den and heard a dog scratching at the backdoor to come inside. Carrie showed up then and opened the door, and an adorable Cavalier King Charles Spaniel bounded inside and into her arms. She cooed and petted, and he licked her in the face.

"He's so cute," I said. "What's his name?"

"Charlie. You know, King Charles?" She put him down and he immediately came to me for more petting. With one arm hanging onto the wet clothes, I bent over and patted his head.

"You scared to go home?" She took my clothes, went into the kitchen, and put them in the dryer that was behind louvered doors.

"No," I lied, following her.

It was awkward, trying to talk to my replacement, but she had rescued me. From what, I wasn't sure. I'd resented and tried to dislike her for so long that it was difficult for me to admit that I appreciated her going out in a storm to help me. How in the world could I tell her that? It would be like confessing to a major sin or eating the last chocolate. On the other hand, if I just said it outright, it would lessen tensions and we could get down to talking about what was wrong with Jason and why that guy was following me.

"Thanks for rescuing me," I said. It didn't hurt nearly as bad as I thought.

She shrugged it off, opened the refrigerator door, and pulled out a rotisserie chicken still in its bag. "You hungry?"

"Starved." I realized that it was true. For the first time since the fateful ham sandwich, I was hungry.

She poured a glass of red wine for both of us and sliced chicken, put it on a plate, and stuck it in the microwave. In a few seconds, she put the plate and a couple of Styrofoam containers of potato salad and coleslaw in front of me. I ate. She watched with an unreadable face, but I noticed that she drank her wine very quickly.

"Aren't you hungry?" I finally asked.

"No, I was eating when Jason called."

"So, of course, you just ran out and did what he told you," I said bitterly. But I didn't want her not to answer my next question, so I rushed on. "Speaking of Jason, what's going on with him? And why's that guy following me?"

"All he told me was that he'd made Venom Gallagher mad." She said it as if it would make sense to me.

I stared at her, trying to figure out what she was talking about. "Venom?"

She turned her glass up, let the last drops of wine sprinkle into her mouth, and poured another glass of wine. "You don't know Venom?" She looked somewhat disbelieving. "Asshole. He graduated with Jason and me."

"So, Jason did something to make this guy mad? Isn't that a bit juvenile? What's Venom going to do?"

"Hurt you." She paused, as if trying to think of what to say next. "Or your son."

"Why?"

She stared at me for a while, mirroring my disbelief. "You really are naïve, aren't you?"

"What're you talking about?"

"You don't even know what your own son does, do you?" She emptied that glass of wine and poured another one, for her and me.

Now I was getting mad. Oh yeah, resentment, come back to mama. "Of course I know what my son does. What kind of mother do you think I am?" I quit cutting bites of chicken and lowered the knife.

"Like the *Leave it to Beaver* mom."

"What?" I could feel the adrenaline rush, my eyes narrow, and my hand curl into a fist. She was the one in danger now.

"You need to get a grip on reality, and when you do, have a long talk with your son. Ask him if he's ever bought drugs."

I felt a hot rush of anger, but behind it, icy cold. I remembered the beer and weed just a couple of days ago, and now he was in Chicago. Maybe I didn't know my son as well as I thought I did. A stab of pain hit my stomach and my body shook. My Danny, my baby, bought drugs? And I didn't notice? Where did he get the money? Dear God, what kind of mother was I? What now? No, it couldn't have been Danny. It was that other kid's fault. He bought the weed. He persuaded my son to . . .

"Weed, for instance. You do know what that is, don't you?" Her words were pure, scathing sarcasm.

I pointed the knife in my hand towards her. "I'm smarter than I look."

"And drunker than you think."

I opened my mouth and almost screamed the curse words in my head. What was wrong with me? I almost never cursed, but lately, profane words seemed to trip off my tongue. Maybe I didn't know myself all that well either.

Carrie rolled her eyes and said, "Don't be stupid, Saman-tha. You know where the guest room is. I've had a long day. I'm going to bed." She took the last of the wine with her and shut the door behind her.

No, I wasn't drunk. Not again. Tipsy, maybe, but I did un-derstand that I couldn't drive. I walked back to the bedroom I had changed clothes in and let the information Carrie had just divulged sink in. According to her, Jason was mixed up in something that involved this guy called Venom, drugs, and Danny. Regardless of whether she was telling the truth or not, I had to get to my baby now more than ever.

11

I closed my eyes, clutched the armrests, and prayed that the pilot and co-pilot were on friendly terms, hadn't had fights with their wives the night before, had gotten plenty of sleep, and didn't get drunk. Flying is never easy for me, especially when the plane zooms down the runway, disconnects from the earth, leaves my stomach on the ground, and, even more especially, when it does so on a stormy day. And that day, my stomach was already churning and burning.

I was on my way to Chicago. Jason had left the hospital that morning and had gone to Carrie's house for a while. She'd be the one adjusting his pillow and covers, putting a cold cloth on his head, and getting his medicine and water for him. She'd be the one who had to nag him and tell him he absolutely couldn't cut the grass, work on the car, or go back to work. She'd be the one he'd hold at night and thank for being there for him. I could've been. Should've been. Would never be again.

As the plane leveled, I opened my eyes and relaxed. The space between heaven and earth is always the best part of any flight, but that day, with the dark clouds below and the sunshine above, it was a tonic for my spirit, a fragment of tranquility in my troubled existence.

Michael had driven me to Atlanta to catch a non-stop to Chicago. He had listened while I told him about my fear of Venom, resentment of Carrie, and anger at Jason and Daniel. He'd paid attention as if he cared, but that time he'd offered no words of wisdom. On the drive, he had been unusually quiet. It had occurred to me then that he was always the sympathetic one, and I was always the complainer and whiner. I knew almost nothing about him. It had sparked me to ask him about himself.

"So, have you found a job yet?" I'd asked.

"Not yet." He sounded distracted.

"Are you still staying at your mother's?"

"Yes."

Talk about reticent. "What's she like?"

Instead of answering, he'd asked a question. "What're your plans for the summer?"

In that minute, the whole conversation had reverted back to me. That's when I told him that every summer since I was a teenager, Dad had let me work with him installing cabinets. It not only helped me earn extra money, but it was a relief to be able to do physical work and not have to worry about grading papers or preparing lessons.

When we parted at the airport, he'd said, "Hang in there. It will get better."

Only now, with nothing else to do but think, did it occur to me to wonder why he had been so quiet. Maybe I had complained once too often, or maybe he was finished with his mission with me. Oddly, I hoped he would stay in touch.

Gliding through the sky with the sunshine above me, it was easy to believe that it would get better. Venom would not hurt Danny. If he tried anything . . . I was the daughter of a Marine. Dad had me shooting at cans by the time I started school and had taught me to defend myself and where to kick a man to disable him. Why was I afraid of a slime-ball like Venom? That's when I knew that I'd take Venom down if I had to, and I knew Dad would help.

Then we started our descent through the dark clouds into the cold, rain, and fog of a spring day in Chicago. About an hour later, I was standing outside O'Hare in the cold drizzle and wind, clutching my dusty pink cardigan around me and gazing into a sea of lights and automobiles as I inhaled the smell of exhaust fumes. The cold, wet wind blew frizzy hair into my face, and I shoved it impatiently back behind my ears. Cabs and rideshares stopped quickly, picked up or let out passengers, and departed abruptly. I wished I'd asked Greg what kind of car he drove, as if that would help. I wouldn't recognize a Mercedes from a Buick, but I could've at least known what color to look for.

Finally, a shiny, maroon-colored car pulled up beside me. Greg got out and walked around it as slowly as if it were a clear, sunshiny day and there wasn't a line of impatient drivers behind him. He came up to me, smiling, his arms outstretched, and gave me a bear hug.

When he let go, he pushed me back and held me at arms' length and said, "Hi," as if we'd just seen each other the day before yesterday.

"Hi, yourself," I said, as I pushed my hair back and took a good look at him. He was mostly unchanged. Same dark hair, a little paunchier in the middle and rounder in the face, maybe, but he'd been a little on the thin side anyway so it looked good on him.

He put my suitcase in the trunk, and soon we were heading out of the airport.

"How was your flight?" he asked as we turned merged into the traffic.

I'm not an easy car rider. I hung onto the strap at the top of the window, pressed the imaginary brake as hard as I could, and prayed.

He glanced at me and smiled. "You okay?"

"I'm fine," I said in a terrified squeak.

"Close your eyes," he said. "I'll tell you when you can open them."

I tried, but I couldn't. We drove several minutes without any conversation. We hadn't seen each other in fifteen years, but in those years, we'd talked on the phone, emailed, and Facebooked; we were best buds, could always console and encourage each other. But face-to-face? No words. Nothing.

My mind darted between the speeding cars around us, so close I could stick my hand out and touch them, and anxious visions of Danny buying drugs and wondering what he'd do when he saw me. Would he push me away or be glad to see me?

I could barely manage to breathe. This wasn't the reunion with Greg that I'd imagined.

"You sure you're okay?" Greg asked.

"Uh huh," was all I could say.

He laughed. It was his nervous laugh. I'd seen and heard it lots of times when his ex-wife had criticized him or laughed at some mishap of his. At that time, he'd been a bit accident-prone. It hadn't occurred to me that seeing me again might make Greg anxious. Surely, he didn't think of me as . . . no, he knew we were just friends.

After a while, though still congested, the traffic flowed into a fast-paced, but steady rhythm. I loosened my grip on the strap a bit, took a deep breath, and was able to talk. But what to say? Awkward silence. Greg focused on the road. I wanted to tell him not to expect too much from me during this visit and to go straight to Daniel's apartment. I didn't. I did tell him that his long-ago friend, Daniel, had kidnapped Danny and taken him to Chicago. He didn't seem surprised.

He kept looking straight ahead and said, "I'm sorry, Samantha, but you know he won't hurt him."

"He has no right to my son. And he shouldn't have abandoned us in the first place."

"You should've told him."

"What? You too, Brute?"

"I'm not saying he did the right thing, but maybe you should cut him some slack."

"I want to go to Daniel's apartment right now. I have his address right here." I pulled out the piece of paper Daniel had given me just four days earlier.

"It's late; we can go tomorrow."

"Tonight."

"That the only reason you came?"

I'd never felt so much fury toward Greg as I did at that minute. It clutched my stomach and tightened my throat, and I thought I might open the door and jump out into the angry, rushing traffic. "Yes, and I want to see my son right now."

"For some stupid reason, I thought you might've wanted to see me."

"Of course, I wanted to see you." It was the truth, but it wasn't something I could even contemplate at that time.

"I can tell." Sarcasm oozed from Greg's words. "We'll go tomorrow."

I didn't remember him ever being such a jerk. "Give me one good reason we can't go now."

"For one thing, you're soaking wet, and another, you should let him know you're coming. Why don't you call him before we barge in?"

Barge in? The man had my son, and Greg didn't want to barge in? I couldn't argue any more. It wouldn't do any good. The man was as stubborn as a mule. Probably why Anna left him. Another awkward silence. Defeated, I sunk into the seat and watched buildings and lights float by against the night sky, visualizing what I'd say to Daniel and Danny when I saw them.

I'd forgotten how huge downtown Chicago was. It could've swallowed up all of Alabama's major cities and still have room for dessert. The next stop would be Valparaiso in Northwest Indiana. About an hour's drive from where I wanted to be. When we drove into Greg's neighborhood, the past came alive. It looked pretty much the same as the last time I'd seen it. It seemed strange to me that while my life had changed from day to day, sometimes minute to minute, Greg had lived in the same neighborhood in the same house and still had the same job as a pharmacist at the local drugstore for the past fifteen years.

When he carried my suitcase to my room for the night— the room that still had the bunkbeds and Star Wars comforters where his small children had slept—I melted a little, but not much. He threw my suitcase on the top bunk and went silently into the kitchen. We'd seemed so close, so connected on the phone. What happened? Maybe it was true that you can't go back home. But this was never home. The truth was that Greg was a stranger to me now. What had I thought that we would be? What had he thought that we would be?

With no idea of what to say or do, I trudged into the kitchen and sat in stony silence at the table. While he made coffee, I tapped my fingernails against the waiting blue mug until he filled it with the caffeine that was sure to keep me awake all night. I didn't care. He pushed the sugar bowl and half-and-half toward me, slid into the chair opposite me, and stirred his coffee. And stirred and stirred. The spoon clanked and the coffee splashed, its warm fragrance calming my nerves a bit. Not much, but a tiny bit. Was I being irrational?

"I've talked to Daniel," he said calmly. "In fact, we've become friends again. We go to bars, Cubs games, that sort of thing."

No, I was not being irrational. It was my turn to stir and splash. I took a deep breath and willed myself to speak in a civilized tone. "Why didn't you tell me?"

"I don't know."

Yep, he was definitely at the top of my mad list. "You knew, didn't you?" Okay, civility gone; tirade rushing in. "You knew he was going to Parkville to get my son? Why didn't you tell me?"

"I didn't know he'd take Danny. I thought he just wanted to see him."

I tried not to yell. My mind wanted to have an intelligent, rational discussion about this, but my emotions overrode my brain. "I'm not believing this." I began searching the house. "Where the hell's my purse?"

"Samantha," Greg said, following me. "Calm down. Let me explain."

"I'm leaving. I'll get a room somewhere for tonight. I'd rather wait there than stay another minute with a man who betrayed me. You were the one person I thought I could trust. How could you?"

He stopped. "Look, I'm sorry. I honestly didn't know he'd take Danny. Do you think for one minute I'd let him do that and not tell you?"

I stopped, turned toward him, and said in as hateful a voice as I'd ever said anything, "Yes."

"I didn't know, honestly," he said.

"How many times have you gotten off the phone with me and called and reported it to Daniel? Were you the one who gave him my number? My address?"

"It wasn't like that. Please, let's sit down and I'll explain." He ran a hand through his hair. "You can't go out in the middle of the night. It's not safe."

Another deep breath. I was able to quit pacing, but my heart still raced, and my insides still trembled. I sat at the table and stirred my coffee, yet again.

Greg sat beside me and tried to place his hand on top of mine. "He told me he was going to Parkville to talk to you. That's all. He never mentioned taking Danny. I didn't even know about that until you told me."

I jerked my hand away. "You sure as hell weren't surprised when I told you."

"No, I wasn't." He paused, probably trying to figure out his next lie. "Ever since he found out he has a son, he's been obsessed with seeing Danny and spending time with him. Things haven't been going so great for him since his parents died. He's lost most of the money they left him on one bad investment after the other. His wife left him, said she wanted someone who could give her a baby. He's been in rehab but can't quit drinking. He's pretty much alone. He needed a friend, but he didn't want anyone to know how bad off he was."

"I can be sympathetic to all that, but Danny is not some tool for Daniel to use to make himself feel better. He is my child. First thing in the morning, I want to go get my son. I'll find a room somewhere to stay tomorrow night, but I won't stay here a second night, and I sure as hell won't stay at Daniel's."

I couldn't sleep that night. Occasionally I dozed off, but mostly I lay there with images of Daniel and his messed-up life in my head. He and I had once been so carefree, and so had Greg and Anna. Yet here we were, our lives in shambles. Except for Anna. Never again would I blame her for leaving that no-good traitor.

12

The next morning, I was a mess. My eyes were red and swollen from lack of sleep, my hair frizzed around my head, and my face was splotched. When I walked into the kitchen, still wearing my baggy red pajamas, Greg was frying bacon and had eggs ready to scramble. For a few minutes, we didn't say anything.

He set the finished product on a plate in front of me and poured some orange juice. "I'm sorry I didn't tell you about talking to Daniel," he said.

"You should be." I paused and added, "Why didn't you at least warn me?"

He set his plate and orange juice on the table and sat down opposite me. "I should have. You know I'd never intentionally hurt you. I love you."

I was hungry but couldn't eat. I took a sip of juice. It burned my stomach. "I could've loved you, too. In a way I did. I used to wonder how things could have been different."

"No, I mean I really love you. I loved you fifteen years ago, and I've never stopped."

I took one bite of eggs and swallowed. It felt like a rock hit my stomach. "Then you don't know anything about love." I pushed my plate away and tried to sip my coffee. It wouldn't go down either.

He got up, jerked the dishes from the table, and dropped them into the sink. "So shoot me. I befriended a guy who needed it."

"Why didn't you tell me?" I tried to be calm, to understand.

"Would you have understood? No, you'd have slammed the phone down and never talked to me again."

"You don't know that." But he was right. I probably would have.

"I needed to talk to you, didn't want to lose you. I guess somehow, I figured one day we'd get together. I never told Daniel I still talked to you." He was pleading for understanding.

I couldn't give it to him.

"We should call Daniel and let him know we're coming." His words were quiet, emotionless, as if he were accepting defeat.

But I knew better. Greg didn't give up easily. He'd strike again. "I loved you, Greg, like the friend you were and, who knows, maybe we could've turned it into something more. I used to wonder and dream about it. But not now, never again. It's not that you befriended Daniel when he needed it. I get that. It's that you didn't trust me enough to tell me."

"I made a serious mistake. I know that. Haven't you ever done something you regretted for the rest of your life? Wouldn't you want forgiveness and another chance?"

I wanted to tell him that this weekend was one of those mistakes I'd always regret, but I didn't. Going around and around arguing about this wouldn't get my son back. I didn't answer him.

After considerable pleading and threatening to walk to Chicago or steal his car and drive, Greg relented to go to Daniel's apartment. We couldn't get either of them on the phone, and we couldn't get into his fancy apartment building, so we waited in the coffee shop across the street for them to return.

It was about three o'clock before I saw him. My son. Across the street. I jumped up and ran. Horns blew. Tires screeched. Drivers stuck their heads out windows and cursed. I darted through traffic and around cars and reached Danny just as they got to the door of the building.

As if he were in a faraway land, I heard Daniel say, "What the hell?"

But I focused on only one thing. I grabbed my son from behind, jerked him around, and hugged him. I cried and told him I loved him, and I couldn't let go. Passersby probably thought I hadn't seen him since he was a baby.

"Mom." Danny tried to pull away from me. "Mom, let go."

He wasn't glad to see me. He didn't hug me or thank me for rescuing him. He was trying to get away from me.

Greg caught up with us and put his arm around my shoulders. "For Pete's sake, Samantha, give him breathing room."

I let go. Daniel led us to his apartment in the sky and of-fered us something to drink. The apartment was nice, but not as fancy as I thought it would be. I guess I'd expected gold-plat-ed faucets or something like that.

We sat in wrought iron chairs on his balcony overlooking Lake Michigan.

It was a beautiful day with a few high white clouds and lots of sunshine, if a bit cold and breezy. Danny couldn't quit talking about the planetarium and science museum and how much he loved Millennium Park and the Art Institute. He knew how much I liked art, and he wanted to show me. "Please, Mom, let me stay."

When he finally took a breath, I said, "I came to take you home, and I won't leave without you."

Danny looked at me, then at his dad, then back at me. Not with those sweet pleading eyes like when he was little and want-ed something. They were his dad's eyes when he was angry in-side but didn't want to talk about it.

"You're going home," I said firmly. "Tomorrow."

Daniel moved his chair closer to mine. "We need to talk."

"Oh really?" I snapped. "I guess that would explain why you never answered your damn phone. I've been out of my mind with worry!"

Greg said to Danny, "Let's go inside."

When we were alone, Daniel said, "Okay. I should've called you back. But you never called me back either. So we're even. What's your next gripe?"

My blood boiled at the word "gripe" being used to describe the absolute hell I had been through in the past week. "We're not even. You took my son away from me—"

"*Our* son," he interrupted.

"I'm the one who wanted him—always wanted him. I'm the one who raised him, and I'm the only one with custody. I don't know what kind of person you are anymore. I can't trust you or know that he's safe with you."

"Maybe so, but that doesn't mean you understand him. That you're the only one that knows what's best for him. If only you knew the things he's told me—the kinds of conversations we've had."

"That doesn't excuse what you've done!" I shouted, standing up. "Why couldn't you just have your conversations in Alabama? Why did you bring him here?"

"Danny asked me to."

"He's a teenager! You're not supposed to do everything he asks!"

Daniel stood up as well and glared coldly at me. "I didn't even know he existed until a few weeks ago. All of a sudden, he was in my life, and he was an absolute mess."

"So, you just said 'Oh, you're mad at your mom? Sure, I'll take you away from her.' Did it not occur to you how I would feel to learn he had been whisked off to the other side of the country? I should've had your ass thrown in jail! I still can!"

He wasn't cowed by my threats. "Did it not occur to you that I might want to know I had a son?" he shot back with just as much force. "I made the decision to bring him here, because he needed a break from all the chaos." Then, more calmly, he said, "You had agreed to me being in his life. Him coming here was inevitable anyway."

I took a few steadying breaths, as if to prove I wasn't chaotic. "I'm taking him home. His life is with me. His home is with me. Next week is the last week of school, and he's missed too much already."

"I know."

"You know?" I'd had a comeback ready for his next argument, but it stopped somewhere between thought and mouth. Had he just agreed with me?

"I'm moving back to Alabama, but I want to keep him here until my lease is up. The end of June."

What was he up to? "Have you lost your lease or something? Can't pay the rent? I know you have a drinking problem."

"Drinking? I haven't had a drink since rehab. I've gone through too much to start over again. Look, I'm coming home, I'm going to find a job, and I'd like to be a part of Danny's life. Danny wants me in his life too."

That was odd. Greg had said Daniel couldn't stop drinking. One of them was lying. "A job? Doing what?"

"I don't know yet, but I'd appreciate it if you'd talk to the principal of Danny's school and ask if he can take a test or something to pass this year, and I promise I'll have him home by the end of June. Is that so much to ask after missing most of his childhood?"

I rubbed my eyes, trying to clear my head. It was becoming too much to process. "I need to talk to my son," I said resolutely. "I'm not agreeing to anything yet."

Danny and I went into his room in Daniel's apartment and sat on the edge of the bed. The room was the kind of room I could only dream of giving him, with modern, nice-looking furniture, a closet full of new clothes, and a computer on the desk. He sat in silence, staring at me with those angry eyes and daring me to say the wrong thing.

For a few minutes I didn't know what to say, so we stared at each other in an awkward reticence that I'd never felt with my son. Who was this young man? My son was a kid with shaggy hair and raggedy clothes. This young man had on neat, clean jeans and a collared shirt tucked in. He even wore a belt.

Finally, I asked, "Has your dad been drinking while you've been here?"

"No, Mom. Of course not."

I believed him. He wasn't a liar. Like Jason, tactfulness wasn't his strong suit, and he could be blunt and truthful to a fault. If his Daniel had been drinking, Danny would admit it and then try to explain and give me reason after reason why.

"So . . ." I changed to another subject. "You've been talking a lot with your dad."

He nodded, looking down at his hands in his lap.

"What do you talk about?"

"Different stuff," he mumbled, then silence.

"Do you talk about Jason?" I asked.

I watched as Danny winced at the name of the man who had been his father figure for a whole third of his life. I let out a sigh. "I guess Daniel's very understanding, huh?"

Another nod.

Against my better judgment, I said reluctantly, "I'm thinking about letting you stay."

Danny suddenly gave a whoop of joy that cut me to the core. His arms came around me in a fierce hug, and I couldn't help but relish in his joy. He started showing me pictures on his phone of all the cool places he had gone, talking a mile a minute about the excitement of the city, the museums, and how he wanted to go to college in Chicago. Stunned, I realized it was the first time he had mentioned anything about wanting to go to college.

I went out on the balcony again, this time alone. I needed a clear head. Now that I had found Danny and was certain he was safe, I could spare the energy to worry about the other problems in my life. I recalled Carrie telling me about Venom Gallagher. I thought of the silver car outside of Jason's house and the mysterious circumstances that led to him ending up in the hospital. A shiver went down my spine.

I needed to go back home and finally move out of Jason's house. It wasn't safe for Danny there. For once, I saw the necessity of keeping my son far away from all of that until it was sorted out. And also . . . I had to admit to myself that Daniel was not doing a terrible job of parenting. A few weeks here would not be the worst thing for Danny. The resolve of what I had to do cemented in my mind as I soaked in the breeze coming off the lake. Even so, my heart broke as I thought of how much I would miss him.

I had another talk with Daniel before leaving. "I'm allowing Danny to stay with you until the end of June," I said. "But only under the condition that you answer your phone every damn time I call you." I jabbed my finger at him as he opened his mouth to speak. "And before you say another word about my 'gripes,' just remember that he is still my baby, and I will go to hell and back to make sure he's safe. Even if that means taking up my gripes with the police."

His eyes widened. Whether it was at my threat or the strict tone I'd suddenly taken, I wasn't sure.

"You won't see very much of your son once you get saddled with kidnapping charges," I said, driving my point home.

13

Michael picked me up at the Atlanta airport, but he acted more like a chauffeur than a friend. He nodded and said "Hi" as he threw my suitcase in the trunk of his car and on the way home said almost nothing. He still looked sort of neat, but his beard had to be a couple of days old, and his beige shorts and faded t-shirt were wrinkled. I almost laughed as I wondered if his aura was fading, but for some reason I couldn't bring myself to ask. It would have been mean-spirited after he had been so kind to me, and I figured we were both too caught up in our own internal worries to be convivial.

When we got to Jason's, Michael declined to go in with me. I wondered again what was wrong with him but dismissed it from my mind. At least Venom's car was nowhere to be seen.

My weekend trip made it official. Jason's house was no longer home. It felt like it had the first time I walked into Gram-

Dirty Pink

ma's house after she died. The fake-crystal salt and peppershakers Jason and I bought at Wal-Mart, the homogeneous
beige towels from Target, the matching t-shirts with jumping
dolphins that we'd bought on a trip to Orange Beach were now
sacred, shattered memories. I touched the cool, smooth surface
of the saltshaker, picked up Jason's dolphin t-shirt from the top
of the washer, and inhaled the odor of masculine sweat. I threw
it and the towels into the washer and started it. Throw out the
old; start the new. That was me. Nothing permanent. Ever.
My mind hummed the tune of "Another Suitcase in Another
Hall." Nothing like an Andrew Lloyd Webber as a soundtrack
to self-pity. I found the song on my phone and played it while
I packed.

I found the box I'd started packing a few days ago and
stuffed some more clothes in it. When it was full, I was as tired
and wrung-out as if I'd run ten miles. I went to the back porch
and gazed at the trees, roses, gardenia bush, and the patch of
flourishing mint Jason and I had planted. Together. The bird
feeder was almost empty, but that didn't stop the birds from
pecking the ground or the squirrels and chipmunks from dart-
ing around looking for the birdseed. If only Pepper were here.
She'd make the house feel more like home than a mausoleum.
Even she had a friend now; I pictured her running and playing
with Carrie's dog, Charlie.

I had a sudden urge to hear Jason's voice, so I decided to
call him.

"How're you feeling?" I asked after he answered.

"Better," he said. "Going back to work tomorrow."

"Light duty, I hope."

He laughed. "Yeah. I'll be carrying tools for your dad."

There was an awkward stretch of silence, and then I said, "I'm back from Chicago. At your house, actually. Just doing some packing. I was wondering when you were coming back home."

"I don't know. Did Danny come home with you?"

"No. He's staying with his dad until the end of June."

"Good," he said. "That's the best thing for him."

"Why?" I asked, suddenly suspicious. "Why would you say that?"

Jason paused, as if trying to think of an answer. "So he can get to know his dad."

I wasn't fooled. I knew Jason didn't really think that; he didn't even know Daniel. He knew Daniel had left me. He had sympathized with me when I told him my story of abandonment, and he had even called him those expletives he reserved only for the people who made him mad beyond his ability to think. I remembered Venom and the silver car that had followed Jason and now me and nearly asked him if that was what he was actually concerned about. But then I recalled how angry he'd gotten the last time I'd drilled him about it and decided not to.

"The best thing for my son is to be with me, and you know that," I said abruptly. "I'll get my stuff out of your house this week."

"Maybe you can stay with your mom and dad for a while."

"Maybe," I said. "Goodbye, Jason."

We hung up, and just like that, it was the end. The end of my most recent life, and the beginning of who knew what. I debated about whether to stay at Jason's that night or to call Mom and Dad and tell them I was coming to see them, maybe for longer than any of us wanted. The more I thought about it and procrastinated, the later it got, and then the decision was made for me.

While closing the blinds in the bedroom for my last night in Jason's bed, I saw it. Fear rushed into my stomach as I realized Venom's car was parked across the street. I couldn't tell if anyone was in it or not. Maybe he just parked it there to scare me. Or maybe he was there and was planning to break in when I went to sleep. I pulled my gun from the top of the closet and put it under my pillow, just in case. But I didn't sleep. Every creak of the house sounded like a bomb going off. The wind rustled the bushes and twigs snapped. I imagined I could hear the sound of footsteps outside, and the German shepherds next door, barking relentlessly, sounded even more vicious than normal. I sat straight up in bed.

It wasn't my imagination. Someone really was outside. At that moment, I knew why most people believe in God. I prayed like a whiny toddler, "Please, God, help me." I heard my dad's voice in my head. "Get a grip, Samantha. Remember what I taught you. Remain calm. In an emergency, panic can get you hurt or killed."

I took a deep breath, picked up the gun, crept to the window, and pushed one of the blinds up a little. There he was—a huge, lurking figure in the dark. I couldn't see his face, but I knew it was Venom, and he was walking between the two crape myrtles toward the front door. I wished Pepper was there or that the dogs next door weren't fenced in.

Still staring out the window, my hand reached behind me for my phone that was always on the bedside table at night. Well, every night except that night. I couldn't turn on the lights, but I had to find the damn thing. My hands groped across the bed, under the bed, under the nightstand, on the dresser. Surely, I hadn't left it in the living room. Again. Outside, the footsteps were getting closer. My heart pounded and my insides trembled, but I held the gun steady, released the safety, and walked quietly to the living room.

I aimed it toward the front door. As soon as it opened, I would pull the trigger. I'd never shot at a living thing, and I hated to do it, but I would. When I was a little girl and Dad tried to make a hunter out of me, I'd run through the woods shouting, "Run for your lives!" His training wasn't in vain, however. I was ready to stand my ground and defend myself, even though I was scared. My mind could think of only one thing. Shoot.

Footsteps advanced. Silence. For what seemed like a long time but was probably only seconds, I stood ready, heart beating so hard I could feel it in my chest, the back of my neck, and my temples, but my arms and hands were steady. All thoughts were obliterated by fear and anger and self-preservation. Suddenly, a bright light shone through the front window. Headlights. Footsteps running away. A bang at the door.

I couldn't say anything. My throat tightened. My hands tightened on the gun. I was ready. The doorbell rang. *What?* Stupidity set in. What kind of bad guy rings the doorbell?

A voice called out, "Samantha? You okay?"

Gun still pointed at the door, I tried to get my bearings. Venom was playing with my mind. *Don't be fooled, Samantha.*

"Samantha, it's me, Michael."

Banging on the door. I kept my fingers on the trigger. I couldn't move. A voice in my head kept saying, "Shoot, Samantha. Shoot."

"It's Michael. I came to help."

I stepped to the door, released the lock, and flung it open. It was Michael.

But fear and confusion wouldn't let me lower my gun.

He held up his palms and spoke to me in a whispered voice, as if loud talking might set me off. "He's gone. Ran away when I pulled up."

Oh, yes, the headlights. I relaxed a little, but not much. "What the hell?" I said. "What are you even doing here?"

"I felt an urgent need to come over here," he said. "And when I turned into the driveway, I saw a guy running from your front porch, jump into his car, and drive away."

"You just happened to feel a need to visit me in the middle of the night?" Who did he think I was? Some idiot girl who had to have a man defend her? Venom, the guy who sold drugs to my son, could've been dead in the foyer where Michael stood. Anger and murder filled my soul, churning out every rational thought, and I couldn't let them go, not even for this gentleman whose only motive to help me.

"Go home, Michael," I said. "Leave me alone. I just want everybody to leave me alone."

He took a cautious step toward me, then another, and reached out and took the gun from me. "I'll sleep on the couch," he said. "You go back to bed. Try to get some sleep."

I let go. The adrenaline that had propelled me into action was quickly draining from my body, and I had no words or feelings left, only total exhaustion. I admitted deep inside that it was good to have someone there at that moment.

The first rays of light streaming around the blinds and the aroma of coffee brewing woke me up. I'd slept only intermittently between weird dreams of being underwater with fish talking to me, dreams of running from strangers down dark city streets, and dreams about looking for Danny and not being able to find him. I slipped into a pair of sweats and stumbled into the kitchen, poured myself a cup of coffee, and headed for the back porch.

I found a barefoot Michael sitting on a bench that Jason and Dad had built, sipping coffee and staring at the bird feeders on the small hill. A couple of sparrows were pecking at the dwindling supply of birdseed on the ground. I couldn't leave the poor little things with nothing to eat, so I set my mug down, went to the garage, grabbed the bag of birdseed, and lugged it up the hill. "Maybe, Jason'll be home before this runs out," I said to the critters hiding in the trees as I refilled the feeders.

"You have a kind heart," Michael said when I returned to the porch and sat next to him.

"For birds and chipmunks, maybe," I said. "Humans? Not so much."

"I noticed," he said. "I thought you were going to shoot me last night."

"I honestly think I could have."

"You didn't know you had it in you, did you?"

It was as if someone had pierced me with a needle and all the air left my body. He was right. I wasn't just angry and fearful; I was filled with a rage I hadn't known existed in me, and I knew if Venom tried to hurt Danny or me again, I could and would defend myself and my son, no matter what it took. If I'd been honest with myself, I would've admitted that a part of me wanted Venom to try again so I could take him out, but the other part of my soul knew I'd feel guilty just thinking that. "No," I admitted.

"None of us know what we're capable of until we're tested."

I looked into his deep-blue eyes and wondered what he was capable of. Was he really only interested in helping damsels in distress? Were his motives sinister, or was he just a lonely guy who needed to be needed?

"What if you knew that Venom has a name?" he asked. "It's Richard Gallagher, and his mother was drunk for most of his childhood, forgetting to buy groceries or make sure he got to school. She beat him and told him it was his fault his father deserted them and that she hated him and wished he'd never been born."

"Did you just make that up?"

"Do you still want to kill him, Samantha?"

I thought about it for a few minutes. I did feel sorry for Venom, but lots of people had terrible childhoods and didn't resort to crime. "I did want to kill him last night, but not right now. If he ever sells drugs to my son again, I might."

"Can you find it in your heart to pray for him?"

"No."

"Think about it."

It was too early in the morning and I had too much anxiety inside me to think about anything much. Last night's fear and anger hadn't left but had taken up residence deeper inside my soul. I really wanted to know this man who kept showing up in my life and what his motives were. I longed for a straight answer from him.

"Who are you?" I asked, "And how do you know when I need you? Are you stalking me? Am I your only project, or do you have other people to save?"

"Like I told you, I get this feeling—"

"I don't believe you. I've never believed you."

"I can't help you with that," he said.

"Don't you have any emotion at all? You know . . . anger, joy, sadness?"

"We all have hidden thoughts and feelings we don't show to anyone."

I couldn't help it. "Even Jesus?" I blurted out.

He smiled. "I have to go," he said. "Don't you have to get to work?"

"Oh my goodness, yes."

It was Monday. Finals week. It was always chaotic at best, and I'd almost forgotten. I rushed to the bathroom, humming in my head the lines of an old Boomtown Rats song about how they hated Monday mornings. I knew how they felt.

14

At least it was a warm, bright morning, full of sunshine and promise. As I drove to work, I thought about the graduating class and wished I could recapture some of their elation and enthusiasm. When I graduated from community college, I thought I could conquer the world. I'd thought of how I would go on to get my master's degree and teach other young people and help them learn and grow and achieve their dreams. Some of my friends who'd graduated at the same time in cosmetology, nursing, auto mechanics, and other two-year courses had made more money than me, but I'd never been sorry I went into teaching. Of course, it would've been appreciated if I'd made a more livable wage and gotten better health insurance, but, oh, how I'd have missed the excitement of graduation.

By the time I pulled into the parking lot, I was feeling better and a bit more optimistic, like I could handle whatever happened to me. Until I saw Venom's car in one of the parking spaces.

No one was inside the car, but there were two young men standing next to it. One of them I recognized as one of my students. A small, skinny guy with mostly average grades. I realized the other, larger man must be Venom. My student handed something to Venom, and they bumped fists as they departed. Only a couple of weeks before, in my naivety, I wouldn't have even noticed the transaction, but now I knew it was a drug deal. The resentment I'd managed to suppress on my drive to work resurfaced in my mind, and I had a gigantic urge to ram Venom with my car. Again and again. Instead, I parked on the other side of the lot.

As I walked to my office, I took in the details of his appearance for the first time. He didn't slouch or slump, have long, unkempt hair or a beard, like I thought a drug dealer might. Venom looked like he could be a student. He had reddish-blond hair cut short, was medium-height with a big chest and arms, and was dressed in a clean shirt and jeans. In the brief glimpses I'd had of him in his car, he'd seemed huge and dark and hulking, but he wasn't at all like that. And he was smiling. Not at all unhappy or miserable because he had to sell harmful substances that could alter the minds and health of his customers, or even kill them.

When I got to my office, there were three students waiting to see me. All of them wanted me to change their grades. I knew this would only be the first of many times this week that I'd have to explain why they got the grades they did and that they couldn't be changed. In my current state, it was harder than usual to maintain a controlled, even tone as I explained that my job was to prepare them for the workplace, and that I wasn't doing them any favors by making it too easy.

During the exams, I had the students put their cellphones on their desks where I could see them and, while grading papers, frequently checked to be sure they weren't cheating. When the day was over, I was as tired as they were. But I had a dilemma I hoped none of them did. Where to spend the night? I sat in my car and wondered why I didn't want to spend a few days with Mom and Dad. After all, unlike so many people I knew, I was fortunate enough to have parents who loved me, wanted only the best for me, and were always there when I needed them. Even if I'd done something stupid that they'd warned me about.

As I knew I would before all the internal wavering, I drove to the house I still called home, the one I had grown up in. It was a modest house in a friendly, blue-collar neighborhood in Parkville, with beige aluminum siding and dark brown shudders.

By today's standards, my parents weren't what anyone would call "successful," but to me, they were the most successful couple I knew. They'd managed to keep their marriage together for forty years, despite being the total opposite of each other. He was a republican; she was a democrat. He was Alabama; she was Auburn. He was a bit on the messy side, leaving tools, empty glasses, and sometimes various pieces of clothing around the house; she was a neat freak, with a place for everything and everything in its place. I'd heard and seen them argue and scream and carry on about politics or football, and an outsider might think they were headed for the divorce court or murder and mayhem. But I knew that after all the arguing, they'd go on with their activities as if it had never happened. And if the stand-off happened at night, they'd put their arms around each other, laugh and whisper, and go to bed.

Usually when I came to their house, I went in through the garage and appeared without any forewarning. But that night I'd forgotten my key and, reluctantly, like an abject failure of a daughter, rang the doorbell. The TV went silent. Footsteps marched toward the front door.

"Who could that be?" Dad called out. "You expecting anybody, Ellie?"

When he opened the door, his expression of surprise gave way to open arms and a big hug. "Come on in, baby," he said as he picked up my suitcase with ease, as if it weighed no more than a cardboard box.

Mom ran to take Dad's place and hugged me and held on for a few seconds. "Oh, honey, I'm so glad you're here." She took my hand and led me to the kitchen. "I've got some chocolate pie. You want some?"

Of course I did. I nodded and sat down at my place at the table.

"We've been praying for you to come home," she said, setting the pie and a fork in front of me. "We didn't like the idea of you staying at Jason's house all by yourself. You know, I never liked you living there."

Yes, I was home. I closed my eyes, inhaled the aroma of the chocolate, tasted its sweet creaminess, and was brought back to my childhood and all the memories of eating in that kitchen.

"Did Jason show up for work today?" I asked as my dad joined us.

"Yeah," he answered. "He couldn't do much, but he was there."

"Did y'all talk about me?"

"A little."

"What'd he say?"

He hesitated, as if trying to think of an answer. "Well, I told him I didn't like the way he had treated you, and he said he was sorry. That's it."

"You're still friends, right?"

"Maybe."

"Don't be mad at him, Dad," I said. "Things just didn't work out."

"If you ask me, things worked out just the way they were supposed to," Mom said as she positioned the cover over the pie and placed it in the refrigerator. "Living like that, not even married, is never right."

I got up, rinsed my plate and fork, and stuck them in the dishwasher. "I think I'll go to my room now. I'm tired and still have lots of papers to grade." I hugged them both and said, "Good night, and thanks for letting me stay."

My room was the same as it always had been, except a lot neater. The French provincial furniture and canopy bed that'd been there my entire life were polished and gleaming, the walls were painted Mom-and-Dad beige, and the curtains and bedspread had changed from the bright red I'd chosen as a teenager to a more sedate and boring pale green. Pictures of my brother and me in all phases of our childhood, teenage years, and young adulthood were grouped on the walls and on both end tables. I was a baby, smiling toothlessly at the camera, a child holding our cocker spaniel, a teenager in my bright blue prom dress, a young woman holding one of my degrees. There were also photos of Danny in all his stages of growth and of him and me together.

I sprawled on the bed as I had so many times before, but this time I was grading papers instead of writing one.

The next couple of days flew by in a chaotic flurry of exams, grading, and conferences with unhappy or downright angry students and sometimes their parents. At night, Mom, Dad, and I settled into an amiable routine that was familiar and comforting to me. Mom and I made dinner together, which we all ate in the living room, and then we cleaned the kitchen while laughing and sharing our day's events while Dad watched television. At ten o'clock exactly, they went to bed, which helped me get all my grades in by the Thursday deadline.

A dark, cloudy sky and an intermittent drizzle or shower wasn't enough to dampen spirits on graduation night. Whenever I put on my black gown, draped over my shoulders with the hood and its white band for my history degree and the crimson and white for the University of Alabama, and put the square mortarboard on my head, I always got a thrill of achievement and of ceremony. Unlike some of my colleagues, I loved graduation.

As it always did, my heart swelled when I heard "Pomp and Circumstance" being played by our band and saw our students looking strange and familiar all at once in their own finery and black cap-and-gown ensembles. I walked with my head high, proud of all the obstacles I'd overcome to be a faculty member here, proud of my students for all they'd accomplished to get to this day, and proud of the fact that I was a small part of that achievement. Despite all that was wrong with my world, in that moment, I remembered that there was so much right as well, and that I could overcome what needed to be overcome.

I went home that night to the place where I knew I would always be welcomed and loved, and it felt right and comfortable.

15

The next morning, as I drove to Jason's house to get more of my stuff, I was still feeling the lingering effects of excitement and optimism from graduation. As always at this time of year, I looked forward to working with Dad during summer break. Working with Jason might be uncomfortable, but we would manage it.

I thought back to memories of lifting out the old, unsightly cabinets to reveal the empty holes, carefully measuring and inserting modern, beautiful cabinets, and stepping back to admire the new and improved kitchen or bathroom. In my mind, it was a metaphor for the students who came to my class, usually unprepared and undisciplined for college. The ones who paid attention and worked hard graduated with better life skills, which gave me a feeling of having done something worthwhile.

As I turned the corner and approached Jason's house, however, all the enthusiasm drained from my body. He and Venom were standing face-to-face in the driveway, shouting, fists waving but not making contact. My first impulse was to hit the gas pedal and keep going. I didn't want to talk to either of them, but I did want to know what was going on. I parked on the street and walked slowly and deliberately toward them. The garage door was opened, and I saw Carrie's bright red Mustang, not Hayley's Corolla, in the garage.

In my meanest school-teacher voice and facial expression, I demanded, "Which one of you is going to tell me what's going on?"

They glanced at each other and then at me, and Jason said, "It's none of your business."

None of my business? My son had bought drugs from that Venom creep. I'd been stalked and scared out of my wits, and it was none of my business? I didn't plan it; I didn't think about it. On its own, without any forethought on my part, my fist clenched and landed right on Jason's face. I turned and was about to do the same to Venom, but he ducked, and I missed.

Jason yelled, and for a minute I thought he was going to hit me back. Instead, he said, "Get your stuff and get out of here."

Venom just smirked.

I stormed into the house and stuffed and slammed the rest of my clothes, dishes, and pictures into cardboard boxes. The two men talked in hushed tones as I went back and forth from the house to my car with the boxes.

As I walked past them with the last box, I said coldly to Jason, "Dad'll come later today and get my couch and chair and Danny's stuff." I tried to sound as nonchalant as I could. I was gratified to see that Jason's eye was red and starting to swell. Good. I hoped he had a black eye. I never did see Carrie. I guessed she was scared to come out and face me.

Jason said nothing, but Venom started walking in step with me and said, "May I carry that for you?"

I ignored him.

"I'm sorry if I scared you that night," he said. "I was . . . I was looking for something. I thought you had it. I wasn't going to hurt you."

An apology? A polite drug dealer who used proper English? No, I would not be taken in by him. Clearly, he just wanted to sweettalk me into not reporting him to the police. Something I should've already done.

"I don't believe you," I said. "I don't know what's going on with you and Jason, and I don't care. Just leave me and my son alone."

Before he could reply, I tried to shove the box into the trunk of my car with all the others. It didn't fit. I cursed and crammed and rearranged boxes, desperately wanting to slam the trunk shut and drive away in a huff. Venom, without saying anything, took the insubordinate box from me and placed it in the back seat of the car. I did have the satisfaction of squealing tires as I drove away, and I felt a muffled sense of triumph for some reason.

When I got home, I told Dad what had happened and asked him to talk to Jason and help him. "I think he's in some kind of trouble."

"You're out of it now," he said. "Leave it alone."

I stared at him with the expression that'd gotten me ice cream cones and out of trouble when I was little.

Dad sighed helplessly, as he'd always done. "Okay," he said. "I'll talk to Jason."

Dad was on the job. I could quit worrying now. I spent the rest of the day looking at apartments and rental houses, and, unbelievably, I found the perfect house for me—a small, white, 1950s-looking, three-bedroom, one-bath house with cedar shake siding. It was on a long, winding country road in the middle of several acres of rolling hills and was surrounded by trees. It even had a creek behind it at the edge of the woods. It was an oasis in a crowded, chaotic world.

The owner was an older, retired gentleman with a slightly wrinkled, worn and pleasant face and thinning gray hair. He lived in a two-story colonial house nearer the street. He told me that he and his wife had started out in that small white house when they first married and had raised three children there, all boys. They were grown now, and his wife had passed away. The kitchen had a 1970s look, copper-colored stove and refrigerator, real porcelain sink, and a faded green Formica table with silver sides and matching chairs. The bathroom had a pink bathtub, sink, and tile, all perfectly preserved from the 1950s; it smelled like Avon and Ajax.

As I stood there, I could feel their warmth and love and envisioned the family sitting around the table, laughing and talking as they ate their dinner. Maybe the planets were about to go back where they were supposed to be—and not a minute too soon.

That night, Michael called and told me my aura was glowing brightly. I called Danny to ask how he was doing and to tell him about our new home. He was still too excited about Chicago to care much about our new house in Parkville. He told me about swimming in the pool at Daniel's apartment and lifting weights in the exercise room and that he was getting really strong. Daniel had also been keeping me updated every day on Danny's many activities. I wasn't sure if he was just rubbing it in or if he was genuinely trying to appease my concerns. I'd heard nothing from Greg since my visit with him.

The next week, Dad and Jason helped me move into my new home. It wasn't difficult. Since the kitchen was furnished, all I had to move in was a sofa and chair, a television set, two bedroom suites, and Mom and Dad's old washer and dryer because they suddenly "needed" new ones. Dad and Jason carried all of it into the house with the ease of a little girl arranging furniture in a doll house. I took care of the small things: pictures, dishes, clothes, and small porcelain figures of children and dogs my grandmother had left me.

During the entire move, Jason didn't speak one word to me. He and Dad talked, mostly about work and football, and Dad barked orders at Jason and me, but the three of us acted like acquaintances or distant cousins you had to be around but couldn't wait to get away from. Cordial but reserved.

I was glad when they left, and I was able to organize my own kitchen. I threw a sunshiny yellow and white tablecloth on the table and hung matching curtains on the window over the sink. Organizing the bedroom was bittersweet. No problem with who got how much closet or drawer space. No argument over what color the comforter should be. There was plenty of room for me and my stuff. More than enough room. I hung pictures of family on the walls and set some on the dresser and chest. The ones of Jason and me I stuck in the bottom drawer of the dresser. I couldn't bear to get rid of them. Not just yet.

Living in the little white house in the woods was like a fairytale come true, and Jason turned out to be the big bad wolf, trying to huff and puff and blow my barely-emerging optimism away.

On the first day of my summer job, I rode with Dad to a house in the next town where we were to install new cabinets in the kitchen and all three bathrooms. As soon as I slid out of the truck and my feet touched concrete, I saw Jason. I smiled and, as sincerely as I could, said, "Good morning. Thanks for helping me move."

He glared at me, turned away, and went into the house.

For the rest of the week, the only things he said to me were work related. "Bring me that tape measure" or "Grab that end" as we moved a brand-new cabinet from truck to kitchen. In fact, he said little to anyone, never smiled, performed his tasks as if he were a programmed zombie, and at the end of the day, jumped into his truck and left without so much as a goodbye to anyone. Nothing at all like the Jason I'd loved for so long.

"What's wrong with him?" I asked Dad on the drive home.

He shook his head. "I honestly don't know. Acts like he don't even know me."

"*Doesn't*," I said, correcting him.

"Yeah. Don't even know me. After all I done for him."

"Have done." Oh, my goodness, I was my mother after all. "Has he ever mentioned Venom to you?"

"After you told me about that snake and how he was stalking you, I asked him outright if he knew him. He said he'd gone to high school with him."

"They're up to something. I just can't quite figure it out."

"I don't know," he said, "but I told Jason he'd better stay away from you, and if that Venom came near you again, I'd kill both of them."

"He knows you don't mean that," I said. "You wouldn't kill anyone who wasn't the designated enemy of the United States."

"Nope. But he don't know that."

"Doesn't."

"That's right. I wish you were still home where I could keep an eye on you. You better call me if you need anything, you hear?"

"Thanks, Dad," I said, "for always being my protector." I leaned over and kissed him gently on the cheek. "I feel safe with you."

Later that night, I sat in a pink plastic yard chair in the backyard, eating a peanut butter and jelly sandwich, drinking sweet tea, and listening to the chirpings of crickets and treefrogs as the sun set behind the trees. It was as if for that instant my world stood still. I was at one with the nature around me and with the Creator. Anger and resentment were replaced with forgiveness and concern for Jason, Venom, and Daniel, and with pure, unconditional love for my mom, dad, and son.

All my life I'd craved alone time and silence. Mom seemed to come alive when she was with her friends, talking and laughing. I liked having friends and family, but silence calmed me. I felt alive with the trees, birds, and ever-changing sky. At that minute, I knew Jupiter and Mars in my house of discontent were finally getting along again.

It all came to an abrupt halt when a car roared down the driveway and stopped in front of my little home. I didn't get up to see who it was. I called out, "Around back, Michael."

"How did you know it was me?" he asked as he sat in the blue plastic chair next to mine.

"Just psychic, I guess. Want some tea?"

He nodded, and I went into the house, poured a glass, and took it to him. He was stretched out in the chair, his eyes closed, barefoot, his heels in the grass and hands behind his head as if sunning, except he was in deepening shadows.

"Great place to live." He opened his eyes and reached for the glass.

"I like it," I said.

For a while, neither of us spoke. We leaned back in our chairs and gazed at the clear, navy blue sky, the almost-full moon, and the stars. It was too beautiful for words. My body relaxed. Harmony. Bliss. Until Michael stood up and pushed the straggling tendrils from the side of my face. *Uh oh.* Before I could think anything, he leaned over and kissed me on the cheek.

Shock waves bolted through my body and drained every thought from my head. I jumped up, screeching, "What do you think you're doing?" The top of my head clipped his chin as I jumped upwards.

He stumbled, lost his balance, and landed on his butt in the grass.

I bent over him and yelled, "Why are you doing this to me? I can't handle this right now. And you should know that, you . . . you . . ."

Slowly, deliberately, Michael stood up and, with his hands on my shoulders, pushed me into my chair. I sat still. Not calmly. But with the petulance of a toddler who wasn't getting her way.

With his hands on the arms of the chair, he bent over me, his eyes squinted, his eyebrows drew together, and his mouth tightened. For a few seconds, neither of us spoke, and when he did, it was with the tone of a stern father.

"I felt affection for you."

I tried to jump up; he held me down. That no-good, just-like-every-other man, SOB. And I had thought he was so different.

"I love you like a sister, Samantha. Like my own sister."

Oh yeah. Cliché way to get out of it.

"I miss her, and for some reason, you remind me of her."

Could I trust this guy? He could be another Jack the Ripper. How would I know?

He let go of me and sat down in his chair. "You know in your heart I only want what's best for you. I couldn't help my sister, but I can help you."

"What do you mean?"

"You're wondering if I'm going to hurt you." His eyes had that wounded puppy look, as if my thoughts had hurt his feelings. Then he said, "My sister died."

"I'm so sorry. I didn't know." Embarrassed sympathy crept into my head. How dense could I be?

He didn't say anything but looked toward the trees, lost in some world in his mind. He must've really loved her. I wanted to ask him about her, but I needed to change the subject, lighten the mood. There was only so much of this ambivalent love stuff I could handle. First, I'd loved Daniel, and he hadn't loved me back. Then Jason. I thought he had loved me, so desperately wanted him to love me. Then there was Greg and his misplaced love, and now Michael, who'd kissed me and said he loved me but that it was brotherly love. So much for peace in my planetary orbit. My Venus had to be somewhere in another galaxy and couldn't find its way home.

"So, is my aura still bright?" I meant it to be funny.

Michael touched my hand. "For now," he said, but his voice was somber, his eyes gazing into mine as if analyzing my soul.

What was it with this spooky guy? One minute I think he's okay, the next he's weirder than crazy Aunt Sadie, the one who drank too much and thought she was the reincarnation of Martha Washington. "What's that supposed to mean?"

"It means I love you and please be careful."

"Of what?" I was getting antsy. I had to get up, move, do something. I stood up and took his glass and mine and started toward the house.

He fell in step with me and said, "I'll call you in the morning, if that's okay."

"Sure." I hugged him, a loose, almost non-touching hug, and turned and went into the kitchen and locked the back door.

As I got ready for bed, it occurred to me that Michael did have emotions. He tried so hard not to show them, but he could be provoked. He was human, after all. But for Pete's sake, the man thought he was Jesus. However, he'd only said that he loved me like a sister. Surely, I could spare him some platonic love.

I went into Danny's bedroom, neat and clean and waiting for him, and I sat on his bed and imagined him there, surrounded by hamburger wrappers, dirty clothes all over the floor, and a mountain of papers and books. I could almost smell his girl-catching cologne. I picked up my phone and called him for another report on his day. After hanging up, I went to my own room and fell asleep, anticipating his return.

True to his word, Michael called the next morning, and he asked if he could buy me dinner. I said yes. Then, surprisingly, Greg called to tell me he'd missed talking with me and to see if I could forgive him for not being honest with me. I was feeling kind, so I forgave him. The most important call of the day, however, was from Daniel. He and my much-missed son would be home in about a week.

On the drive to work, I asked Dad if he could find something for Danny to do. He wouldn't have to pay him much, and I hoped it would keep him out of trouble for the summer.

"I thought about that, too," Dad said. "Good idea. Kids need to learn to work and be responsible and take care of their finances."

"You know, I think it's going to be a great summer." I closed my eyes and saw Danny happily picking up debris from the floor and yard while I worked nearby. Okay, I knew I was dreaming, but, hey, it could happen.

When I slid from the truck, Jason looked up from inventory boxes and scowled at me, but that wasn't the worst of it.

Right there next to him was Venom. My optimism didn't just fade away, it jumped right out of my heart, and the old familiar anger and fear replaced it.

I turned toward Dad. "Did you know about this?"

"About what?"

"That's the guy that tried to break in on me." I pointed toward Venom.

"No, that guy's Richard something or other."

"Richard Gallagher. Venom. The same," I insisted.

Dad stared at Venom, a general inspecting one of his soldiers. "You sure?"

"Absolutely."

Dad straightened his body, squared his shoulders, and marched toward Venom. "You the one that tried to hurt my daughter?"

Venom, dressed in a polo shirt and khaki pants as if ready to play golf instead of sawing and hammering all day, answered, "I may have scared her one night, sir, but I didn't mean to. Didn't know she was there."

"The hell you didn't."

Venom was unruffled, defiant. "I can explain."

Dad stood face-to-face with him, the wrinkles across his forehead squeezed together, his jaw hard set, and his right hand curled into a fist. "You better tell me the truth, boy. Did you try to break in on my girl?"

"No, sir." Venom took a step backwards.

Dad looked at me. "You sure this is the one?"

I nodded. "I'm sure."

He turned back to Venom. "Get outta here! You go near her

again, I'll kill you. You understand?"

Venom, the reprimanded soldier, stood straight and at attention and, in an emotionless voice, said, "Yes, sir." He turned and marched toward his car, giving me one last glare as he did so.

Dad turned his anger on Jason. "You knew who he was?"

I didn't know if Jason was mad at Venom or Dad, but he said "Yes" in the most insufferable tone I'd ever heard him say anything. I didn't know he had that much hate in him.

"Then why'd you ask me to hire him?"

"He was trying to . . ." He turned to see how many of the men who were supposed to be working were listening. All of them started doing something, if only shuffling from one place to the other. "He wanted to change careers."

Dad then uttered the words I'd known he would but didn't want to hear. "You're fired, Jason. I can't have you around my daughter." He turned and roared orders at the other men.

On his way to his truck, Jason stopped and said to me, "He was trying to give up dealing, get a decent job. Thanks for helping." His voice was so sarcastic and hate-filled, I had a hard time believing this was the Jason I'd loved.

I could barely think or move. Jason and Dad had been friends for years, had wanted to start a business together, had been there for each other during the tough times. What was wrong with me? Chaos seemed to be at the center of my gravity. I figured I should go home and stay there until the planets realigned themselves, but Dad wouldn't hear of it. When I told him I didn't feel well, he yelled, "Get to work!"

Without Jason there, I had to work a lot harder, and Dad was a lot grumpier and more demanding than he usually was. He kept telling me to get a move on. On the drive home, we said nothing, but before I could get out of the truck, he leaned over, hugged me, and told me he loved me. I told him I loved him too.

Later, Michael brought some sweet and sour chicken over for dinner. We ate outside and watched the sun's descent into darkness, raked our bare feet across the cool grass, and listened to the insects' nighttime serenade. I told him about the day's events and waited for his prophecy of glad tidings.

When they weren't forthcoming, I asked, "So, what do you think's going to happen to Jason?"

"I don't know," he said. "I think it's going to be a rough ride for him for a while, though."

"But he'll be okay?" I asked it like a child begging for a toy for Christmas.

Michael smiled. "You have a kind heart. Yes, he'll be okay."

"Danny's coming home next week," I said.

He didn't seem surprised. "That's great."

Awkward silence. Neither of us had said anything about it, but his earlier declaration of love was there between us. Had he really meant it or was he caught up in the atmosphere of the night?

As if reading my thoughts, he said, "I do love you, Samantha. I loved my sister, too; I miss her."

"What happened to her?" I asked as kindly and understanding as I could.

"She died in a car wreck."

"I'm so sorry." I tried to think of something additional to say. Something that would express my sympathy but wouldn't be too morbid. Nothing came to my head. I said nothing.

Michael jumped up and, with fake laughter and lightness, said, "Let's go get some dessert."

For some reason, I liked being with him. I was comfortable talking to him, and he always seemed to know what I needed. I slipped on my flip-flops and started clearing up the dinner mess, and he helped.

"Let's go to a fancy restaurant and order one of those decadent desserts," I suggested.

"Or to an ice cream store and get banana splits."

"You really can read my mind."

As we drove, I told him, "You're weird, you know?"

He laughed.

"Well, not totally weird," I amended. "Abnormal. But that can be good. But not too abnormal." No, that wasn't what I meant either. *Keep trying, Samantha, you'll get it.* "You're just so perfect. Nobody's as insightful and calm as you seem to be." I paused and added, "And you're not Jesus."

He laughed again.

"You're delusional. You know that, don't you? Or just plain crazy."

"I get these feelings and somehow know things, and I don't want to, and I never know if I should tell people, and I see lights around people. I never asked for this. Even my mom thinks I'm a nut case." His fingers tapped around the steering wheel. He cleared his throat several times and started to say something but then didn't. He looked straight ahead, his eyes never wavering.

"You actually see auras around people?" I asked.

"Not all people. Some. Around you? Yes, but you're special, especially to me."

"But you hardly know me." I almost teared up. My whole life I'd been special to no one except my parents. I'd wanted to be special to Daniel and Jason. I'd so desperately wanted them to love me, and I'd held on so tightly. Now, here was this love, unbidden. It had just come to me. Platonic love. How strange was that? "We've both changed since you were a student in my class. I'm not that scared, innocent, girl-trying-to-be-a-teacher anymore, and you're even crazier now than you were then."

He pulled into the parking lot, got out, and came around the car where I was already out and closing the door. He held my hand in his as we walked inside.

16

That night, sleep came to me in the form of nightmares. Images of Venom's and Jason's angry faces stalked my mind and wouldn't let go. They surrounded my house and threw rocks through my windows and set fire to the woods. They were in my backyard, drinking beer, laughing, threatening, and chasing me.

I sat up, turned on the television, and flipped through the channels, trying to find something funny. Anything to take my mind off those two men who were no longer a part of my life but kept haunting it. I settled on an old episode of *Friends*, but I couldn't concentrate. How could Jason turn on me like he had? What was wrong with him? With me? I tried to switch thoughts. Danny would be home in a few days. Everything would be okay when he got home.

I heard something, hit the mute button, and listened. Lights hit the blinds. It was probably nothing. Someone going the wrong way, turning around in my driveway. At the same time, the car's lights went out and my phone rang, Carrie's name and telephone number lighting on the screen. I didn't answer it. She sent a text to say she was at my front door. I ignored it. The air conditioner cranked out cold air, but I was cozy and warm under my comforter. She banged on the door. I willed her to go away. She beat harder and yelled something. I swung the comforter from me and my feet touched the worn carpet. Whatever she wanted, it had better be good.

"What do you want?" I shouted as I opened the door

"To talk to you."

Her face and eyes were red, and her hair looked like it hadn't been brushed in weeks. There were mascara-black smudges under her eyes and she smelled. I couldn't think of anything to say. What happened to her? Why was she here? Surely, she had friends or family somewhere. Or maybe she didn't want anyone she cared about to see her looking like last year's vegetable garden.

Finally, three words came to mind. "Is Jason okay?"

She nodded and sobbed a little. "Well, sort of. Please can I talk to you? Please?"

My heart softened a little. "Alright. Come in. Want some coffee?"

She nodded and followed me into the kitchen.

"So . . . Jason," I said as I measured coffee and water into the pot and pressed the blinking blue button. "Did he leave you, too?" I deliberately asked it with sarcasm, but when she sniffed and nodded, I wished I hadn't.

She pushed her dirty hair from her face. "He's been—I don't know, drinking and taking pain pills, and he's mad and mean and I can't stand him anymore. I told him to give up the pills and alcohol or me. He chose the pills and alcohol."

"So what's that got to do with me?"

"I don't know, but it started when he broke up with you."

"Why are you here?" My head throbbed, I was cold, and the air conditioner was still running. If I drank the coffee that was brewing, my head would feel better, but I'd get no sleep at all.

The coffee pot chugged and stopped, and I poured some of the brew into a mug with a growling cat on the front that turned into a purring cat when hot liquid was poured into it. Just like me in the mornings.

"Why did your dad fire Jason?" she asked as she stirred milk and sugar into her coffee with shaking fingers.

I sighed. "It's a long story. Tell Jason that Dad'll take him back. All he has to do is apologize and say he won't ever again do anything to hurt me."

"Of course it's all about you, isn't it?"

"With my dad? Yes."

"And with Jason."

That surprised me, but the pain on her face said that she believed it. "No," I said. "He made it clear that he wants you, not me."

"What's so great about you anyway? Even Venom wants you."

What? That stopped me, mind and body. No. Venom was a snake. He wanted to hurt me. When finally I could speak, I said, "What're you talking about?"

"Venom was stalking you to keep Jason in line. If Jason obeyed Venom, then you stayed safe. But now he's still fixated on you even though Jason broke up with you."

"And you know this because?"

"Jason said so."

None of this made any sense to me. "What the hell's going on between Jason and Venom? Is Jason buying from Venom?"

"I don't know."

"And why are you here?"

"I want Jason back. I want you to tell him you don't love him and never have and never will."

My cup hit the table so hard the hot liquid spurted out and dropped onto my beautiful yellow tablecloth. Anger didn't describe what I felt. Fury was close. "I love Jason. He loved me. Until you."

"You say you love him, but if you want him to be happy, you'll tell him that you don't. How's he ever supposed to be happy with you when you're so boring? You're a teacher, for God's sake." The derision in her voice was the trigger, that and lack of sleep and my terrifying suspicion that she was right. She didn't know what hit her—until the cup fell to the floor and hot coffee dribbled down her face. But she did know who.

She and I jumped up at the same time, and our chairs crashed backwards to the floor. She grabbed my frizzy hair; I grasped her dirty hair. I tugged; she tugged. Pain. I thought I heard my roots pulling away from my scalp, but I couldn't let go. Even though she was about to snatch me bald-headed. I kicked her in the shin. She kicked me back. My legs came out from under me and I was sort of dangling, and the more I struggled to get free, the worse it hurt. I let go. She could take me in a fight. Even in my righteous rage, self-preservation took over my brain.

"Done!" I shouted. "Now, go home." For a second during which I didn't breathe, she looked like she might give in to her desire to beat me to a pulp, but, slowly, she backed down. Still, I could feel the simmer of her anger as she stomped out.

With one hand rubbing my throbbing scalp, I slammed the door behind her. The wicked witch of Parkville. And to think I'd started to like her. I'd taken only a few sips of my coffee, but still I didn't sleep well.

The next morning, I had to force myself out of bed and got showered and dressed in a sort of walking unconsciousness. Coffee helped some, but I was grumpy and tired and longed to go to the beach, by myself, and lie in the sunshine until my world settled down. On the way to work, I asked Dad to call Jason and ask him to come back to work.

"He was trying to help an old friend," I said.

"Friends of mine don't hurt my daughter."

"Please, Dad. He was just trying to help Venom get a decent job."

I knew he hadn't really wanted to fire Jason. He had done it for me. "Oh, all right," he said. "But he'd better not hurt you again, you hear me?"

"Of course I hear you. The people in Wisconsin hear you." It was the same thing Danny always said when I screamed at him. And he would soon be home. Everything would be back to normal then. Hopefully.

Jason came to work about noon, said "thank you" to me as he walked on by, and stayed as far from me as possible the rest of the day. All that day I debated whether or not to tell him about Carrie's nocturnal visit. On one hand, he might get mad and leave her, but, on the other, he might think she actually did love him and rush home to her. What did it matter to me, anyway? He obviously didn't love me. But he could've if not for . . . *No, don't go there, Samantha.*

After work, as he hurried to his truck without speaking to anyone, I caught up with him. "I need to talk to you," I said.

"No," he said. "You don't."

"It's about Carrie."

He stopped, turned around, and glared at me. I stared back. Like two kids, neither of us let our eyes waver. After a few seconds, his body relaxed, and he almost softened into the Jason I used to know and love. "Is she okay?"

"I guess," I said. "She came to see me last night."

"Want a ride home?"

"Yes."

"So, what did Carrie say?" Jason asked as he cranked up the air conditioner as high as it would go, knowing how I hated cold air blowing on me. He glanced at me. I guess to see if I was properly shivering and miserable as he eased onto the tree-lined residential road that led to the highway.

I was tempted to tell him about her attacking me, but I wanted to show Jason I was over him. So instead I said, "She loves you, really loves you. You need to do whatever you can to make up for whatever you did to her."

"Is that what she said?"

"No, she said she's worried about you."

"I'm a grown man. I can take care of myself."

"Why'd you break up with her?"

"She was getting on my nerves. Told me I was taking too many pills, drinking too much. All the time."

"Aren't you?"

"Dammit, Sam, I hurt like hell. Yeah, I take pain pills, so I can get through the day, and I have a beer or two at night to relax."

"You're not exactly easy to be around when you drink too much."

"Why do you care?"

"I don't." I was lying. I knew it; he knew it.

"So, is she okay?" he asked.

"No. You need to call her and tell her you're sorry."

"I am," he said. "But I'm not going to quit taking the pills. I have to have them, and I have to drink a little at night to be able to sleep. Can't you understand that?"

"What I understand is that you're addicted to alcohol and pain pills. I'm surprised your doctor still prescribes them for you."

Jason didn't say anything. That's when I made the connection. "Venom's getting the pills for you, isn't he?"

He still didn't say anything. He didn't have to. His expression was that of a little boy, not angry that he did the deed, but angry that he got caught. The rest of the drive home was quiet and uncomfortable. I didn't know what to say, and he looked too mad to say anything, but I could tell his brain was stewing with anger and resentment and he couldn't wait to get rid of me, so he could get home and take his pills and have a drink. In spite of myself, I hoped I hadn't made it worse for Carrie.

When we pulled into my driveway, I said to him, "Why on earth did you ask Dad to give Venom a job? Didn't you know he'd be mad?"

"Yeah," he said. "Uncle Joe asked me to help him. You know, get him an honest job."

"Uncle Joe?" Not once in five years had I heard of Uncle Joe.

"Venom's uncle," he said. "He's a sick old man. Raised Venom when his mom and dad checked out. What could I say?"

"Checked out?"

"Deserted him. For drugs and alcohol."

"And you know all this how?"

"Mind your own business, Sam," he said. "And leave me alone."

I slid out of his truck and marched into my house without looking at him or saying goodbye. How I ever thought I could love that man was beyond me. I wished I hadn't asked Dad to give him his job back. Yet I couldn't quit worrying about him, wondering where the Jason I loved was. Had our lives together been a lie? Was there anything I could do to help him? When Michael called, I didn't answer, couldn't talk to him or anyone. I just wanted to take a bath and wash away all thoughts of Jason. It didn't help.

17

Danny came home that weekend. I'd kept my phone close to
me all day while he texted updates about where he and his dad
were. Indianapolis, Louisville, Nashville, Huntsville. When
they passed Cullman, I drove to town and bought Danny's favorite dinner, fried chicken with rolls and potatoes, and had it
on the table when I heard a car in the driveway. I rushed outside and waited impatiently for him to gather his iPad, head-
phones, and a cup of something from McDonald's. When he
finally got out, I grabbed and hugged him. He hung back, his
hands clinging to his electronics. The cup fell and splattered
chocolate shake all over his shoes and the ground.

"Jeez, Mom," he said. "It's only been a few weeks."

I ignored him and held him in a mom-grip. He struggled
and twisted until that kidnapper, Daniel, in his authoritative
voice, commanded me to let go. Not a chance, buster. But as

I turned to stare daggers and scream at him, my son slipped from my arms. Sneaky tears tried to leak from the corners of my eyes. I wouldn't let them. Instead, I silently willed myself to calm down and, after a few deep breaths, I was able to speak, but didn't know what to say. I'd expected my son the child. He was still my son but now almost grown. He somehow looked taller and had filled out even in a few weeks, and was it my imagination or were there a few dark hairs on his face?

"You act like I was gone to combat for a year," he said as he carried a suitcase I didn't recognize into the house and found his room. His demeanor was firm and calm, and he didn't run, jump, or dance as he surveyed his new home. I realized he hadn't done that in a while, but it had crept up so gradually. Now it glared at me.

Daniel and I stood in the living room staring at each other. I didn't know whether to thank him for bringing Danny home or to start shouting at him for taking him away in the first place. Daniel said nothing but shifted his weight from one foot to the other. I held back a dozen curse words and a few witch's curses.

Finally, I said, "What did you do to him?"

"What do you mean?"

"I can't quite put my finger on it," I said, "but he's different. Neater, calmer."

Daniel laughed, the one I remembered from long ago. "I may not have been a father for very long, but I know how to have a man-to-man talk."

There it was, my invitation to guilt. My sin of omission. Mom had told me so many times that God held me accountable, not only for the things I'd done, but also for those things

I'd failed to do, like telling this man he had a child. "Fast learner," I said.

I thought he'd tell me he had to get home and leave, but he just stood there, expectantly, and so did I. The air conditioner growled and started churning out its cold air and I was standing under one of the vents.

He sniffed at the air. "Lemon pie?"

"No," I said. "Lemon oil. I doused it on the windowsills and baseboards to keep the roaches out."

"Guess you don't have any pie, then."

He was getting on my nerves. If I did have pie, I wouldn't have offered him any. I wanted him to leave. "Don't you have to go home now?"

"I guess I'll go find a room for the night."

A room? He had a home in Mountain Brook. "Why?" I asked.

"Why what?"

"Why not go home?"

"Long drive. Too tired," he said, paused, and added, "Mind if I crash here tonight?"

"You're crazy if you think—"

"On your *couch*."

"No, absolutely not. No. Go home."

"If you think I'd sleep with you, you're the crazy one," he grinned as he plopped onto the couch and relaxed on the cushion. "Let me rest a minute and I'll go."

Like he used to, he was playing me. What was he up to? He did look tired. "Oh, alright, but just this one night. You got that?"

"Got it." He said it, but I was sure he didn't mean it.

"You're as worthless as you ever were," I said, looking at him in disgust.

He rolled his eyes. "And you're as pleasant as you ever were."

"If ever I get my hands on Brianna for telling you about Danny . . ."

Danny walked in. "Y'all think I can't hear you?"

In unison, we turned to look at him. He stood in the hallway, leaning against the wall. "Mom, why do you have to spoil everything?"

I couldn't speak, much less answer his question. Had Daniel managed to turn my child against me completely? Tears bubbled up in my eyes and ran down my cheeks, but I tried to remain composed.

"Don't talk to your mother like that," Daniel said authoritatively.

To my surprise, Danny ducked his head and mumbled, "Sorry, Mom."

I felt like I'd been beamed to another planet and these people were imposters, including me. We were all pretending to be Samantha, Daniel, and Danny, but who were we really? Danny walked over and sat on the couch beside his dad. They looked so much alike. Danny wasn't as tall as his dad yet, but he was getting there.

My shortcomings as a mother hit me again with as much force as ever. Why and how did I fail at the most important task I'd been given? My son had needed someone, and he'd turned to a stranger instead of me. What if he was better off without me?

I didn't want an answer to my questions. I turned and went to my room and shut the door. I heard the two men in my living room whispering, but it had nothing to do with me. I ignored their knocks on my door, turned on the TV, and drowned them out. Finally, they quit making noise, and I drifted off into a sleep filled with dreams of Danny running away from me yet again.

When I woke up, it was still dark outside. I turned over and tried to go back to sleep but couldn't. My mind kept going over and over the scene with my son the night before. Images of Danny in Chicago, going to museums with his dad, walking along the shores of Lake Michigan, eating at a pizza place downtown, all rolled through my mind. They'd bonded in ways that I'd never been able to. At least not since Danny had become a teenager. Where did that leave me? An outsider. In my own son's life. Like that day at the hospital after Jason got hurt. I felt the rejection of everyone at that moment and even wondered about those who supposedly loved me.

It was still dark when I got up, showered, and dressed in my work t-shirt and faded jeans. Then I made coffee and went outside to sit in my backyard and watch the sunrise.

The air was moist and heavy and clung to my skin. An owl let me know I was disturbing its early morning tranquility. I sat in one of the plastic chairs, inhaled the fragrance of dewy grass and wet forest, sipped coffee, and watched the changing early-morning sky. This was the way the world should be. Peaceful. Beautiful. I closed my eyes and blocked out all negative thoughts. For about thirty seconds.

If I had a choice, I would stay there all day, but Dad was depending on me, and soon I'd have to face my son's father and act like I didn't hate him. I questioned to myself if I truly did hate him. Maybe I just hated how he seemed to make up for my own inadequacies as a parent. Why was I feeling sorry for myself, anyway? Because I now had to share Danny with his dad? Or because he liked Daniel better than me? I knew my son loved me; he was just confused right now and being a teenager. *Let it go, Samantha. Let it go.* My life was a mess. I just wanted to be alone. In my backyard. Forever.

Footsteps sounded behind me and a hand patted my shoulder. I jumped and splashed hot coffee all over myself. "What the hell?"

"Sorry," Daniel said, sitting in the opposite chair with his own cup of coffee. "Didn't mean to scare you."

I regained what dignity I had left, brushed at my clothes as if that would erase the damp spots, and sat down. "It's okay," I said. "I like being scalded early in the morning."

"Thanks for letting Danny stay with me these last few weeks."

"Yeah, well thanks for kidnapping him."

"Can't you ever let anything go?"

Obviously, I couldn't. "Why don't you go back to Chicago? Everything was fine before you showed up."

"Danny wasn't fine. You would've known that if you'd tried to listen to him."

I stood up, threw what droplets were left in my cup at him, and marched toward the house.

"Well, that's certainly mature," he said to my back.

He was right. I hated that. Hated him. But I had to talk to him. I took a few deep breaths as I walked into the kitchen, poured another cup of coffee and walked back to the chairs and table and sat down. "So, when are you going home?"

"I'm not. I'm going to sell the house in Mountain Brook and buy a smaller place here in Parkville."

"Greg told me you're down on your luck a bit."

"Yeah," he admitted, and then paused, lowering his eyes to the ground. "I was wrong." His eyes came up to meet mine again. "I shouldn't have taken off with Danny before we had the chance to really discuss it. And you were right. You could've had me arrested, and it would've been no one's fault but my own."

Unable to speak, I just swallowed more coffee. He was finally saying what I had wanted to hear, but instead of feeling justified, I just felt more confusion.

"I could blame my impulsive decisions on the hard times I've gone through, but as a father I need to take responsibility for my actions. I'm going to get a job, a house, and I want to spend time with my son," he said.

What could I say? I was defeated. If Daniel stayed true to his word, I had no more arguments to make. Danny had made it clear he wanted to see his dad. If I tried to prevent it, I'd lose him for good. "Good luck with that," was all I could manage.

"So, is it okay if I stay with you and Danny while I find a job and sell the house?"

Panic. Utter overwhelming panic struck my heart. "What? No!" I said, putting my foot down. "What're you thinking? We obviously can't get along with each other, and Danny doesn't need to see his parents kill each other."

While I was at work that day, Daniel moved in to the tiny bedroom across the hall from Danny. So much for putting my foot down. He did, however, inform me that most of his stuff was in storage and would stay there until he found his own pace.

That night, I lay in bed, wondering why I was such a pushover. Had I actually wanted Daniel to stay with us? Maybe, so we could be a sort-of family, if only for a few weeks. Maybe longer. No, that was the kind of thinking that'd gotten me into trouble in the first place.

Between Daniel and Jason, I'd had several short-term relationships, but I had left all of them before they got too serious. Memories of being stranded, alone and pregnant, never left me for very long. If only I could've found someone like my dad. In the world of men, I figured he was an anomaly. He was strong, always the protector and problem-solver.

One time, when I was about seven or eight, we pulled into the driveway and saw an intruder running from our house. Before I knew what was happening, Dad was standing in the driveway, policeman stance, with a gun pointed at the man's back. He didn't shoot, said he could never shoot a man in the back, but I knew I was safe with him and that he would always protect me. He was a John Wayne tough guy. When he gave orders to his crew at work, they obeyed. Inside, though, he was as soft as a newborn puppy. He hugged Mom and me every day and told us he loved us, but we knew better than to get on his bad side.

I'd probably ruled out all the men in the world because they couldn't be like Dad. No one could.

18

To say that Dad was upset about my new roommate would be an understatement, and Mom was worse. Grudgingly, they agreed to come to a backyard barbecue for the Fourth of July. Michael declined the invitation. On a hot, sunny afternoon, we walked along the path beside Turkey Creek, shaded by the canopy of trees. When I told him about Daniel staying with me for a while, to my surprise, he didn't say anything.

So I gave him my rehearsed speech, the one I'd presented to Mom and Dad: "It's just until he finds a job and a place to live. He sleeps in the room I'd planned to use as a study to prepare lessons and grade papers."

As he held a small tree limb for me to go under, he said, "Kind of awkward isn't it?"

"Yeah."

"It'll get easier."

I'm not sure why, but that irritated me. Maybe because I wanted him to be more normal, not some all-knowing, creepy fortune teller. "How do you know that?" I snapped.

"Does it matter?"

"Because you don't know. No one can predict the future. Couldn't you try to be normal?" I walked off the path, down a narrow trail, and sat on a large rock by the flowing water. As I'd expected and wanted, he followed me and sat beside me. "Why do you keep calling me?" I asked. And why did I keep answering?

"Because I love you," he said.

"No, you don't." I took off my shoes and socks and let my feet dangle in the cool water. "You think of me as some kind of project or something."

"I care about you and think I can help you get through this."

"Through what?"

He started to say something while he was taking off his own shoes and socks, but I interrupted him. "We're having a barbecue at my house for the Fourth. Why don't you come?"

"Is Daniel going to be there?"

"Yeah, I can't seem to get rid of him."

"No, I better spend the day with Mother."

"Well, if you have time, come by anyway."

"Maybe," he said as he jumped down into the creek and splashed water on me.

What else could I do? I jumped into the ankle-deep water and splashed him. We leaped across the tops of the rocks jutting up from the bottom and slid down the small waterfall, again and again, laughing and squealing, like I did when I was a kid. It felt for a few minutes like having a brother again. I stuffed all the unsaid questions down into the deep part of my brain, where they'd surely reside until one sleepless night when they'd pop up and annoy me and make me question everything that had been said or should not have been said.

Michael climbed out of the creek, turned to take my hand, and froze, as if he'd suddenly turned to stone. It scared me. I thought he'd seen a snake in the water beside me.

"What's the matter?" I said, twisting around as I snatched my hand away.

He came to life again and almost imperceptibly shook his head and waited for me to get out. Carrying our shoes and socks, we walked back to the area with benches and tables and sat in the sunshine to let our clothes would dry. Our laughter had stopped, and he was quiet and sullen.

"You sure do change moods fast," I said.

"You'll be okay," he said, as if he were trying to convince himself. "This time next year, you and Daniel will be fine."

"You've told me that before."

"You have to be careful, though. Take care of yourself."

"Is this about Daniel staying with me? You don't trust him, do you? Nothing's going on with us. He's just staying there until he finds a job and a place."

"He has a house."

What could I say? He did have a house. He just didn't want to live in it. That was a little fishy and I knew it. I really was gullible.

The Fourth was another hot, sunshiny day, and we'd picked three o'clock, the hottest part of the afternoon, to start our meal. Dad put a watermelon into the flowing water behind my house, picked out a lawn chair and a beer, and waited for his food to arrive. Daniel worked at the grill while Mom and I set the table with red, white, and blue decorations.

As Mom placed a pitcher of sweet tea in the center and cups filled with ice in their proper place, she said, "This is wrong, Samantha. Just plain wrong. Living with him again. What's going to become of you? And poor little Danny?"

I didn't answer. I couldn't. In her mind, everything in my adult life had been wrong, and there was nothing I could do or say to change it.

She went on, "Even your father thinks it's wrong"

"Why? Because I'm helping my son's father get back on his feet?"

"Because he thinks that you'll wind up supporting him like his parents did, and so do I. And then he'll leave you, like he did before. He's worthless, baby. You know that."

I didn't tell her I'd had those same reservations but kept stuffing them down in the crevices of my mind. Daniel and I had been getting to be almost-friends, could sometimes even talk to each other without arguing. We had established a routine during the past week. I went to work, and he cleaned and cooked and made sure Danny stayed out of trouble. At night, we ate dinner, and he and Danny sometimes went to the ballpark or movies, and sometimes I went out with Michael.

"You know what I mean," she said in that huffy, superior way of hers.

"And you don't know what you're talking about."

I turned around and marched away from her, went into the kitchen, got the steaks, and took them to where Daniel stood at the grill.

Danny had invited his latest girlfriend, and they spent most of the afternoon walking in and out of the woods. Mom said little to any of us and nothing, not one word, to Daniel. Dad, on the other hand, talked to him about college football. The more they drank, the chummier they got, and by the end of the evening they'd gone over and ranked every Alabama team and player from Joe Namath to the ones who would play in the fall. Of course, Bear Bryant was at the top of their coaches list. Saban was next.

Michael dropped by later that evening, and Mom became even more remote. Dad was happy that he had another man to talk football with, and Daniel busied himself with cleaning up. Danny and I took his girlfriend home.

The next few weeks were the closest to normal I'd had since April. Although I didn't want to admit to myself how much I liked that Daniel was doing the housework and spending time with our son. On my last cabinet-installing day, Dad and the crew took me out for dinner. We all had a good time, and when we parted, I hugged my co-workers and told them I'd genuinely enjoyed the summer with them, and I kissed Dad on the cheek and told him I loved him.

All except Jason. When I came to him, I hesitated. We'd said very little to each other all summer, even though we'd worked side by side. I never knew what mood he would be in.

He hugged me, though, and said, "I'll miss you."

It felt good. I was so close to him yet way too far away. I didn't answer. I backed away and waved goodbye to everyone.

I came home that night to find the kitchen in a mess. It had been an emotional day for me, and I'd wanted to be alone and think and calm my insides. I didn't need this. Obviously, my so-called honeymoon with Daniel had ended, and Mom was right. He was settling into his old habits, and I was going to end up supporting him.

I stomped into the living room where he was watching TV with a beer in his hand. "So, how's your job and house hunting going?" I asked, putting my hands on my hips.

"I'm looking, okay?" He kept watching the screen.

"Where'd you look?" I asked.

"Internet." His voice was curt, obviously wanting me to stop questioning him.

Did he think I was still the same naïve girl I had been the last time we lived together? If he did, he no longer knew me. I'd gotten tougher than I'd shown him, and I wouldn't take any crap from him anymore. "Did you send in any applications? What kind of work do you do, anyway?"

He finally turned his face towards me, and I could see the anger in his eyes. "I can do any kind of work I want to."

"Then why don't you go do it and get out of my house?"

"Okay, I will." He jumped up, marched out the back door, and slammed it.

I couldn't help but notice that he hadn't taken his wallet or put on his shoes.

It was August and hot and humid, and I will always wonder why the powers that be decided that this was an appropriate time to go back to school. To me it was beach and swimming pool time, but I couldn't help dreaming about my new classes. Based on past experiences, I'd probably have at least two older women in their early to mid-sixties, and they'd be good students, a few thirty-somethings, also good students, and then the kids. A lot of them would be totally unprepared for college and would need lots of help, and a couple of them would be almost brilliant. I would try my best to help all of them get the education they needed to begin their next paths in life.

Before the first week of classes began, however, I would have to sit through in-service day, which was tedious at its best. I'd at least get to see and talk to all the teachers I'd missed throughout the summer, as well as some I hadn't missed at all. Last year, the president had talked and talked about state-level stuff that had little relevance to me and how I taught, but she did tell us about some new things going on at our school.

I sat in the next to last row at the back of the room and worked on my syllabus. All around me, other faculty were playing games on their phones, getting some work done, or just plain dozing off. I felt guilty. The president was doing her best to keep us up-to-date, and we were like the bored students in our classes. I sat up straight and tried to listen, but my mind wandered again, this time to Jason, wondering if he and Carrie were back to together or not. No, mind back on the president. *Listen, Samantha. Listen.*

My phone vibrated. Greg the traitor. We hadn't had any of our soulmate conversations since my visit and most likely never would again. I knew I'd miss them, but I could no longer trust him with my thoughts and feelings. Before my trip to Chicago, we'd been able to tell each other anything on the phone; in person, not so much.

I read the text he had sent: "I'd like to fix things between us. I have a few days off. I'll call when I get to Birmingham."

Wow. I hadn't expected that. He didn't even ask if I wanted to see him—which I didn't. That wasn't the Greg I'd once known and loved as a friend. Maybe I'd just text him back and tell him not to come, but I didn't. I thought I heard the president say "pay raise" and diverted my undivided attention to her. Just my luck. She'd moved on to test scores. And on and on and on. All day. Maybe I could've paid better attention if it hadn't lasted so long.

When it was finally over, I walked, almost comatose, to my car. The weather had turned from hot and sunny to hot and stormy. Small clouds of fog steamed up from the asphalt as the first few raindrops touched it.

I pulled into a gas station on my way home, and by the time I slid my credit card into the machine and lifted the pump handle, the rain was coming down in sheets. As I stood there, inhaling the smell of gasoline and rain, the wind whipping through my hair, I thought I recognized Venom inside the convenience store. I stared. Was it really him? It was. I suddenly noticed his silver Honda parked not far from where I stood. My heart thudded at the thought of him walking outside any second and seeing me.

I shut off the pump and jerked the nozzle out of my car. I wasn't sure how much gas I had managed to get, but I wasn't staying a moment longer. I peeled out onto the road and tried to peer through the heavy rain. Even with my windshield wipers beating as hard and fast as they could, I could barely make out the narrow, two-lane road that led to my house. I forced myself to slow down and then looked at my rearview mirror to make sure I wasn't being followed. Nothing there. I breathed out a sigh of relief.

My eyes turned back to the road, and I suddenly noticed two spots of light headed toward me. Directly toward me. The rainfall was so thick I couldn't tell if the other car was in the wrong lane or if I was. I swerved to the right, skidding off the road, down a slight embankment, and landed in a ditch. Later, I would remember none of it. The next day, when my car was found, the cabin was intact, the windshield wasn't shattered, and the airbag had been deployed, but I wasn't there.

19

I woke up in the middle of a nightmare. In a cold, dank fog. Pink walls inched toward me. I ordered them to stop, but they kept coming.

Okay, Samantha. Wake up, my mind said.

"Why?" I asked. "What day is it?"

My hand automatically reached over to the other side of the bed to shake Jason, but there was no other side of the bed. I tried to sit up, but I was made of cement. I lay back and went to sleep again. The nightmares kept repeating. I floated to the edge of reality and tried to climb out but always slid backwards into the fog with the pink walls.

Finally, my eyes opened, but the connections in my brain must have died, and I was still in a dream where nothing made sense. Where was I anyway? I was in a lumpy bed, lying flat on my back and looking up at a dirty, popcorn ceiling with water spots and an overhead light that had only two lightbulbs burning. The other two were as dead as the insects that covered the bottom of the bowl. Like coming out of that deep, drug-induced sleep after having my tonsils out, I was groggy. Discombobulated. I could almost smell wet grass and feel pebbles of rain on my face, but my mind couldn't grasp any thoughts to go with it. Where was Danny? Where was Jason? Whatever was happening to me right now, it was all his fault.

Two things did connect: I had to go to the bathroom, and I had to have coffee. Like I'd done every morning for the past five years, still mostly asleep and guided by habit, I sat up and dangled my feet over the side of the bed, waiting for my brain to engage. It didn't. But I had to pee, so, like always, my feet hit the floor and started toward the bathroom. What the—? Who put that desk there?

"Jason?" I called out as I teetered backwards. My hands thrashed around for something to grab onto. I heard glass on the other side of the desk hit the floor and shatter. I landed on my butt in a puddle that smelled like pee. Dammit to hell. "Jason? Danny? Get in here. This isn't funny anymore."

Nothing. No sound, except the hum of an air-conditioner that cranked out enough cold air to make a penguin happy. I sat there, shivering, wondering what was going on. I heard my mom's voice in my head saying, "Samantha Grace McKenzie, get up from there; your son needs you." Her translucent head sort of bobbed around me.

"Mom?" Had I been to some kind of wild party and got drunk and passed out? No, of course not. I'd given up that stuff when Danny was born. I reached up to her, but she was gone.

Now what? I was in a room with hideous, dingy pink walls laughing at me and the gray and pink tile floor freezing my butt. I had to get to the shower and put on clean clothes, but where was the shower? Or clean clothes? Where was I? Had I ever been in a room like this one? It was one room divided into sections. One area was the bedroom, with a maple bed and a white children's chest of drawers; one was a sitting area with two dirty-beige couches in an L-shape facing an old-fashioned TV set. A dark-green coffee table held books and magazines. No, I'd never seen anything like this before.

I didn't know what to do or how to think. I slid out of the puddle to the edge of the bed, slipped out of my wet undies and t-shirt, and wrapped myself in the comforter. I pulled my knees to my chest, put my hands on my forehead, and cried, like the time when I was about six years old and lost my mother in a store. Back then, I sat on the floor in front of the bicycles and waited. Yes, I'd just wait here, and she'd come find me.

It seemed like every nerve in my body jerked and pounded and screamed. My head hurt, my chest was heavy and tight, my stomach sloshed and growled, my intestines felt like they were fighting each other, and my heart raced and throbbed in my ears. I was so very cold. Coffee. That's what I needed. A jolt of caffeine. My hands, with all the force and agility of a ninety-nine-year-old woman, pushed at the floor. I must've gained fifty pounds. My body didn't budge. Hanging on to the bedpost, with lots of moaning and groaning, I stood up. Nothing was familiar. It was quiet as a tomb.

As clearly as if he were right there, I heard Dad's Marine-Sergeant voice command, "Get moving, baby girl. Remember, always do something. You can't get out of there by standing around, feeling sorry for yourself."

"Do what?" I said out loud, looking around for him.

The room spun, and so did my head and stomach, but I let go and landed on the floor again. Now what? I tried to go into downward dog and push myself up. My elbows wouldn't lock; I sagged in the middle, but at least I got into sitting position. And there she was again. Mom's translucent, disembodied head again bobbed around me. Dad and Danny joined her. I was dying. Over and over my mind called out "Mom!" and waited. But I never felt the touch of her hand on my forehead or hear her soothing voice.

But if I were really dying, where was that peaceful floaty feeling? Or bright light? Oh no, I was in Hell. I was in Hell, and it was pink. What in the world had I done this time? Nothing happened. No burning stench. No fire. Dad and Danny disappeared. But Mom, the nagger, had the determination and stubbornness of Granny's old mule, Horace, and when she set her mind to something, she never let go.

I stood up and, tottering like an old lady, looked around to try to make sense of where I was, and then I saw the golden staircase to the sky. Well, actually, it was a rickety wooden staircase that led to a door at the top. Trying to hold the comforter around me and run at the same time, stopping to catch my breath every step or two, I made my way to the staircase, up the stairs, and twisted the doorknob. It broke off in my hand. There was a deadbolt above it, but I had no key.

"Help!" I screamed as I pounded and kicked the door. Vibrations of pain jerked though my hands and legs. I shouted, pushed, kicked, and tried to hit it with my shoulder like I'd seen so many times in the movies. "Ouch!"

I sat on my butt on the top step and cried and screamed and shouted and told God He'd better get me out of this place or else. Or else what, though? What can you do to God? I held onto the rail, made my way down to that ugly room, and searched every surface for my phone and purse. When I couldn't find them, I kicked the bed I'd woken up in. More hurt for my feet and legs, and a lot more curse words.

I didn't know where I was or what to do. I was lost, might never see my son again. Where would I go? What would I do? What would happen to me? To Danny? Fear and panic welled up inside me. At the store that day, as if by magic, my mother's hand took mine. But in that hazy-pink room, when I called out for her, the word raced from my brain to my throat and stuck there. I climbed into the bed and curled into a fetal position.

For the longest time, I cried so hard my body shuddered and my nose stopped up and ran. I wiped it and my eyes with the pillowcase, no pride left. For a second or so, I thought I saw Mom hand me a tissue and heard her say, "Stop that sniveling right now." My arm struggled to reach toward her. Nothing. No one. I tried to remember all the awful things I'd done. Maybe I deserved this. I'd never robbed or killed, never did drugs, and didn't even cheat on my taxes. I loved my students and wanted what was best for them. But I'd also loved two men and had lived with them without being married—not at the same time, of course. Mom told me I'd regret it one day.

When my crying was depleted, I took a deep breath and started searching again for anything that would give me some idea of what was going on and how I could get out. In one corner of the room was a door and behind it a bathroom filled with everything a woman might ever need in the way of toiletries. I raked my hand across the tiny pink sink with its narrow countertop and sent toothbrush, toothpaste, lotions, and a paper cup flying to the floor. No phone. I stomped on the cup. Again and again. When it was crushed into shards of red and white plastic, I sat on the toilet seat and tried to retrace the last things I remembered. Like in those detective shows, I asked aloud, "Ms. McKenzie, what's the last thing you remember? What day was it? What time?"

And I answered myself, "Let's see. I went to in-service day. When? Wednesday." But nothing else surfaced in my mind.

Maybe if I meditated it would help me remember more. I took several deep breaths and thought the word "peace" over and over until my mind and body calmed a little. Michael's words, "This time next year, you and Danny will be fine," soothed me. Yes. I could believe him. I trusted Michael. I still didn't believe he was Jesus, but maybe he was an angel.

I went back to the other room and lay on the twin bed with its elaborately carved head and footboards and tried to put things together. Danny. I was on the way home to my son. I had to get there. Where was he now? Surely, with Mom and Dad or Daniel. If he was alone and I didn't come home, he'd call one of them. Of course he would. Visions of him at home alone filled my mind. No, he wasn't calling his grandparents. He was drinking beer and smoking weed and listening to that loud noise he called music. A bunch of kids were with him; they were partying in my house. While I wasn't there. The place was a mess. Someone took my framed "Water Lilies" print right off the wall and dropped it.

Okay, Samantha, get a grip here. Think peace. Oh, yes. His father was there. At my house. Living with me. No, not exactly living with me. Staying there. He was one of the kids drinking too much, smoking weed, and he was trying to cook something. In the kitchen. The stove on. Drunk. No. Daniel was more grown up than that now. He had not shown that side at all since he met Danny.

There had to be a way out of this nauseatingly pink prison. I had to get home. "Okay, God," I said aloud. "You win. If You'll take care of my son, I'll do whatever You want me to, but You got to tell me what it is."

Nothing. No thunder. No lightning. Was it dark or light outside? Again, I took several deep breaths and thought "peace," but I didn't calm down. I decided to walk around and search again until I found my stuff.

The walls had probably at one time been a bright little-girl pink. I was in a little girl's room. Not mine, though. My little girl room had been painted a pale blue and had two big windows trimmed in glossy white, with plantation blinds and no curtains. This room didn't even have windows and was the ugliest, dirtiest shade of pink I'd ever seen. I felt like I'd taken a trip with Captain Kirk and landed on Planet Pink, where little girls ruled, decorative taste was outlawed, and walls didn't like strangers.

On the right side of the bed was a dusty maple desk, its top decorated with assorted stuffed bunnies, dogs, and kittens that looked like they'd played hard and been severely injured.

In another corner of the room was a small almost-kitchen with a diminutive refrigerator, stove, sink, and a small, free-standing white cabinet. The cabinet was full of all kinds of canned goods, boxed potatoes, and rice and macaroni dinners. The refrigerator had an eight-pack of canned sodas. On the small table beside the sink, topped with a white and pink checked tablecloth, was a bottle of pain pills. Hydrocodone. Who left them there? Why? Were they for me? My head hurt so bad I thought it might burst and so did my neck and shoulders and back and . . . One. I'd take one.

I also got a drink from the fridge and a box of crackers from the cabinet then went to the sitting area. I sipped the soda, ate a few crackers, and swallowed one of the pain pills before turning on the TV. The local weatherman stood in front of a map and explained that a tornado warning had diminished into a strong thunderstorm that would hit the Birmingham area in about ten minutes. I realized that wherever I was, at least I wasn't far from home. I prayed for my family's safety during the storm, even though I was still mad at God.

I crept back to the bed and again escaped into sleep. I woke up to the sound of footsteps over my head and crashes of thunder.

I sat straight up and shouted, "Who's there?"

The footsteps stopped. I made my way to the top of the stairs and banged on the door. No one answered but the footsteps sounded again. I yelled as loud as I could.

A woman's voice shouted malevolently, "Shut up!"

I banged again and again but grew tired, and there was no other sound. I went back downstairs, turned off the TV, and lay on the bed. I closed my eyes and listened to the silence I'd so often craved in my hectic life. No more. It wasn't comforting. It was eerie. I fell into a dank, dark well. The only light was way over my head and the longing to get to it intense. I tried to grasp the slippery sides, but my fingers slid, and I sank deeper.

20

I woke to the smell of coffee and an old lady looking down at me.

"Would you like some coffee, dear?"

My brain quickly scanned its archives for some explanation, but finding none, my mind jerked awake and I sat up. "Who are you?" I demanded.

"You're going to be fine now, Susie," she said with a voice full of sweetness. "It's me, Mother, and I'm going to take good care of you."

"Huh?"

"I knew you'd come back. You don't have to worry anymore. I'm here now. I'll take care of you." When I said nothing, she nudged me. "Susie? You still like milk and sugar in your coffee?"

Caffeine. Maybe if I drank it, I'd be able to think again. I sat up and reached for the white mug as she handed it to me. I gulped the brew, and it burned my tongue and throat. I gagged. It was hotter than burnt grease and bitter. I jumped from the bed, still naked and clutching the comforter around me, and sprinted as fast as my aching body would go toward the stairs. The deadbolt still locked. I kicked and cursed before charging back down the stairs to where the old lady sat calmly sipping her coffee.

"You tell me right now where I am and why I'm here, and get me outta this place or I'm going to choke the life out of you."

"You should sit down, dear." She patted the chair next to her. "You don't want to exert yourself too soon."

She stood and walked over to the TV, turning it on. She was tall and heavy-set with sagging skin; her gray hair was pulled into a French twist on the back of her head with not one stray hair sticking out. Her lips were thin, her skin pale, her eyebrows and eyelashes gray and almost non-existent. Her eyes were the dull blue-green of the horizon on a cloudy day. Somewhere on her body had to be the key to the bolted door. I could take her in a fight. Although she did appear sturdy, and I still felt like I was in a painful fog.

I decided to try a nicer way. Mom had always said that you can catch more flies with honey than vinegar. As calmly as I could, I asked, "Who are you? Why am I here? Where is here?"

She patted my hand. "I know, Susie. I know how much you miss her."

Suddenly, a picture of me flashed on the TV screen, and the news anchor was asking anyone with any information about my whereabouts to please call the number on the screen.

Absolute panic raced through me, revving up my heart and brain and making my legs jerk and my skin quiver. For the life of me I couldn't figure out what was going on. But I had to find out. "Where's my phone?" I yelled. "I've got to call my son and my parents. They're worried about me."

"Don't you worry about a thing. Everything's good now," she said as she put her cup and spoon in the sink and started up the stairs.

I rushed to grab her from behind. She turned around and slapped me in the face with a force that knocked me backwards. I grabbed the handrail to keep from falling and sort of dangled for a few seconds. As if nothing had happened, she continued her ascent. When I regained my energy and gripped her arm, she turned and shoved me down the stairs as if I were no more than a ragdoll. While I lay on the cold concrete looking up at her, hate, murder, and mayhem filled my heart. She reached the top of the stairs, unlocked the door, and disappeared on the other side. The lock clicked into place. I never saw the key. I'd be waiting for that witch next time she showed her face.

As it turned out, I had to wait a long time. I searched every inch of that ugly room several times. In the closet were some clothes that looked like they'd been hanging there since the moon landing, and in the chest of drawers were sweatpants, sweatshirts, and cotton underwear—more my fashion style. I went into the bathroom and used the old, tiny shower to wash my hair and body, wincing as I delicately rubbed my sore, tender skull. Then I put on clean clothes, cleaned the broken glass and pee off the floor, and ate some more food from the kitchen. I'd used up a whole hour.

The clock on the TV said it was seven a.m., and as the day went by, I watched the various programs. After the news, the

Today Show aired, and then *The Waltons*. At noon I watched as my photo was plastered all over the screen again. Still missing. Family still worried. Why didn't they at least use a good photo of me? Oh, wait, I knew the answer. I didn't take good photos. I found peanut butter and peach preserves in the pantry and made myself a sandwich for lunch. My supply of sugary, carbonated drinks was getting low.

A few times I muted the TV and listened for sounds, anything that would signify life above or around me. Nothing. Finally, sometime during *Little House on the Prairie*, I heard footsteps and banging above me. I climbed the stairs and, for a few minutes, shouted and banged at the door, but gave up.

During the evening news the old lady appeared again, this time carrying a tray with heavenly aromas surrounding it. My stomach was somewhere between queasy and ravenous, and I couldn't remember the last time I'd eaten a real meal. Steak, a baked potato with sour cream and butter, and a salad with an array of dressings. She set the table much like Mom always did, with plates, silverware, and napkins in their proper place.

"So, Mother," I said, trying a new tactic as I cut a small sliver of steak and stuck it in my mouth. "Want to go shopping today?"

You'd have thought I'd eaten half a cow. That one bite of meat awakened the gases in my stomach, and they growled and sloshed around and tried to climb out of my throat. I burped, long and loud.

"I think you better stay here," she said. "Doctor's orders."

"What doctor? What're you talking about?" I couldn't help it; I grabbed her by her lacy collar. "Tell me right now what's going on. Who are you, and why am I here?"

She didn't move or say a word. After a minute or so, I let go.

"I don't talk to impolite people. You know that," she said as if that should satisfy my unfounded curiosity.

I willed my insides to quit trembling and my hands to quit wanting to get a chokehold on her neck. "Let, me rephrase," I said in a honeyed voice. "Who are you and why am I here?"

"I forgot the name, you know, of your doctor. Do you remember it?"

This woman was really getting on my nerves. "No, I don't know."

"Your doctor, dear, you know, the one that treated you after . . ." She let the word drop, and in her condescending voice, said, "Told me you'd been sick and got confused and needed lots of rest, and I promised I'd follow doctor's orders exactly."

"After what? And what were his orders?"

"The accident, dear," she whispered as if it were a shameful secret. "And that I should take good care of you. Not let you out of this room."

Using my best baby-talk, I said, "Have you watched the news this morning, Mother? Didn't you see my picture on the little screen? I'm missing. From my family. They want me back."

She was totally oblivious to my distress or my predicament. She was the one who needed a doctor. "Yeah," she said. "Not a good likeness, though."

I couldn't eat anymore, and I couldn't stand to be in that room with that old lady one more minute. I went into the bathroom, slammed the door and kicked the toilet, the bathtub, and the closed door. My foot throbbed. I sat on the toilet seat—and screamed, a real horror movie scream.

When I went back into the other room, Mother was gone along with the remainders of dinner. I took another pain pill from the bottle and lay on the bed. As I waited for sleep, I could almost see my beautiful backyard and the sunrise behind the trees, feel the cool damp grass beneath my feet, and inhale the fragrance of my yellow roses and gardenia bushes. My son and I sat side by side in those plastic lawn chairs, and we laughed and talked. The yearning to hug Danny and tell him I loved him and hadn't abandoned him was so great I thought I'd burst, and I needed Mom and Dad to hug me and tell me it would get better. Surely, they were looking for me. The way we'd looked for Jason. I wondered who the school had gotten to take over my history class. Probably someone already overworked who longed for me to be back as much as I wanted to be there. I could feel the pill kicking in and finally slept.

It became a routine. Every day, I fussed, fumed, cursed, kicked, and screamed, but the reticent whoever-she-was never lost her cool. One morning, while I was in the shower, washing my hair with some cheap shampoo I'd never heard of, I heard Michael's voice say, "Remember, this time next year you will be fine."

"How do you know that?" I shouted out loud.

He didn't answer my question, but either he said, or I thought he said, "Meditate. Pray. Write it down."

While I was rinsing watermelon-smelling conditioner from my hair and thinking how great it would be to write what I was feeling and what was happening just in case I did somehow get out, I heard Mom say, "Write your prayers in there, too." Of course, Mom. I'd give it a try. I'd try anything and everything, even though I was sure my merit points with God had already been used up. As I dried off and slipped into some clothes, I smelled coffee and bacon and heard footsteps on the other side of the door.

Mother had brought my favorite breakfast, French toast with lots of bacon, real butter, and real maple syrup. Also on the tray were six ballpoint pens and a collegiate-lined notebook with a bright red cover. Thoughts and words failed me. I just plopped into my chair at the table and picked up the notebook and examined it as if it were made of gold—a priceless piece of art.

"Cat got your tongue?" Mother asked as she carefully stirred sugar into her coffee, her spoon barely clinking against the white mug.

For some reason I noticed her hands had little knobs on the joints. Arthritis, I thought, like Granny had. Why had this woman, my jailor, brought me a notebook? I hadn't even asked for it yet. Coincidence. That's what it was. Sure. Coincidence. As clearly as if he were standing right there, I heard Michael say, "We'll find you, Samantha."

"You might at least thank me for cooking your breakfast," Mother said, her words laden with irritation and harshness. "You're the most ungrateful child. If you don't sit up and eat, I'm going to take it all back to the kitchen and throw it away."

That brought me back to reality. "Thanks," I said in a falsely bright, cheery voice. "For my breakfast and the notebook."

"You're welcome," she said, but she didn't sound like she meant it, and her bad mood was evident.

When she opened her mouth to take another gulp of coffee, I could see her stained teeth and a couple of gold ones in the back. On her forehead, wrinkles clung to each other. I didn't know what to say to get her in a better mood, but I figured if I asked her some questions about neutral things, maybe she'd let her guard down.

Instead—I don't know why—I blurted out, "Are you a nurse?"

She shook her head and downed a piece of syrup-drenched French toast. "Don't be silly. You know I'm not." She stopped, moved her lips a little, and almost smiled. "But sometimes I felt like one. Remember all those scrapes and cuts y'all used to get?" Her expression changed from anger to sadness. Her eyes gazed at her hands as they clasped, and her thumbs rubbed each other.

I tried again. "Sure. My sisters and brothers and me?"

Her face lit up. "Y'all were a handful."

Bingo. "How're the grandkids?"

"You know, after you went away, I didn't get to see them much." She gazed at the door at the top of the stairs, as if it might give her a clue as to where her children and grandchildren were and why they didn't come see her.

"How come?"

She shook her head. "You'd think they lived in Timbuctoo instead of across town. I guess Nathan's busy with his work and, you know, his wife doesn't like me all that much."

She had a son named Nathan who didn't visit her. Okay, that was a start. "I'm sorry. Must be hard on you."

She nodded but said nothing, and her eyes scanned the room as if trying to remember something important.

Grab it, Sam, run with it. "My room looks the same as it always did," I said.

"It was Georgie's room, too."

Was. She was grown. Maybe Georgie didn't visit her dear old mom either. Maybe there was a reason Mother's kids didn't like her.

"Guess she's all grown up now, huh?" I asked, fishing for more.

She gave me a quizzical look, like I was the crazy one. "She's dead, Susie. The sooner you accept it, the sooner you'll get well." Without another word she got up, left the tray, and walked up the stairs and out the door without looking back.

I sat at the table, opened my notebook, and started writing as quickly as my fingers would move. It was gibberish. Illegible. My sentences ran together, my verbs and nouns didn't go together, and my words and meaning were incoherent. I ranted and raved about the old lady and what a bitch she was and asked God why He allowed me to be imprisoned like this. Did He hate me? Would I ever get to go home? Would Danny and I be a family again? Self-pity was rampant, hope non-existent.

It didn't matter. So what if I couldn't read what I'd written? When I stood up and closed the notebook, I felt a little better.

21

Mother didn't bring me dinner that night. My mood see-sawed between elation that I didn't have to talk to her and disappointment that I wouldn't get to eat one of her tasty dinners. Her pot roast with potatoes, carrots, and onions was almost as good as Mom's and made that intense longing for home and family bubble up inside me. That night, I envisioned Mom, Dad, Danny, and me sitting at their dining room table, eating, laughing, and talking. Would I ever do that again? Why hadn't I appreciated those times with the people I loved most in the world?

There had to be something somewhere that would give me a clue about the old woman and why I was here and how I could get out. I had searched every inch of that basement, and found nothing useful.

I sat on the sofa, trying not to let despair take root, and decided to watch the nightly news, but I couldn't find the remote.

I looked under the books and magazines, around and under the cushions, and, finally, pulled the couch out and hit pay dirt. There was a short, wide box. I picked it up and opened it.

Inside were lots of pictures of a young, beautiful girl with auburn hair about the color of mine and freckles across her nose. There were photos of her as a baby, a toddler, and a child, but there were no adult pictures. Underneath them were several newspaper clippings dated July 1990. Georgie was ten when she accidently drowned in the swimming pool at the home of her grandparents, Wilbur and Rose Gilbert. She'd been in the pool with her six-year-old brother, Alan, while her grandparents had been inside the house getting ready for a Fourth of July party. Georgie's mother, Susan Gilbert, wasn't home at the time. No mention of Georgie's father. The boy had yelled for help and tried to save her.

Rose Gilbert. That must be the old woman. Now I knew her story, but how did that help me?

When I turned on the news, I saw Mom and Dad, their faces as sad as I'd ever seen them, and the next scene was of a search party combing through the woods behind my house. The reporter was interviewing them; they answered in broken, tired words that there was a $25,000 reward, their entire life savings, for any information that would help them find me. Then it was over. No, no, not yet. Show Danny. Where's Danny? Is he okay?

One morning, after about three days of isolation, Rose came in with a box of corn flakes, a carton of milk, a Keurig coffee maker, and a box of little coffee pods.

"Thank you, Rose," I said, grabbing the coffee maker and plugging it in. "Next time, bring me hazelnut. It's my favorite."

I couldn't believe how energized I was at the prospect of being able to make my own coffee.

She gazed at me as if she couldn't believe it either. "That's 'Mother' to you."

"I know, Rose," I said. "I found the box under the couch."

"Georgie is never coming back, Susie. The sooner you accept it, the sooner . . ." she stopped.

The sooner what? If I accepted it, would she let me out of here? Her eyes moistened. Could it be she had a heart, after all? My mind groped for just the right words, but the only ones that came out of my mouth were, "I know."

"I'm so sorry. Can you forgive me?" Her words were strung together, a plea for hope and charity.

With all the sincerity I could gather inside me, I hugged her and said, "Yes. If I were Susie, I'd forgive you. We all make mistakes. Unfortunately, sometimes they're so bad, they can't be undone."

She hugged me, too. "Oh, Susie, I knew you'd come back."

"My name's Samantha," I said. "I'm not Susie, but if you let me go, I promise I'll help you try to find her."

For a few minutes she stared at me, probably trying to figure out if I was telling the truth or not. "No, I already lost Georgie; I can't lose you, too."

"I'm not your daughter!" I screamed, immediately wishing I hadn't.

Rose turned away and marched up the stairs. I heard footsteps stomping around and cabinet doors slamming. Oh, God, please help me get out of here. I had to get home to my family, my history class. I had to get out of this place.

In a few minutes, she came back downstairs, this time carrying a black leather belt in one hand and stroking it with the other. "Remember, Susie. Remember what happens to little girls who lie to their mothers."

No, I didn't. My mom may have been strange at times, but she didn't believe in hitting children. "Yes," I lied.

"Good." She hung the belt on a nail sticking out of the wall beside the bathroom door. "I never liked whipping you, but I had to teach you manners, turn you into a good person."

"Was I not a good person?"

She shook her head. "Rebellious. Don't you remember all those temper tantrums? Sneaking out at night, taking my car without permission, driving it drunk, all the times you talked back and disobeyed, you ungrateful child? I should've made you mind." She calmly took the belt from the nail and snapped it between her hands. "Tell me you don't remember running off with that no-good, sorry bastard?"

No, but I understood why Susie did. "I'm sorry," I said, but there was not much honesty attached to it.

Rose noticed it, too. "No, you're not. You're sorry you got caught."

"No, I'm genuinely sorry." Whatever had happened to Rose, Susie, and Georgie must've been horrible, and I really was sorry that I had somehow gotten caught up in their mess.

That seemed to satisfy her. She mellowed a little. As we sat at the table with our coffee, a talk show came on the TV with a man sitting on a couch in front of an audience, and Rose's eyes lit up.

"Have you seen this show?" she asked, and I shook my head no. "He's an amazing psychologist! One time, he had this mother and daughter on the show, and they were screaming and arguing right there on stage, but by the end of the episode, they'd reconciled and were going to some ranch somewhere to get help. Isn't that something?"

"So you think we should go on his show?" I'd have agreed to go just to escape the basement.

"Of course not. We're going to be fine now."

She left not long after that and took her belt with her, but not before she pulled a gun out of the pocket of her long, denim skirt and told me, "You're home now, Susie, and you can't ever leave me again. You understand?"

Yep, I understood.

After that day, I was Susie and she was Mother. For how many days or weeks I didn't know, but I kept biding my time, waiting for the right minute to overtake her, grab her gun, and get the hell out of Dodge. I had no phone, no calendar, only the television to tell me what day it was and whether it was rainy or sunny, cold or hot, and whether they were still looking for me. I was sure Mom, Dad, and Danny were, but the rest of the world had probably gone about their own lives and forgotten about mine. There were no more pictures of me on the evening news and no mention of any search parties.

Every day, Rose came down those stairs, toting her gun and brandishing her belt, and every day she disclosed a little more of herself. Right before Halloween, she brought a bag of assorted candies and said, "Trick or treat."

I took one of the small chocolate almond bars and asked, "You have many trick or treaters?"

"No." She shook her head. "Too far out in the sticks. Remember how we used to drive to those neighborhoods in Trussville?" She got that far-away reminiscent look.

"Those were good times, weren't they?" I ventured.

"Yeah."

"Georgie liked to trick or treat, didn't she?" I knew I was treading on thin ice.

Sometimes my innocent comments about something mundane, like the time I mentioned that I liked hiking in the woods, pushed her into hysteria. I guessed that trick or treating wasn't a threat to her sanity, though.

"I remember her last Halloween," Rose said wistfully. "She dressed up like Darth Vader. I wanted her to be a princess or Wonder Woman, someone pretty, you know, but she insisted on Darth Vader. Said she wanted to be scary. Every house we went to, they thought she was a boy. She thought that was funny."

"She was special, wasn't she?"

"She was. You should've been here, Susie. It wasn't right, you not being here. Remember how smart she was?"

I nodded. "And pretty."

"I wish you'd seen her that last year. She was so much like you'd been at that age."

That startled me. Susie hadn't just run off and left her mother; she'd run off and left her child. Why? "Where was I?" I blurted out.

"You don't remember?" She was visibly upset by that. Her pupils got larger and the dull blue of her eyes was just a small ring around the black; the green part had disappeared. Her eyebrows shot up, and her hands trembled.

I shook my head.

"How could you not remember, you Jezebel?" She got up and jerked the belt off its nail. "You don't remember the drugs, the alcohol, or running off to who knows where with that . . ."

She let out a litany of descriptive words, none of them virtuous, and with each one, her voice grew louder and higher. She held the belt up like a pitcher about to throw his fast one. Fear enveloped me. I was ready for fight or flight; my hands came up in fists. I scanned her baggy khaki pants for the bulge in her pocket. It was there. If I could just duck and dodge the belt, I could grab the gun. Amazingly, her arm lowered, the belt dangling at her side, and she sat down.

"I'm sorry, Susie," she said, whimpering like a scolded puppy. "I promised I'd never hit you again if you came home, and I won't unless you make me."

"I can't believe she left her daughter with you." Emphasis on you. It just came out; I didn't mean to say it like that—didn't want to upset her again.

But it didn't seem to register with her. "Me neither. I never laid a hand on her, Susie. I didn't. I promised, and I kept that promise. It wasn't my fault. Georgie loved me; I loved her." She broke down and sobbed, her head on her arms on the table. "I never hurt her. I didn't."

I stroked her hair and purred, "I believe you." And I did. Sort of. But I couldn't help but notice how close my hand was to her gun.

I patted her back and told her what Mom always told me, "It'll get better, Rose. It'll get better." My hand inched closer to the gun handle poking out of her pocket.

She sat up straight and looked me in the eye. "You're not Susie, are you?"

Thank God. Thank God, this nightmare was almost over. "No, my name's Samantha McKenzie."

"But you look so much like Susie. Are you sure?"

I couldn't help but smile. "I'm sure."

"You know, I still can't let you go," she said.

The anger that resided just below my skin erupted. "Why the hell not? I'm not Susie. I've got a son, a family, a job. I've got to go home."

She looked at me as if trying to figure out who I was and what I was doing there. As if she didn't know where she was. "Your doctor wouldn't like it. Why, just yesterday—" She stopped, blinked, and then said, "You are Susie." She looked around as if trying to figure out who or where she was. "I . . . I don't know. But you're not safe out there." Then, she turned her eyes toward the couch, nodded, and said, "Yes, Doctor, I'll follow your orders."

Panic was a mild word to describe what I felt. I was imprisoned by a lunatic. I grabbed the end of the belt and jerked. "If you don't let me out of here, I'm going to shoot you with your own damned gun."

She didn't move, but her hand clutched the belt with an iron grip. I tugged; she held tight. Her big black pupils stared over my shoulder at the love seat, and her head nodded. I glared at her. Absolute terror, exhaustion, desperation, and fatigue settled into my body and bones. I could take her down if I just tried a little harder.

I let go of the belt, reached for the bulge in her pocket, and screamed, "I'm not Susie!"

Rose may have been old and crazy, but she was fast. Her trance suddenly broke, and she was on her feet and had that gun out and pointed at me while my words were still spewing from my mouth. We stood face-to-face, both of us pumped with adrenaline and anger. My posture dared her to shoot me.

"I'm a crack shot, Susie," she said in a tone of utter cruelty. "You know that."

For a minute, I figured I could wrestle the gun from her, but an image of Danny flashed through my mind and self-preservation, that great motivator, took over. I had to think, calm down, and do what I had to do to get home to my son. Even if it meant groveling to this despicable witch.

"Look, Mother," I said. "Let's sit down and talk and make up. How about it?" I had to get out of there, but I preferred to be alive when I did.

"I'd like that." She stuck her gun in her pocket.

"So, is Nathan coming for Thanksgiving?" I asked, hoping that would put her in a better mood.

It didn't work. That pensive, sad expression that I hated to see crept over her face. Her thin lips pouted like a child's, her eyes stared at her hands, and her fingers intertwined themselves over and over. "Probably not," she said. "He never does. None of you do. Except Michael. For some reason he started coming by to see me. Even stayed a while with me last spring."

My mind quit listening to her. It listened to my friend, Michael, the one who, since spring, had always known when I was in trouble. I could hear his voice asking me where I was, to give him a sign, and telling me that I would be okay. My thoughts answered him, "Why don't you know where I am? I don't."

"He was a mess when he got home," Rose continued. "All dirty, not a cent to his name. I got him cleaned up and straightened out, and he run out on me, just like the rest of you."

Reality suddenly hit me. Dirty? Cleaned up? Spring? Michael? My Michael? Surely, he wasn't behind this. No, of course not. Just a coincidence. His last name was Larsen. Michael Larsen. Not Gilbert. But my Michael had also stayed with his mother last spring.

Rose must not have noticed the panic that overtook my mind. She kept on talking. "Said he wanted us to make up, and I told him I'd like that fine. We were nice to each other for a while. He wouldn't change his name back, though. I told him if he wanted to freeload at my house, he'd have to go by Gilbert, the name he was born with. Guess he thought it wasn't good enough for him."

"I can't believe it." No, I wouldn't believe it. He was my friend. He'd been in my history class; he'd been one of those students who'd actually listened to me. He wanted nothing more than to help me. No, it couldn't be.

"What does he go by now?" I asked in my totally compliant, defeated voice.

"Larsen." She rattled on and on about her son's shortcomings, like my world hadn't collapsed underneath me, like I understood what she was saying. "He was always the good kid, the one who seemed to love me. But it turned out that he was just another ungrateful child. He moved out, got himself a job. Haven't seen him since. Just like all my kids. They don't need my money; they don't bother to come see me. Ungrateful, every last one of 'em."

I couldn't say or do anything. Did Michael know his Mother held me hostage? Was he in on it? His mother said she hadn't seen him since he moved out. But still . . . I wanted to go to sleep and not wake up until this nightmare was over. I wanted this strange, evil woman to go away and never come back. I had to get away.

I went to the counter, took another pain pill, dropped onto the bed, and wadded that pink comforter around me. But sleep, my only escape, didn't come. I turned and twisted and sweated, and, occasionally, slipped into a semi-sleep where Mom smiled and touched my forehead and Grandma pulled crackling cornbread from the oven, buttered it and gave it to me. I was a kid again, my world simple and happy. But Rose managed to ruin even my dreams. She stomped into the kitchen and shot Grandma in the back.

When I opened my eyes, I was sitting straight up in the bed, screaming. At least the wicked witch was gone. Hopefully, someone had poured water on her. Good riddance.

I tried to walk around, but my legs were rubbery, and my mind wouldn't focus on anything except that it wanted to go back to sleep again. I took another pill and sat down at the table to write in that red notebook. My fingers ached as they moved fiercely across the paper and images of torments for Rose and Michael and visions of escape for me rushed from my mind through my fingers to the paper.

"Where are you, Michael? You damned stalker!" I shouted to the walls that enclosed me. "Say something sweet and optimistic; tell me you love me now!"

Maybe I'd gone as mad as Rose. But I heard his voice, calm and peaceful, whisper, "I love you."

Was I hearing things? Was he upstairs? Was he trying to torture me, drive me crazy? I stood up, slammed the notebook shut, and knocked the table and chairs over. "You and your mom can go to hell!" I screamed. "You hear me? You and your good deeds go straight to hell and burn forever!"

When my body quit shaking and I could stop it from running, throwing, and hitting things, I sat on the bed. Defeated. Alone. And so very tired. I ate some crackers and opened a can of soda. Funny, I'd never noticed how good the salt and sugar together tasted. I ate and drank slowly, the only pleasure left to me, and took two more pain pills. I had to go to sleep. To sleep until . . . what? Until I died? Yes. Until then.

As I drifted toward that semi-conscious state between awake and asleep, I was lost in a fog, searching for my home. Mom and Dad's home. Searching for my son. I could see him and hear him calling me. Michael, his body translucent, walked toward me, arms outstretched, and said, "I do love you, Samantha. Just remember, this time next year . . ."

22

Michael was wrong. There would be no "this time next year." Why should I go home anyway? Danny was better off without me. Mom and Dad would take care of him. Daniel Sr., that no-good, irresponsible coward was no match for them. Jason didn't love me. Greg did, but I didn't love him. And Michael. My friend. Who was he? Seemingly endless days of haze, stupor, crackers, soda, and pills set in. Sometimes I was back with Jason, sometimes I was in Valparaiso with Daniel, and once in a while I was at home with Mom, Dad, and Buddy.

Occasionally, I thought I saw Rose and heard her tell me to get up out of bed and eat something. Why? I'd never leave that pink room, and I didn't care. Maybe one day I wouldn't wake up. And everyone would be better off. On some days, I woke up enough to press the button on the remote and watch the television. The people on the little screen were my only company, but sometimes they shouted insults and hit and fought and shot each other, and I didn't like to see it, so I clicked them out of existence. When I had to go to the bathroom, I stumbled and held onto the wall and fell back into bed when I was done. Most of the time, my world was a misty nightmare with the hope of death as my only escape.

One morning, I pressed the button on the remote, and a group of cartoon elves were singing Christmas carols. Every commercial boasted great presents for the whole family, and a smiley-faced Santa told me I'd better stock up on Christmas goodies now. Suddenly, I was in the screen and in the store with those happy people. Danny showed me the phone he'd been wanting. Mom and I dashed through a sleety rain from store to store, scooping up the latest bargains for Dad and Danny, including the phone. Why, God, why? What would Christmas be like for my family this year? Would they miss me? I had to go home, but my stomach was queasy, and I was so, so tired, and I couldn't remember the last time I'd seen Rose or when I'd quit trying to escape. I tried to picture my home. Where was it? At Jason's? No, that wasn't right. Where was Danny? Did he still miss me? Oh God, I missed him. Why couldn't I get out? Or better yet, why couldn't I just die and get it over with?

Rose came down that morning with a box of cereal and sat down at the table without bothering to set it properly. I tried to sit up but instead pushed the pillow up a little and lay back on it.

"How is he?" My mouth felt like cotton, and I knew my words were muffled and incoherent.

But she thought she knew who I was talking about. "I don't know. Haven't seen Michael lately."

I wanted to tell her I didn't give a damn about Michael. "Dan . . . ny?" The word I tried to say was disjointed even to me.

"I'm going to invite him for Christmas," she said as if she were proud of herself for coming up with such an original idea. She gave me a pill and a glass of water and said, "I want you to get well so the three of us can have a real old-fashioned Christmas like we used to. You know, turkey and dressing and presents."

I held the pill between my thumb and forefinger and gazed at it, as if it could tell me what I should do, how to get away. I had to stay awake and escape, but I wanted to go back to sleep—forever. What was the use of trying, anyway? My mind conjured up a picture of Danny nibbling on chips and onion dip while Mom mixed her famous sweet potato casserole. I could almost smell the turkey roasting in the oven.

"I'd like that," I mumbled. "Let's go shopping, you and me." Neither the voice nor the words sounded like me. They were inaudible, far-away sounds, coming from someone somewhere else in the galaxy.

"Nonsense," Rose said. "You're not up to it. We'll have Christmas right here."

"Got to go home." I struggled to push myself up and get my legs to move.

Rose's hands on my shoulders felt like bricks hitting me. I fell back onto my pillow. "When will you quit talking like that, you ungrateful child? You are home. When will you get that through your thick skull?" She slapped me across the face. "Forget Christmas. Michael and I will have a fine time without you."

While she marched up the stairs, I prayed for God to give me the strength to kill her, and I swallowed the pill and washed it down with the water. After that, I returned to life in the dirty pink haze and quit trying to figure out was real and what was not. Those people on the screen? Did I know them? Who were they and why were they screaming at each other? Were they there in the room with me? Why didn't they take their fight somewhere else?

Sometimes, I thought I was still stranded up north, a brand-new human being growing inside me while I worked as a receptionist at a lawyer's office. The rent was due; I didn't have enough money to pay it. The power company had threatened to turn off the electricity. When I was nauseated and throwing up, there was no one there to hold my hand and tell me it would get better, except Greg. He gave me enough money to go home. I felt the cash as it passed from his hand to mine and heard my voice say "I'll pay you back. I promise I will." I heard the drone of the engines with Bruce Springsteen in the background as I drove that long stretch of I-65 south toward home and Mommy and Daddy.

Mom and Dad came to visit a lot, their voices and faces often watery, wavy, and distant. In the background I heard music and people talking, telling us whether it would be rainy or sunny, who got shot the night before, or other stuff I didn't want to know and didn't understand.

I was a little girl in the backyard with Daddy standing a few feet in front of me, the childhood aroma of fresh dirt and recently eaten apple on my hands. He tossed a softball to me. It touched my hands, but they couldn't grasp it. He said, "Good try, baby girl." I picked it up and tossed it toward him. I caught a grasshopper and let it go then watched a robin pluck a worm from the earth and take it back to her hungry babies. I was a teenager, mortified as Dad, in his Marine uniform and sergeant voice, told my date when I had to be home and how he'd better treat me right or else.

Often, I felt Mom's hands on my forehead and smelled the vanilla aroma of her body lotion, except somehow its scent was a little off, more flowery and spring like. My best friend Brianna and I, about twelve years old, sat at the table eating Mom's homemade mac and cheese, the enticing aroma of it mixing with that of the lemon cleaner she poured onto a dish cloth. While she rinsed dishes, stuck them in the dishwasher, and wiped counter tops, she lectured us on the necessity of good manners and proper English and how important it would be to us when we were applying for college and entering the workforce. She stepped on the trash can pedal; its lid popped up with a clink, and she threw a paper towel in the white plastic bag and sat at the table with us.

"And another thing," she said. "If I ever catch you drinking or smoking pot, there'll be hell to pay." No, that wasn't right. Mom never cursed. Or did she mean the literal Hell? "If you're ever out and drink or take drugs of any kind, I want you to promise me right here and now that you'll never, ever try to drive or get in the car with anyone else who's been drinking or doing drugs." Did I promise her? Why couldn't I remember?

My sweet baby Danny, enveloped in his baby-lotion and strained carrot scent, often came to see me. He smiled a toothless grin as I read Dr. Seuss to him. He took his first wobbly steps, fell over, pushed himself up, and started again. He brought me a homemade valentine with a lacy, white paper heart glued onto red construction paper. On Mother's Day he gave me a few scraggly yellow irises he'd picked from our next-door neighbor's yard. I felt his little arms hug me as I bent to accept my gifts with gratitude.

Jason held my hand, told me he loved me, and led me out of that pink basement, but Venom grabbed both my wrists and dragged me back to my prison. Michael told me to keep the faith. Things would get better.

The days and scenes ran together, rain blurring a sidewalk drawing. Hawkeye or Trapper John sometimes turned into Daddy; the villain on *Days of Our Lives* turned into Rose, or Daniel and Michael grabbed my son, dragged him away and locked him in a basement. My mind spent a lot of time asking, *Is this for real?*

One day, I saw a man walk through the door at the top of the stairs. Was it Michael? Was he real or not? In a thin fog, he slowly descended the stairs, his body translucent and glowing, and I wondered if he'd died, or had I?

The apparition took my hand in his and said, "I'm here to help you, Samantha."

God, please let this be real.

He washed my pills down the sink. I yelled and screamed and cursed. Those pills were the only things that kept me sane. I wanted to tell him to stop, but I couldn't quite get any words out. He held me in the shower and let the water run down my hair and body while I screamed and kicked. Susie's nightgown stuck to my skin.

When he turned off the water, he handed me a towel and a pair of sweats. "You probably should get out of those wet clothes." He left and shut the door behind him.

I tried, but my stomach wouldn't cooperate. I held the towel around me and threw up until all that came up was bitter bile. Every time my stomach calmed a bit, Michael's and Rose's faces filled my mind and hate welled up inside me. I'd get even with them, someday, somehow. From sheer force of will, I finished drying off, slipped into the dry clothes, and opened the bathroom door. My spirit went from fight or flight to abject self-pity. I'd been dreaming again. No one was there. No one knew where I was. No one would ever rescue me. I lay on the bed and tried to sleep, but it didn't come.

I heard something. Someone snoring? I opened my eyes, scanned the room, and saw him or at least the shadow of him. He was sprawled out on the couch in the sitting area, his mouth slightly open and his hair totally disheveled. Strands of it stuck out like he'd been struck by lightning and big clumps of it lay across his forehead. He reminded me of the young man I'd taught not that many years ago, young and innocent. Little had I known then that he was a traitorous stalker. If I had a fork, I could've stabbed his eyes out. No, I couldn't. Deep inside I was a wimp. I just wanted to see daylight again, to go home and hug my son, and listen to Mom tell me she'd told me so. Whatever "so" was.

The musty odor always present in my prison was overwhelmed by the aroma of freshly brewed coffee. I didn't remember making coffee. Did Michael make coffee for me? Why? He was up to something. Maybe he'd put something in it to put me back to sleep. At that minute, it seemed like a good idea. Go back to sleep. Forget everything for a few minutes. But why, God, why? Why Michael? What did he get out of keeping me prisoner? I almost lapsed into self-pity, longing to lie down and cry and sleep and never wake up. But I couldn't, wouldn't. That anger inside me took a stand. Caffeine first, revenge later.

Sitting up was a challenge, but getting myself off the bed almost did me in. My legs inched their way to the edge and over, my feet touched the cold floor, and I sat there for a while, slightly bent, my arms closed around my gurgling stomach, and breathing hard with the effort. If only the room would quit spinning. I put my weight on my feet, slid off the bed, and wobbled toward the table, thankfully only a few feet away, and fell into the closest chair. But the coffee pot was on the counter. I reached and stretched as far as I could, but my arms weren't long enough. I tried to push myself out of the chair, but I felt like I weighed a ton.

What in the world was wrong with me? Why in the world had I become obsessed with coffee? My jailor was asleep. I was awake. Two forks were lying there beside the sink. If I could just get to them. Okay, maybe I wouldn't stab him. Maybe I could search him for the door key while he was still asleep and get out of there.

I tried to push myself up on the edge of the table. Bad mistake. The table attacked me, and salt and peppershakers, two empty mugs, and a glass of water all slid toward me. I tried to get out of the way and fell smack dab on my bottom on the cold floor.

I cursed as water doused my face and shoulders and dribbled down the top of my sweatshirt. The glass shattered, but those sturdy mugs just bounced and landed right next to me. Empty. Still no caffeine.

That woke him up. He bolted upright and cursed, looking around the room like an escaped prisoner searching for cops. Uh oh. Something was wrong with this picture. The red-blond hair. The booming, adamant voice filled with anger. It was not bland, unemotional Michael. I stared at him as he marched toward me. No, it couldn't be. Adrenaline shot through my body. Venom. It was Venom who'd kept me in this God-forsaken hellhole and sent Rose to torture me.

"You low-down, good-for-nothing, son-of-a-bitch!" I screamed.

He didn't answer but bent down and lifted me effortlessly out of the broken glass, the muscles in his arms barely moving. Fear, absolute terror, raced through my body and mind. How could I possibly win in a fight with him? I couldn't even take an old woman down.

"I'm gonna get you of here," he said as he dropped me on the bed. "Don't try no more funny stuff, you hear? I won't hurt you."

He just stood beside the bed and watched while I screamed, cursed, and tried to sit up. So, I did to him what I'd so often done to Rose. I lay back, shut up, and pretended to sleep. I heard him walk to the kitchen area and set the table upright. Liquid splashed into a cup.

Pure hate seethed inside me. How dare he drink my coffee? With all the meager strength left inside me, I rolled over and off the side of the bed, again landing on that damnably cold floor. I couldn't help it; I screamed again.

He came over and gently took my hands in his and helped me up. "No need for all this," he said. "I told you I'm going to get you out of here." He helped me back into the bed. "Right now, I want you to sleep it off."

Defeated again. I wanted to hit him in the head with a skillet. I sent him a mental message to take his shoes off and walk through the broken glass. It didn't work. I gave up. He'd probably kill me, and I didn't know why. Mom, Dad, and Danny would never know what happened to me. If only I could've gotten away from that witch Rose. If I'd tried harder, I could've taken that gun from her, shot her through her acid heart. What now? Just lie there and wait for him to torture me? I could almost see Danny's face and smile, but I heard Mom's voice as it said, "You can do anything you set our mind to," and felt her hand caress my forehead. No, Mom. Not this time. The enemy was big and strong and mean. And I was so, so tired. There was no fight left in me.

My ethereal dad sat beside me and told me to "catch him off-guard," while Michael said, "Remember, this time next year you will be fine."

"You people don't understand." I don't know if I said it or thought it. "I'm tired. I can't go on. I just want to die."

Danny walked through my vision, searching for me and calling, "Mom, where are you? I need you." He walked across the high school stage in cap and gown with his diploma, scanning the crowd for me. He stood at the altar, watching his beautiful bride walk down the aisle and whispered, "I wish you were here, Mom." His dad stood by his side.

No, I couldn't, wouldn't give up; I had to get home to my son. He needed me. But how? Definitely not by lying in bed feeling sorry for myself. My Marine dad had taught me better.

"Get up," he commanded. "Do something. My daughter's not a quitter."

Okay, Dad. You got it. You're right. I can do it. I opened my eyes and willed my stomach and abdomen to quit sloshing and gurgling, took deep breaths, and tried to think "peace." Michael, luminous and transparent, sat beside me and said, "You will get through this."

But not without caffeine. My throat hurt and my voice squeaked, but the word, "caffeine," could've been heard in Wisconsin. Venom pressed a button on his phone and looked toward me. "Coffee, pills?" was all I could get out.

"No more pills. Not today, not ever. Didn't you see me wash them down the drain?" His voice wasn't mean, but it was loud and edgy. He was nervous, too. Uh, oh. Not good. Anxious people did stupid things.

No pills. I had to somehow compose myself. Think. "Please. One." At this point in my life, I wasn't above begging, but my whiny voice, the one that worked so well on Dad, didn't do a thing to him.

"No." Emphatic and final.

While the coffee pot gurgled, he helped me out of bed and to the table. I eased into a chair. The coffee maker moaned and coughed, and he handed a cup to me. My stomach vehemently protested when I tried to drink it. I closed my eyes. What now? What would he do to me? Had he already hurt my son and parents? Would I ever know? That's when it hit me.

He'd said something. Was it what I thought it was? "What did you say?"

"No more pills, that's what I said. I want you to know what's going on."

"No, you said you were here to take me home?"

"No, I said I'm going to get you out of here." He rinsed his cup, dried it, and put it in the cabinet, and wiped off the counter. A kidnapper who cleaned up after himself?

I so desperately wanted to believe he was telling the truth, but I couldn't. He was the devil. In the distance, sirens wailed and carried on and kept getting closer and louder, but I ignored them. All I could think about was getting that pill and getting out of that dungeon.

"It shouldn't be long now." He walked up the stairs, turned, said, "I'm sorry," and disappeared on the other side of the door. He left it open.

Stunned was a mild word for my emotions at that moment. Elation, panic, fear, hope, and a hundred other emotions fought for control of my mind and body. I'd barely been able to get from the bed to the table; how could I get up those stairs? Everything inside me literally quivered. My hands shook, and my legs were gelatin salad, but by damn I'd get up those stairs or die trying. I pushed myself up into a standing position and, like an old lady, stood there a few seconds to gain my balance, and let the pain subside a little. Holding on to the chairs, bookcase, and bed as I went by, I crept toward the stairs. When I grasped the railing, visions of freedom and sunshine filled my mind. As I took my first step up the stairs, the wail of the sirens grew louder and louder and stopped. So close.

Why? What had Venom said? He'd heard the sirens. It wouldn't be long. No, no, no. Go away. Leave me alone. I had to go home. A loud clanging and commotion outside. Banging on a door somewhere. I tried to hurry. My right food had to be steel covered in concrete. It didn't budge. Upstairs, Rose screamed. Venom told her to shut up. My right foot landed on the second step. A man in a uniform, someone I didn't know, entered the doorway and ran down the stairs toward me.

"Please," I whispered. "Don't let them take me. I want to go home."

He had a kindly, round face and gray hair and spoke with a firm but gentle voice, "Yes ma'am."

Before he could say anything else, two more men and a woman stood around me, taking my pulse, sticking a stethoscope on my chest, talking to each other, and telling me I'd be okay. No. I wouldn't. I had to go home. It all happened so quickly, I barely had time to think. I was on a stretcher, heading up the stairs.

Then I saw her. On another stretcher, her face all blotched and wet with sweat, and her gray hair tangled like a wet mop around her head. She held onto Venom, crying and begging him not to do that to her. Served her right. I hoped they were taking her to the guillotine. They shoved her into an ambulance, slammed the door, and that was the last time I ever saw Rose.

I closed my eyes and didn't listen to or answer any of the questions the paramedics asked me. More than anything in the world, I wanted them to go away and leave me alone. If only I could see my son. A longing so fierce it made my heart ache rose up inside me, and, like when I was a child, I refused to do or say anything until they took me to my mom and dad and son.

In the emergency room, I was no better. I cried and carried on and told them I was healthy and had to go home and they should leave me alone. They ignored me. The strange thing was, I knew I was being irrational and childish, but I couldn't help it. It was like it all happened in some other dimension, somewhere outside me, and I couldn't get back to my world. Finally, the nurse injected a needle into my hand and my body relaxed.

When I opened my eyes, I knew something was wrong. I was still in another world. I tried to clear the stupor in my brain and locate those detestable pink walls, inhale that musty basement odor, and hear my tormentor's steps clomping down the stairs. I smelled disinfectant and medicine and heard voices, real human voices, whispering. I blinked a few times and saw faces bending over and staring at me.

"She's coming around," one voice said, and it sounded like my father. I was dreaming again, and the volume on the television was way too loud.

If I could just capture that dream and hold onto it and live inside it for the rest of my life. It was vivid, in living color, the same one I'd had almost every day since the beginning of my stay in Rose's dungeon; my dad was there to take me home. I was filled with the longing of a sailor at sea when he spots land.

"I love you, baby," Mom said, and her words were as strong and clear as if she were right there with me, and I could feel her hand caressing my forehead like she had when I was a child.

"Me too," Danny said, and I could feel his arms try to hug me, but they were loose and quickly pulled away.

It seemed so real that the intense desire for my home and family overtook my brain and my prayer was loud and sincere. "God, please let me go home."

"As soon as you're well," God answered.

My beautiful dream vanished, and blackness settled in.

23

Bright lights pierced my eyes and woke me up. My head throbbed and spun, and my stomach was uneasy, like I'd been riding the Tilt-A-Whirl at the fair. Maybe I'd died and was on my way to heaven.

As I tried to sit up, I called out, "God, are you there?"

"Right here," He answered, putting his hand over mine and patting it.

Something bit into the top of my other hand; I slapped at it. God's hand gently pulled mine into His. Slowly, my surroundings materialized. I saw the overhead light and the IV pole and its bag of whatever flowing through a tube into a needle attached to the back of my hand. Machines beside me blipped and bleeped in numbers, colors, and lines. The room was white and cool, and a landscape of trees, cattle, and grass was on the wall. My dad sat beside me holding my hand.

"What?" My voice was raspy, and my throat ached and burned, and no other words would come out of it.

"You're safe now, baby girl," Dad said.

"Am I alive?" My words were those of a toddler learning to talk, barely discernable.

A chorus of voices laughed and said "yes" in unison.

I smiled, closed my eyes, and prayed that this dream would never end.

The next time I woke up, I knew where I was and why. I had vague memories of the basement, Venom, the ambulance ride, and the emergency room. It wasn't home, but the people I loved most in the world were there with me. Overwhelming gratitude filled my heart and mind.

Dad and Danny slouched in chairs, Danny's fingers dancing across his phone. Dad was snoring lightly. Mom sat upright, her eyes closed, hands on the side of my bed, probably praying.

"Good morning," I said as cheerfully as my hoarse voice would allow.

They all jumped like reprimanded soldiers and quickly gathered around me.

"Good morning yourself, sleepy head," Mom said as she pushed a button on the side of the bed, and it rose into sitting position.

"Hi, baby girl," Dad said, but he got so choked up he couldn't say anything else and squeezed my hand.

Danny looked up from his phone and ran to the bed. "Mom, you're awake."

It wasn't easy, but they all, one at a time, managed to get their arms around me and hug me and tell me how glad they were that I'd been found. It was exactly as I'd envisioned it. Tears and laughter and hugs, everyone talking at once. I could hear the rapid-fire questions. From Mom: Are you okay? Are you sick? Are you hurt? Can I get you anything? From Dad: How did this happen? What did they do to you? From Danny: Were you scared?

But I couldn't answer any of them. Words and thoughts cluttered my mind, tumbling over each other.

"Okay, y'all, give her a break. Let her catch her breath," Dad said, and Mom and Danny pulled up their chairs and sat on either side of my bed. Dad stood there and held my hand. Each of them seemed to be searching for something to say.

"It's okay. I know. It was Venom," I said, though I still couldn't believe it.

That no-good, drug-dealing weasel had saved me. A hazy, pale memory of him walking down the stairs flashed through my mind. Then I saw Rose caressing her belt as if it were a baby, fingering her gun, threatening me, heard her dreaded footsteps on the stairs, and smelled her sickening, flowery perfume stench. Panic started burning my stomach and rose through my heart to my throat. I wanted to throw up but coughed and choked instead. I pushed the white sheet and blanket off me and tried to get out of bed.

Dad gently put his hands around my shoulders and made me sit back on the pillows. "It's over," he said. "You're safe now."

"How?" I asked.

"Venom told the sheriff's deputies he went to visit Rose Gilbert and found you in her basement and called 911," Dad said. "They were both taken in to custody. He's being held on suspicion of being involved with the kidnapping and also for drugs."

"We got a call and they told us you were in an ambulance on your way to the hospital. We got here as quick as we could," Mom said shakily.

"How?"

"We don't know all the details yet," Dad answered.

I reached for the glass of water that was on the tray beside my bed but knocked it over and splashed water all over Dad. He jumped back and knocked the IV pole over. Mom jumped up to grab it before it hit the floor but fell backwards into her chair with it laying across her. While Mom struggled with the pole, Dad picked it up, set it in its place, and started examining my hand. It didn't hurt. I'd been holding the needle in place. For the first time in months, something close to a laugh escaped me.

Mom got up and also examined where the needle entered my skin, asking if I was hurt over and over. Neither of them knew anything about medicine. Still, they hovered and tried to look like they knew what they were doing.

Immediately, a nurse came into the room, examined the same needle and insertion point, and said to my parents, "You people have got to be more careful and quieter, or you'll have to leave the room. We can hear you down the hall."

Fighting words for Mom. Her body straightened; her expression turned hard and cold. "You will never in this lifetime or the hereafter get me to leave my daughter when she needs me. And for your information, she's been kidnapped, returned, and asleep for almost twelve hours. The noise you hear is a joyful noise. You got that?"

"Be quiet or else," The nurse huffed as she marched out the door.

We never saw her again. A few minutes later, a different nurse and a doctor came into the room. The nurse took my temperature and blood pressure as the doctor scanned my chart and smiled at me.

"Good morning, Ms. McKenzie," she said cheerily, as if she were talking to a child. "How're you feeling?"

I thought I felt better than she looked. Her eyes were red as if she'd been drinking too much and under her eyes were smudges of mascara.

"I'm fine," I said. "Are you okay?"

She laughed. "Long night and morning." She studied my chart again and said, "You've been taking a lot of hydrocodone? Was it prescribed for you?"

I shook my head. "No."

"Where did you get it?"

"From Rose."

"Rose? A drug dealer?"

I had to think a minute. Did she sell drugs? Or just buy them? I had no idea. "Don't know."

She studied the chart again. "If you're up to it," she said, "a couple of sheriff's deputies want to talk to you."

I didn't want to talk to anyone, let alone police officers; I wanted to go home—to my mom and dad's home and sleep in the bed I'd slept in as a child and forget the last few months.

But I said, "Okay," just to get it over with.

In all my visions and anticipation of my homecoming, I'd never imagined what it would be like beyond the first few minutes. The next few days weren't hell; hell was that pink, musty basement. They were, however, purgatory. Doctors and nurses, needles and medicine, and countless tests involving machines that looked like they'd been imported from outer space. But the questions, the continual probing of my memory, that was the worst. And they started that first morning, when those two sheriff's deputies walked into the room—before I'd had a chance to relax and enjoy my release from prison.

One of the deputies, a stout, gray-haired one with a pen and pad, questioned me about every aspect of my confinement and especially about the car wreck and how I got to the house that became my prison. He was the male counterpart to Rose, except that he wore his belt and gun around his waist—in plain sight.

"I know you're tired and confused right now," he said as he stood beside the bed looking down at me. "But what can you tell me about the car wreck? Anything you can remember will be helpful." He talked in that same tone of voice Rose did when she was trying to be polite, right before she exploded in anger.

I thought for a few minutes. Rain. Headlights. Nothing. I shook my head. His voice, his face, his hair, so much like Rose. He was Rose. I had an overwhelming urge to grab his gun and shoot him and run screaming down the hall.

"Can't remember."

"Do you remember how you got to Ms. Gilbert's house?"

"No." I couldn't lie still. My insides agitated like a washing machine with a full load. My hands twisted around each other; my eyes stared at his gun. I could reach out and touch it.

"Were you buying drugs from Ms. Gilbert?"

"No."

His phone rang. He went into the hallway, talked in a whisper, and finally came back into my room.

"Did you know about the newspaper clippings? What did Ms. Gilbert tell you about the death of her grandchild?"

"Yes." I gave him my meanest stare with eyes squinted and eyebrows drawn together.

"Did she tell you how her grandchild died?"

What did Georgie's death have to do with anything? I didn't want to talk to this man. I wished he'd go away. "She drowned in the backyard swimming pool. It was an accident," I said, hoping that would satisfy him.

It didn't. What was wrong with him? Did he think I had kidnapped myself? Or drowned the girl? I had to get away, get out of there before I exploded. "Leave me alone," I tried to scream, although it came out more as a moan as I threw back the thin, white blanket and tried again to get out of the bed. My head throbbed and spun around, and I was so dizzy I couldn't stand up. As I fell back onto the pillows, I heard the deputy call out, "Ms. McKenzie!"

He was cut off by my dad. "Shut the hell up! You ask her one more question and you're going to be laying on the floor with a knot on your head and that pen and pad stuck up your—"

"Craig!" Mom said sharply.

He paused and then said, "Ass."

The deputy left but didn't give up. He and his sidekick came back to my hospital room every day of my three-day stay. On the last morning, when I couldn't barely stand that room and bed any longer, the doctor came in and announced that I could go home.

"Today?" I could hardly believe it. "Today? Right this minute?"

"Soon," she said, pausing and looking me in the eyes. The way I did when I wanted to be sure a student was listening. "Considering what you've been through, you're in pretty good shape. The nurse will come in and give you prescriptions to help with drug withdrawal. You need to go see your primary care physician as soon as possible." She reached into her white jacket pocket, pulled out a card, and handed it to me. "We've made an appointment for you with Dr. Sawyer. I want you to keep it. She'll help you get through the healing process, including recovering from your addiction to painkillers. We've already started easing you off them."

I read the business card carefully. "A shrink?" I squealed. "I'm not some stupid drug addict. I don't need a damned shrink!" My words had gotten louder and shriller.

"Hydrocodone withdrawal is no picnic in the park, Ms. McKenzie. You've been through a horrific ordeal, and Dr. Sawyer can help you."

Every nerve in my body twitched and jumped to attention. In a voice that was a lot louder than I meant, I said, "I don't need your help or anyone else's."

And that was when Dad walked in. "Yes, you do, and you're going to get it," he said as he marched to my bedside.

I looked at Dad with my pleading, puppy-dog eyes. This time it didn't work. "I'll go with you the first time," he said. "But you'll sure as hell go."

The doctor looked at Dad with a "thank God you're here" expression and started talking to him as if I weren't in the room.

After the doctor left, the nurse came in and gave Dad the prescriptions and instructions for my care when I got home. I was wheeled through the landscape-lined halls, on my way to freedom and home.

24

"Please, Dad, just drive by."

He looked at me as if I'd lost my mind. "Are you crazy? Why?"

"I don't know why." It was the truth, but for some macabre reason, I wanted to see the house, my prison, where it was, and what it looked like from the outside.

For a few seconds, he stared at me as if trying to figure out whether to take me back to the hospital or go home. Finally, he glanced at his rearview mirror, turned his head to check the traffic, and pulled out of the parking lot. "Bad idea. Plus, your Mom'll kill me if she finds out."

He was right, of course. She'd start in on her pop-psychology tirade and find a hundred reasons why it would hurt me mentally and emotionally. "I won't tell if you won't."

He glanced at me, didn't say yes or no, but I knew he'd take me to that hateful house. We were both silent as he drove the familiar back roads. My brain was rolling the malevolent tapes that grew while I was in Rose's motel. The words I'd have used on her, the ones that told her how ugly and evil she was, played over and over and over. Images of a little girl lying face down in cool blue water flashed through my brain, and when I turned her over, it was me.

No, I had to stop it. I was on my way home. Joy. Elation. Relief. That's what I should be feeling. I rolled the window down and inhaled the fresh air of early winter and admired the beautiful, bare trees as I'd never done before. So many times, I'd grumbled about the cold, but now it felt so good, and the open window and cold wind whipping through my hair calmed my runaway thoughts. Smoke rising from chimneys, two boys kicking a football, and an old woman raking leaves were as beautiful to me as the Taj Mahal or what the earth looks like from space. *Rewind, Sam. Start over. Thank You, God.*

Before Dad pulled into the driveway, I recognized the house. I'd been totally out of it when I went into it and mostly out of it when I came out. But I knew that miserable, old pile of wood.   It was a big, two-story, menacing thing with peeling, dirty-white paint and faded green shudders, a wrap-around porch surrounded by over-grown boxwoods. A perfect haunted house for a horror movie, and it sat not even a hundred yards or so off the road. The inner peace and tranquility I'd managed to muster for about ten minutes gave way to the ever-present anger and resentment. Why had they not found me? I was right there. Beside a road. Surely Dad, Jason, or Daniel had driven by that house. Michael had probably been inside while I was in the basement. I stared at it; it stared back. The windows on the second floor were evil eyes and the door was a sinister smile.

Why hadn't I heard from Michael? He hadn't been to see me in the hospital, nor had he called. That fact made me even more sure that he had conspired with his mother to keep me captive in that house. But why? What was their connection to Venom? I wanted them all to burn in hell, yet I was sorry for Michael because he was born to the mother from hell and for Rose because she'd lost a child and grandchild. I'd probably be crazy, too, if it'd happened to me.

We'd only been there a minute when I said, "Let's go home, Dad."

Backing out of that driveway and speeding away from that house, I hoped, was the start of a brand-new chapter in my life. But what was the chapter about? One more time I'd go home to Mommy and Daddy and be their little girl? I'd been there before. So what? A few days at my parents' house would be great. In that pink prison, I'd longed to have Mom hover over me, Dad protect me, and my son to spend time with me.

Anticipation began to take over my brain. Again, I noticed things I'd never have paid attention to before my incarceration. The odor of the car mixed with the vanilla fragrance of the air freshener Mom stuck between the seats. The sound of the engine as Johnny Cash, Dad's favorite singer, sang about Folsom Prison. The winter blue of the sky. Sunshine sparkling on the shiny specks in the asphalt as we raced over it. I was like a child again; everything seemed new. As we turned onto the street where I grew up, I was a five-year old waiting for the arrival of Santa. I didn't know what day it was, but the sun was only half-way up on its ascent in the sparsely clouded sky. It was morning, a great time to start my new life.

And just like that, we were in front of my childhood home. The car had barely stopped before I had the car door opened and was barging through my parents' door, and Mom, on the other side, was rushing toward me. I was home. Finally. This time it was for real.

Mom had done what she always did when she was anxious, excited, or mad. The house was filled with those familiar aromas of home and family, the ones I'd dreamed of so often, bacon sizzling in the skillet, coffee brewing, and cinnamon rolls baking in the oven. All those mornings I'd taken for granted, hadn't given a second thought to, now filled me with nostalgia and a childlike Christmas-morning euphoria, and the words that had been forming inside my mind started flowing effortlessly: "I'm so glad to be home. I love y'all so much. I can't believe I'm home."

A few glorious minutes later, Danny and I sat at the table to await the arrival of our food and catch up on our lives without each other.

"Where did you stay while I was . . . gone?" I asked him.

"With Dad during the week. Here on weekends."

"How'd that work out? Were you okay? Was he good to you?"

"I was fine. And no, he was worse." He didn't offer any details, and I was glad he didn't extol the virtues of his father. I wanted to ask if his dad had any women in our house but restrained myself. I'd find out soon enough.

"Is he still at our house?"

"No, he sold the Mountain Brook house and bought one not far from us."

While I listened to my son talk on and on about his schoolwork and which teachers he didn't like, how his dad let him drive sometimes, and how he had a new girlfriend, I gulped Mom's perfect coffee and watched her cook. Though his mouth was talking and smiling, his eyes were sad. They didn't crinkle and sparkle. I couldn't help it; I had to. I reached over and hugged him as tightly as I could.

For just a minute, he hugged me back, then he pulled away. But he was smiling, and I thought I saw moisture in his eyes.

The perfect day. The day I'd dreamed about. Never again would I take my family for granted. I'd always, every day, tell them I loved them. "I love you, son," I said.

And he uttered the words every mom longs to hear, "I love you too, Mom."

The next two days were bliss. Mom treated me like I was the queen, and I enjoyed every minute of it. She did all the cooking and cleaning and wouldn't let me help. She made my favorite foods, including chocolate and lemon cream pies.

My bliss dissipated the day the doorbell rang. Dad answered the door, and soon I heard an exchange of male voices trying to argue quietly. I knew it was Michael; Dad didn't seem to want to let him inside.

"It's okay," I called out. "Let him in." But it wasn't okay, and I didn't know why I didn't tell Dad to slam the door in his face. I was sure Michael must have known by now that his mother kept me prisoner, but I didn't know if he'd been in on it. I needed to know.

"Hi, Samantha," Michael said. He sounded anxious and insecure, more like the college student I once taught than Jesus.

For the last few weeks, in all the imaginings of my mind, I'd pictured him as hateful and mean like his mother. I'd forgotten how calm and gentle he really was, but that was maybe just the surface that he wanted me to see. I glared at him.

"Why are you here?"

Dad spoke before Michael could answer. "He's been searching for you all this time. Never gave up. Wouldn't let us either. Every time we felt like we couldn't go on, he kept telling us we'd find you."

So, he'd taken them in too. I looked at him for a while, gauging his truthfulness and character. What was he? A kind but dumb guy who had no idea his mom was a monster? Or was he just like her?

"You didn't have a flash of insight, some vision of me in your mom's ugly pink basement?" I tried to sound mean and sarcastic. "You could find Jason, someone you didn't even know, but not me?" I walked up to him and hit him in the chest with my fists, over and over and over, until Dad pulled me away. "Why?" I screamed. Rage, tears, and sobs erupted inside me and escaped into a volcano of flailing arms and kicking feet as Dad held me onto me, his arms tight around my waist.

Mom spoke soothingly, "Calm down, sweetie."

"And you didn't even come see me at the hospital!" Still screaming. Still flailing and kicking.

"I told him not to," Dad said. "You just needed your family then."

My fury turned to my father. I kicked him in the shin and stomped his foot. He let go.

"I was protecting you! You're my little girl."

Being his little girl just about summed up my life. I'd taught young adults, helping them grow into self-sufficient, responsible adults. When would I do the same? Then, my teenage self charged right in. "I hate you! All of you!"

I turned and marched out the back door. And ran. As far and fast as I could. I wanted to hurt Rose and Michael and watch them squirm in fear. Of me. I wanted to ask them why. What was in it for them? I had no idea how long I ran. It couldn't have been very long or far in my weakened state, but when I got home, my legs were barely able to put one foot in front of the other. I was tired, cold, and hungry, but the volcano inside me had quietened a bit. The prodigal daughter, I crept into the house, saying nothing as I poured myself a cup of coffee and sat at the table with Dad and Michael.

"You should go now," Dad said to Michael.

"No, I want to talk to him and get it over with," I said.

Michael stared straight at me. "I'm sorry," he said.

"Sorry?" My brain tried to come up with something hateful to say or do to show Michael how mad I was. Instead, I asked Dad, "Did he tell you who he is?"

"A former student," Mom explained as she took a plate from the microwave and set limp bacon and overdone scrambled eggs in front of me.

"He's the son of the woman who kidnapped me."

For a couple of minutes, we could've heard a grain of salt fall out of its shaker.

Finally, Dad said, "You have some explaining to do."

"I didn't know," Michael said.

"And I'm supposed to believe that?" I asked.

Dad looked at him and commanded, "Start from the beginning, and you better tell it all and tell the truth."

"I don't know how you got to my mother's house," Michael said to me. "But she called me a few weeks ago and invited me to Thanksgiving dinner. She said Susie was there. That was my sister who died. I told Mother to accept that Susie wasn't ever coming back, but she kept insisting that she was back. I wish I'd gone to see her on Thanksgiving, but I had no idea." He looked at me, his eyes pleading for understanding. "I was still looking for you, going over everything in my mind I could think of, trying to figure out where you might be. I must've walked every inch of Turkey Creek twice." He stopped and scanned my face. I figured he wanted to see some sign there that I believed him. I didn't. "I simply couldn't believe my mother . . . my own mother . . . It never entered my mind that she even knew you existed."

Dad cleared his throat. "Get on with it."

"I didn't know until the deputies called me and told me to get down to the sheriff's office. I couldn't believe it. I'd been working with them, cooperating, trying to find you. They interrogated me for hours. I think they're still suspicious of me."

"But you're Jesus," I blurted out, startling Mom and Dad into silence. "You're supposed to know everything. And your feelings, those thoughts that just pop into your head and tell you things? They didn't give you a clue as to where I was?"

Michael ignored my outburst and kept on talking, like a programmed robot that'd practiced his speech. "I kept thinking you were close, but I couldn't figure out where." He took my hand in his and said with what sounded like genuine sincerity, "Sometimes I could see you through a pinkish mist and called out and asked you to give me a sign. I honestly didn't know she knew you. Maybe I should've. She wasn't much of a mother. But she had her good moments. I didn't know she had it in her to be so cruel."

"So what's your mom's connection to Venom and how did he happen to find Samantha?" Dad asked impatiently.

Michael hesitated before saying, "I'm not sure."

"I don't believe you," Dad said

Michael didn't have an answer to that, and for a couple of minutes, questions, belief, and disbelief all hung in the air, no one saying anything. We were like zombies waiting to be told what was real and not real.

The muscles in Dad's face and arms had tightened and were ready to strike with obscenities and blows. "That's it. You didn't go to your mother's for Thanksgiving. You don't know about Venom's connection to her. You haven't told us anything." He wasn't yelling or screaming, but he was using his Marine Sergeant's voice. "Get the hell out of here."

Michael said nothing as he stood up and walked purposefully toward the front door and left.

"There's something he's not telling us," Dad said.

Suddenly, all energy drained from my body. The angry self-pity took over, and the smell of the bacon and eggs made my stomach nauseous. Without another word, I went to my room, lay down, and closed my eyes. But sleep didn't happen. I willed my stomach to stop gurgling, my heart to quit thumping so hard, and my insides to quit quivering.

My thoughts bounced from one fleeting scene to the other. Again, I floated face-down in the cool blue of a swimming pool. Rose chased me with a gun and shot me in the back. Danny, my sweet toddler, ran toward me with his arms outstretched but turned into his father and ran away. Mom told me I'd surely go to hell for all my sins. I heard myself scream.

Mom's soft, warm hand on my forehead woke me from my hallucinations. "You're safe, baby; you're home now."

I opened my eyes, sat up, and hugged her. I could feel the warmth of her arms and the side of her face touching mine and smell the faint aroma of vanilla body wash. She was real. It wasn't a dream. "I love you, Mom," I said. We'd had so many differences in our lives, but I was truly grateful I hadn't had a mom like Michael's.

"I love you, too." For a while she clung to me. "It will get better, Samantha. Time has a way of healing us."

Yes, time and medication would heal me. "Did the deputies search Rose's house?"

"Of course."

"Did they find my pills?"

"I think they found some drugs there, yes."

"Mom, please get me one, just one. Please. I won't ask for anything else. I've got to calm down, to quit thinking. Please, Mom? Please."

"I can't, baby." She stroked my hair the way she had when I was a child.

"My head hurts. Please. Just one."

"We don't have them," she said. "Anything the deputies found, I presume they kept. Would you like some coffee?"

No, I didn't want coffee. I wanted her to go away and leave me alone. I wanted to get rid of the thunderstorm inside my head and the pain and shivering and shaking all over my body. I curled into a fetal ball and cried. This wasn't part of the homecoming I'd imagined. My real mother, the one of my childhood, wouldn't let me suffer like this.

She patted my knee as she stood up and left, closing the door gently behind her. I'd been dismissed.

I jumped out of bed and searched through my original clothes, the ones I'd worn to in-service day last August. They were the only things I'd asked the deputies who searched the house to bring to me. I'd hidden a few pills in them a long time ago. To hide them from Rose. Just in case I needed them, and she didn't come. They weren't there. I turned my pants upside down over my bed and shook them. Only a pen, some old receipts, and a couple of cough drops fell out. Damned deputies. Probably took my pills themselves. My purse and phone hadn't been found. What now? I had to sleep. I needed those pills. I needed to forget Michael. That devil in angel's clothes.

Those images and tapes played in my mind again, the ones that fueled my hatred. Damn Rose and Michael and Venom to hell and back. If I had the strength, I'd choke them to death one at a time. I needed those pills to get rid of the tapes. My brain pulled up Michael's likeness, and I called him every curse word it could think of and meted out justice. He appeared before a female judge and was sentenced to thirty years of hard labor. I looked at him standing behind bars and told him I hoped he would rot there. The thoughts went on and on and on. I saw Michael's face stained with tears, repentant and begging me to forgive him. But I wouldn't. Ever.

I had to stop the tapes, get some sleep, forget. First Daniel, then Jason, now Michael. I hated all men, except my father and Danny, of course.

I had to let it go. I needed something to help me relax. I wanted quiet. Peace. And for everyone and everything to go away. Leave me alone. I frantically searched my room for something, screaming as I pulled the comforter and matching sheets off the bed and stomped on them. I opened, searched, and slammed the dresser drawers, ripped clothes from their hangers in my closet and threw them on the floor. No pills anywhere. I plucked a framed picture of me in my high school graduation cap and gown and threw it across the room. It crashed and sent glass fragments flying. I couldn't stop screaming. All around me were mementos of my childhood. I started throwing all of them.

I didn't stop until I picked up a photo of my brother holding a baby Danny. It was Easter, my brother's last Easter. I hugged the picture to my chest as I surveyed the chaos around me, wondering why Mom and Dad hadn't come in and tried to stop me.

Exhaustion and grief settled into my body and brain. I found my old CD player and a stash of CDs that had been collected and left there over the years. I stuck a pair of earbuds in my ears and listened to Bruce Springsteen and his hungry heart.

25

For the next few days, Mom let me lie in my little girl bed all day and be her baby. She brought food to me and never once told me to get up, get some clothes on, and do something. My emotions bounced from depression so deep I could barely get out of bed to go to the bathroom to agitation that propelled me to run around the room and jump on the bed like a kid. My head hurt. I was always thirsty. I wanted to die. Mom said very little during my outbursts and sometimes patted my knee or placed her palm on my forehead and told me it would get better. She didn't clean my room.

When she, Dad, or Danny came in to see me, they stepped gingerly through the mess, and all of them strained to talk about something that wouldn't upset me. Occasionally, I tried to talk, but most of the time I just listened. I didn't know what to say, and my mind wouldn't bring up the simplest words or thoughts. One evening, when Mom came in carrying a tray of roast beef and potatoes and chattering as if nothing bad had ever happened, I hit the bottom of the tray with my hand. I didn't mean to make a mess. I only wanted her to shut up. She gave me a hurt, disappointed look and stomped out the door, leaving the mess all over my comforter and floor.

A few minutes later, I heard Mom, Dad, and Danny whispering loud enough for me to hear but not loud enough for me to understand their words. Dishes and silverware clanked, and the aroma of chocolate mixed with that of the roast. They were eating dinner, at the dining room table like a real family, and I was the wayward outcast. I ate a few bites off the comforter as if I were in there with them, wondering why Mom hadn't brought any of the chocolate dessert to me. I would've eaten that. I wished I'd died in that old pink basement. Slowly, the sounds and smells drifted away, and I lapsed into a fitful sleep.

When I woke up, I heard Mom and Dad talking and smelled coffee. Like I had when I was young, I lay there and listened, hoping to hear some secret, something they weren't telling me. Were they planning on keeping me here forever? Was I going crazy? Would I ever be able to go home? Why did I think every conversation they had was about me? Maybe they were talking about the weather or their work or Danny's homework. Why did I always think I was the center of their lives? Maybe they had liked their empty nest and were waiting patiently for me to get well enough to go home.

That minute something happened inside me. I knew I had to get well and go home—to mine and Danny's home. The one Dad had faithfully paid the rent on while I was away, where I could be the adult I was supposed to be. I had to go back to work so I could pay my own bills. Optimism. Hope. I knew I could do it. But could I? Resolve wavered. I felt panicky just thinking about being alone. Being separated from Danny while he went to school terrified me. Going through days and nights without the pills to calm my nerves and help me sleep? Never having another one? I imagined my future if I never got better: everyday, unable to get out of bed or go to work; Danny unable to depend on me; Daniel getting custody and never letting me see my son again.

I jumped up, ran into the kitchen, and yelled at my bewildered mom and dad. "I will never, ever let that happen. You hear?" I stomped to the bathroom, turned the knob, and stepped under the warm, soothing water. It would've been better if I'd taken off the t-shirt I'd slept in.

It seemed like my head throbbed less and a bit of energy slipped back into my body. I knew I had to do something, anything, that very day. Alone. To prove to myself that I could accomplish one little thing. Without Mom, Dad, or Danny watching over me and making sure I wasn't going to wreck the house or run away. A walk outside would be good. When I walked out the back door with my notebook, the one I'd kept while in the dungeon, Mom got up from the table and followed me.

It was so cold I thought about going back inside, but instead I trudged through the grass as though I were ninety years old. Mom watched every movement, and when I laboriously climbed the wooden stairs to the deck, she started toward me.

"Don't," Dad said. "She can do it."

And I did. One thing. Maybe tomorrow I'd be able to do another thing. Instead of reading or writing in my notebook, I turned toward Mom and smiled. It felt good. I hadn't done much of that in a while. She put her arm around me as we walked inside.

That night, though, the notebook called to me. Why? Why did I want to read what I thought and felt during that time? Morbid. That's what it was. Especially since I'd made a tiny bit of progress. Yet I had to do it. I touched the cover and ran my fingers over the doodles, arrows, crude drawings of open windows, and the outline of a head and face that was probably supposed to be Danny but looked like a bad cartoon. I stared at it for a long time, trying to remember when I drew it. What had I been thinking? A voice in my head said, "Open the book, Samantha." The voice didn't sound like me or anyone I knew. Whose voice was it? No voices lived in my brain except mine. Hopefully.

Slowly, my hand turned to the first page and the first sentence I'd written: *I've got to get out of this hellhole and find my son.* I didn't want to read anymore, but I couldn't stop. Nor could I quit remembering and reliving. The handwriting was sloppy and almost illegible. I'd written short stories, mostly about lost love, unfaithful, heartless men and violent women, and character assassinations of Rose, Jason, Michael, Daniel, and Venom. I wrote letters to Danny, Mom, and Dad, telling them I loved them and to please forgive me for not being a better daughter and mom.

One letter to Danny brought tears to my eyes.

Dear Danny, my beautiful baby boy. I don't know if you'll ever

*get this or if I'll ever see you again, but if by some miracle you do, re-
member that I didn't mean to leave you, and I carry inside me pictures
of you as a baby, a preschooler, a child growing up, and the teenager
you've become. In my mind I see you graduating from high school
and college and with a little boy and girl, my grandchildren. Always
remember that I love you with all my heart and soul. If I never see
you again in this life, then maybe, like Gramma says, I'll see you in
heaven.*

I had also written letters to God. Mom believed in Him totally; I tried to. I wrote out some of the Bible verses I'd remembered from my childhood. Treat others the way you want to
be treated. Feed the orphans and widows. And I wrote history
lessons for the students I might never teach again. I'd covered
every page with words. Almost every inch of the back inside
cover was filled with question marks and arrows going in both
directions.

I had described the room, Rose, the smells, the sounds
of the television. Over and over, I relived my ordeal. I wanted
to quit reading and thinking, but the images and sounds and
smells played repeatedly in my mind. It was the horror movie
that never quit playing.

26

My decision to get well and become independent again had been knocked dead by the next morning. The nightmares reminded me, once again, how powerless I was. I lay awake for hours, unsure of what was real and what wasn't, wishing I could just take a pain pill and block it all out.

However, Mom wasn't the type to let me go on lying around and feeling sorry for myself forever. She didn't bring breakfast up that morning. Instead, just like when I was a kid, she yelled from downstairs loud enough for me to hear, "Time to get up!"

I didn't respond.

"Samantha McKenzie, get out of that bed right now!"

I pulled the pillow over my head. I was not a schoolgirl, and I would not get up.

Then she pulled out the sentence that always worked, "You better not make me come up there and get you!"

Slowly, my feet touched the carpet, and I sat up on the side of the bed. No pain. No throbbing headache. The shock of having no physical pain gave me the jolt I needed to make myself stand up.

Mom's voice called from the kitchen, "And get dressed. We're going to see Dr. Sawyer this morning. And, for goodness sake, clean up your room!"

I minded her, but in my own time, starting with a slow march to the kitchen. I opened the door to the broom closet, and without saying a word, pulled out the vacuum and marched back to my room to suck everything I could off the floor. Like I did to my mind. Suck up the debris and store it in the dust bag in my brain.

I threw my clothes onto the closet floor and closed the door, rehung the pictures with the frames and glass intact, and took the broken glass from the others and placed them in a drawer. I jerked the comforter that still smelled like rotten roast beef to the laundry room and tossed it into the washer. Like the adolescent I still was, I refused to put on my going-to-the-doctor clothes; I wore jeans and a sweatshirt. I did put a tiny dab of olive oil in my palms, rubbed them together, and brushed it into my frizzy hair so I wouldn't scare anyone.

About half an hour later, I stood staring at the contents of the refrigerator, trying to find something that didn't make me want to throw-up. Mom walked into the kitchen to tell me that Daniel had called earlier that morning to ask about making Christmas plans for Danny.

"It's almost Christmas?" I asked, suddenly aware I hadn't been keeping up with what day it was.

"Yes," she said, laughing a little. "Dad and Danny are going to go get the tree today."

"Today?" My time in the pink prison seemed like some far-off world in another universe and time, but it was probably just a few days ago.

"Would you like to go shopping after your appointment? It might do you good."

"No, I don't think so. Not yet." I pulled a piece of left-over chocolate cake from the refrigerator, but I was interrupted when the phone rang.

It was Jason. At first, my heart leapt. A fleeting image of him hugging me and telling me he loved me was replaced with reality. "I just called to see how you are," he said. His words were awkward, as if he'd been rehearsing what to say.

"Fine," I answered.

"Let me know if I can do anything to help," he said.

"I will. Thanks for calling."

And it was over. The man who'd once professed his love for me could barely think of any words to say to me, and he didn't even mean the ones he did say. It was a courteous gesture, something that said he cared a little but didn't know how to show it.

I'd barely put the phone down when it rang again. This time it was Greg.

"Hi, Sam," he said cheerfully, as if my whole world hadn't crumbled since the last time we'd talked.

"Hi," I said, though I wanted to slam the phone down and go back to eating.

"How are you feeling?"

"How do you think I'm feeling?" I couldn't help it. I wanted to be polite, but it just wasn't in me.

"I know you must be going through hell. If you'll let me, I'd like to come see you. Help you if I can, if it's not too soon."

Was he kidding? It was way too soon. "Maybe later. After the holidays sometime," I said in a clipped voice. "Well, I've got to go. Thanks for calling." I hung up.

After my last bite of the chocolate cake, I took the plate to the kitchen and stuck it in the dishwasher. While there, I figured it couldn't hurt to look through Mom's meds. Just to see if she had anything that would soothe my nerves, though I knew she didn't. Just some buffered aspirin, ibuprofen, some old cold tablets, stuff to put on scrapes and scratches, and various antacids.

I took a couple of aspirin, washed them down with a glass of cold water, and went back to bed to wait. Wait for my mommy to take me to the doctor, like a little girl. Why couldn't she let me be a grown up? Maybe because I acted like a child. She didn't trust me to make the simplest decisions, like whether to go to the doctor or not. I'd show her; I'd get out of my childhood bed and go home. I didn't need a psychiatrist. I needed to be an adult. I'd show her.

Propped up on pillows and looking out the window, I reminisced about my old life with Jason and Danny and how I didn't know then how blissful normal was.

The phone rang again. This time Mom answered it.

I heard her voice float up from downstairs. "Good morning, Michael." She didn't sound nervous. She sounded polite and even almost cheerful. "Yes, that's good. I'll be there." She paused, listening to whatever he was saying, then said, "Great. See you then."

Now that was odd. What was going on and how long had it been going on? My mom and Michael? Friends? Of course not. Yet when she came into my room to force me out of bed, she didn't mention him or their phone call. When I told her I thought it was strange that Daniel, Jason, Greg, and Michael had all called that morning, she said that they had been calling every morning since I had been found. I had no answer to that.

Dr. Sawyer had red hair. Not auburn like mine, but a bright orange-red that looked like a home coloring job gone wrong, but it was cut short and framed her round face perfectly. She was short, stout, younger than I expected, and spoke with the authority of an experienced sixth grade teacher. We had the potential to be instant allies.

When Mom went into her office with me, Dr. Sawyer politely asked her to sit in the waiting room. In a huff, Mom obeyed, but she was definitely not pleased. I liked Dr. Sawyer even more.

"Were you a Marine?" I asked.

She laughed. "No, but I had three stubborn sisters."

Her office was decorated the way I'd have done it. Paintings cluttered the cream-colored walls and sunshine streamed through a large window highlighting a real tree, not a plastic one, that decorated one corner. On her desk and credenza were prayer plants and Chinese evergreens. I sat in one of the aqua-colored chairs and stared at the huge copy of a pond scene behind her desk. All at once, I was in a canoe floating down a stream, my hand over the side and touching the cool ripples as water lilies floated peacefully beside me.

Dr. Sawyer sat in the chair opposite mine and followed my gaze toward the painting. "When I feel flustered, I, too, get lost in that picture."

"Perfect for a shrink's office."

She ignored my comment. "How are you today?"

It was just a remark, a nicety you said to someone to be polite, but I couldn't help my response. It just came right out of my mouth. "You tell me."

She laughed. "You've got this shrink thing backwards," she said. "You get to talk; I listen."

"So what do you want me to talk about?"

"How do you feel? Does your head hurt? Are you tired?"

"Yes and yes."

It was a long, long hour. I didn't know why I was taking my anger out on her, but it didn't seem to bother her. She kept talking and asking questions; I kept giving flip answers. I'm not sure how it happened, but at some point, we were having a cordial conversation about Impressionist painters and which ones we liked best. Her favorite was Pissarro—I told her mine was Monet. By the end of the session, I was blabbing my heart out, pausing only to breathe. I told her about my childhood, Mom and Dad, Daniel and Jason, Greg and Michael, and Rose and the pink basement. She barely got a few words in, and when time was almost running out, I asked her what I'd been asking myself for years, "What's wrong with men, anyway?"

"When I find out, I'll write a book," she said with a wink.

Mom wanted to know everything we talked about, a play-by-play description. She was both annoyed and angry when I wouldn't tell her. She did, however, take me to the phone store where I purchased a brand-new cellphone. Again, I was connected to the world. But there was no one I wanted to talk to or text and nothing I wanted to know.

Later, when Dad got home from work and I was in my room trying to make sense of the words on the pages of a book, I heard him and Mom talking about having lunch with Michael. I could tell they were beginning to like him and that they believed he was a nice guy. Apparently, they felt no need to bother me with their findings. I was livid. Self-pity flew away; my old friends, anger and resentment, came home. I'd show them. I'd get out of this house. Go home. Find out the truth. Be an adult. And I had to start somewhere. I had to go back to that miserable old house.

Mom and Dad thought it was a terrible idea, but I talked them into it, and Dr. Sawyer didn't object. For some irrational reason I couldn't quite figure out, I knew if I went back to the house that had been my prison, I would be cured. If I could go in and walk freely out the door, every tape connected with my incarceration would be wiped from my mind. And if Michael was there to let me in and be my tour guide, I would know once and for all if he could be trusted.

27

"It's so dark," I said as I pushed open the heavy front door and stared into the hallway I'd seen only once—the day they had carried me out.

Michael switched on the lights, but it didn't help much. I inched down the hallway, inspecting each crack and faded spot on the flowered wallpaper and dragging my feet across the faded carpet. To the left was a living room with a fireplace, an old Victorian couch, and a matching chair. To the right were stairs that led to the second story, their centers sinking, dusty, and worn, and at the end of the hall were the stairs that led to the basement. The air was musty and smelled like old lady gardenia, and the pictures that lined the walls were dusty. The whole place was a mausoleum.

I found the door that led to the basement. It was right there. Those hateful walls, those dirty pink walls that had held me, tortured me, and watched me suffer. I couldn't go any further. I turned, pushed Dad and Michael aside, and dashed back outside. They followed me.

"I can't. I just can't." I plopped onto the brown grass, my head in my hands, gasping for breath and desperately trying to get the pink visions out of my head.

Dad sat down beside me and put an arm around my shoulders. "You don't have to."

"I thought if I went inside again and saw that it was just a house, I'd feel better." But it wasn't just a house. There was something sinister about it. Maybe it was the remnants of Rose.

"Maybe later, when you feel better."

"I thought I was better." I couldn't bring myself to move even though I was cold.

While Dad held me tight, those ever-present resentments filled my mind. If I ever saw Rose again, I'd have do her bodily harm, after I tormented her with a gun and a belt. And what about Michael? I couldn't bring myself to believe he had anything to do with it, but I couldn't shake the doubt.

He stood looking down at Dad and me. I stared straight into his blue-green eyes and dared him to lie to me. "Why was Venom at your mother's house? And I want the truth this time."

"Mother was his supplier." He said it with no emotion or inflection.

Dad was on him quicker than a frog on a June bug. "What the hell?" His fist tightened around the collar of Michael's shirt.

Michael coughed and sputtered and carried on like Dad was strangling him. I felt sorry for him. "Dad, stop it. You're hurting him."

Dad looked at me as if he'd been in a trance, then he looked back at Michael and let go.

After coughing some more and catching his breath, Michael said, "I didn't know until the deputies questioned me about Mother's connection to Venom."

"You didn't know a thing about it? You stayed with her last spring and you didn't know a thing about her drug dealing? You expect us to believe that?" Dad bellowed.

It all began to make sense to me. Jason and Danny bought drugs from Venom; he got them from Rose. But what was Michael's role in all of it?

Michael regained his composure. "I knew she was selling drugs, but that's all I knew. I tried to get her to stop, told her I'd help her get into rehab, pay her bills, whatever she needed."

"But you didn't turn her in, did you?" I said.

Michael sat down beside me, careful not to touch me. I looked into his face, searching for some sign of guilt or innocence. I saw anguish. "She's my mother. She wasn't the best mother in the world, but I didn't want her to go to jail. I just wanted to help her. We fought about it all the time when I was with her. I had to leave, but I still tried to help her. She'd lost her daughter and granddaughter; two husbands had left her. How could I not try to at least help her?"

I believed him. He'd tried to help me, a virtual stranger. Yet I couldn't let go of the anger. "It didn't work, did it?"

"No."

Dad, at attention and ready for action, eyed Michael as if he were a mountain lion ready to pounce on me. "You better watch your step, boy. I'm watching you. If you did anything to help your crazy mother or if you ever hurt my daughter, you better run. You got that?"

Michael nodded. "I would never intentionally hurt her."

"You sure as hell better not."

Michael was no longer Jesus wanting to help people. He was just a young man filled with uncertainty. His eyes cried out for help and understanding.

"What's going to happen to your mother?" I asked.

"She's in the psych ward right now. Don't know if or when she'll be able to stand trial." He gazed at his hands while he spoke, and his fingers twisted twigs of dead grass around and around. His eyes were watery.

A sudden spurt of empathy washed through me. He was a victim too. His mother was ding-bat crazy. No telling what she had done to him when he was a child.

"What was it like growing up in a God-forsaken house like this?" I asked.

"The house wasn't always like this. Mother was always—" He stopped and searched for a word. "Stern, sometimes downright mean. But she kept the house clean and cooked and sometimes we had pool parties, and sometimes it was filled with laughter. But she could turn on a dime, and we never knew when that would be. She'd hit us with a belt or—" He stopped again, swallowed, and cleared his throat. "It wasn't the house. It was her."

For a while, we were all silent. Even Dad couldn't think of anything to say.

Finally, Michael looked directly into my eyes and said, "I'm sorry. I should've turned her in, but I didn't know. I had no idea she could do what she did. I really am sorry."

My sympathy was short-lived. "You should have done something," I snapped.

He looked at me, started to say something, but then marched to the car that had been his mother's, got in, and drove away.

Dad took my hand. "Let's get out of here. This place gives me the creeps."

As he drove us home, I said, "You knew about Rose and Venom, didn't you?"

"Not until you were in the hospital." He paused and added, "I think Michael might be telling the truth. I interrogated him about six times in the last few days, as hard and fast and mean as I could, and he passed. Your mom and I had lunch with him. He told us about his sister and about her daughter drowning and how his mother had been cruel to her children, but he hadn't known until he came home last spring about her selling drugs. We both agreed not to talk about any of it to you until you were better. He sure as hell didn't keep his end of the bargain."

And there it was. Everyone keeping everything from me. Because I was his little girl and too weak to handle it.

I suppressed the hurt and anger. "So what's going to happen to Venom?"

"Guess that's up to a jury. At least for now, he's in jail."

For a while, we didn't say anything. I wondered what he was thinking. What else was he keeping from me? Would I always be a baby to him? Somehow, I had to take control of my own life. But how? I couldn't even decide if this year I should wear my silly Christmas sweater with bells that jingled—the one Jason had bought me. I suddenly realized Dad hadn't said anything about Jason since I'd been home.

"So how's Jason?" I asked.

His expression was that of the proverbial deer in head-lights. "Ok, I guess."

I'd hoped he'd tell me Jason was upset and sad and could barely go on without me. "Living with Carrie?"

He nodded, looked over at me, and said, "He looked for you, honey. Every day, for a long time. He worried about you. I could tell."

"It's okay, Dad, you can tell me the truth. I'm a big girl now; I can handle it."

"Truth about what?"

"For starters, I know Jason doesn't love me, never did. You can say it."

"But he does love you. Maybe not like you want, but . . ."

"For Pete's sake!" I shouted. "Stop it. I'm not your baby. In case you haven't noticed, I've grown up."

He spoke over me, "Shut up and listen."

I shut up.

"What I wonder is, how'd that friend of yours up north know you were missing?"

"Who? Greg? Daniel probably told him. They're friends."

"Well Greg and Jason sure aren't friends. I thought they were going to knock each other's brains out."

"Huh?"

"Little girl, you got this whole line of guys wanting to take care of you. You need to straighten this thing out."

"What are you talking about?"

"Jason didn't like Greg or Daniel. Daniel didn't like Jason. And near as I could tell, they all thought Michael was weird, and all of them suspected each other of having something to do with your disappearance."

"What the crap?"

"Hell, if you don't understand it, how can I?"

I felt paralyzed by shock and disbelief.

"I called them all and told them you were home, and they all still want to help you."

"Help me what?"

"Hell if I know."

Did they all think I was helpless, a damsel to be rescued? Forever the needy friend, never the love? I'd show them. I didn't need them. Any of them. Danny and I would be fine, no matter what. Michael had said so.

When we got home, I told Mom and Dad I was ready to go back to my own house. They unexpectedly didn't argue with me but asked if we'd stay through the holidays. I agreed. We all wanted an old-fashioned Christmas, the kind Danny and I had every year with my parents, and we needed something familiar, warm, and comforting in our lives.

Michael continued to be attentive and persistent. He called every day and came to see me as often as I would let him. He didn't try to answer my questions and acted like I'd never asked, but he brought poinsettias for Mom and talked football with Dad. They even invited him for Christmas. Danny invited his dad.

When I was a kid, we'd gone to Grandma's house and all my aunts, uncles, and cousins would be there. The house would be filled with the aroma of baking turkey, cinnamon and pumpkin spice, and a real evergreen tree, and the noise was just a decibel lower than a jet taking off. I'd always looked forward to it the entire year and was never disappointed.

Gradually, though, my cousins and I grew up, Grandma and Grandpa died, and the uncles and aunts spent the holidays with their children and grandchildren. Our family Christmases now were much smaller, but still special It was always Mom, Dad, Danny, and me. My parents decorated, Mom cooked, and Dad, though Danny had quit believing in Santa a long time ago, still put on the same Santa suit that had delighted my cousins and gave out the gifts. He would "ho-ho-ho" then laugh for real, and he had a younger-than-his-age spring in his step. He did the same that year, even giving presents to Michael and Daniel, but not as many as he did to Mom, Danny, and me.

After a couple of glasses of pre-dinner wine, Michael and Daniel acted like friends. Well, that was probably stretching it a bit. They acted like tolerable acquaintances. And I was able, for a while, to forget the basement and Rose with her belt and gun, and my mind didn't pull up images of a little girl floating underwater, surrounded by blood.

I didn't totally trust Michael but had gotten cautiously close to him again. We were able to talk, laugh, and sit at the table and have a pleasant dinner. I pretended I was fine and pushed everything to the back of my mind.

Danny knew, though. "You okay, Mom?" he asked several times during our hour of gluttony, Dad's war stories, Daniel's praise of Chicago, and everyone's absolute admiration of Nick Saban and Alabama football. Well, everyone but Mom.

When it was all over, Michael helped me pick up discarded wrapping paper. "Would you like to take a ride?" he asked.

Danny, sitting on the couch with his head bowed over his new phone, jumped up, put his arm around my shoulder, and said, "No, she wouldn't."

Michael picked up a couple of green bows from the floor and put them on the table for Mom to use again next year. "I understand," he said.

After a few seconds of silence, Danny shouted at Michael, "She wants to be with us, not you!"

For a moment, I was speechless. Why hadn't I noticed how angry my son was? I had been so focused on myself, I hadn't seen he was hurting too. "Daniel Caldwell McKenzie!" I finally blurted.

Immediately, everyone stopped and stared at us. Daniel Sr. and Dad stood up and started toward us.

"It's okay," Michael said. "I need to go anyway."

And he left. I spent the rest of the evening staying close to Danny and trying to lighten the mood again. He, Mom, and I talked, laughed, snacked on cookies, and rehashed some of the funny things we'd done on previous Christmases. Daniel and Dad watched football. I forgot about the pink dungeon, the search for pills, and everyone and everything except my family and having fun with them.

Well, almost everyone and everything. Without warning, an image of Jason flashed through my mind. Dad missed him too. Several times throughout the day, he'd accidentally called Daniel by Jason's name. Or he'd laugh at something and ask me if I remembered the time he, Jason, and I got lost trying to find the job site and wound up somewhere in Fairfield instead of Hoover.

I couldn't help it. I laughed with him and choked back melancholy at the same time.

Greg called the next day. I thanked him for coming all the way to Parkville to look for me and even told him I wanted to be friends again. Then we asked each other about our Christmases. He'd spent his with Anna and the kids. I told him about mine, leaving out the Jason part.

Then suddenly he asked, "How'd you like to spend New Year's in Chicago?"

I wasn't sure how to answer.

He filled the silent gap with, "It'll be like old times, except we won't have Daniel and Anna with us."

I was blindsided. Chicago on News Year's? With Greg? Since my visit last summer, I hadn't felt the same about him. Something inside me felt uneasy even talking to him on the phone.

"I'll think about it," I said.

Days at Mom and Dad's turned into weeks. I was better and wanted to go home, but something inside me, fear, wouldn't let me make the first step. I just kept procrastinating. All of us were getting on each other's nerves. Dad growled about everything, especially Danny's inability to clean his room or wash his dirty clothes. Mom went on a strike and refused to ever cook or clean again until someone started helping.

One morning, I walked into the kitchen to find Mom and Dad having a huge argument about nothing.

"All I said was the eggs had too much pepper!" Dad yelled.

Mom picked up his plate, threw his eggs and grits in the sink, and turned on the disposal. "Next time, fix them yourself!"

Danny sauntered into the kitchen and mumbled, "Jeez, they can here y'all in Wisconsin"

Dad turned and yelled at my sweet son, "Don't talk to your grandmother like that!"

Well, I couldn't let that go by. "He didn't—"

"And you stay out of it," Dad warned, pointing his finger at me like I was a child.

That did it. Time to go home. To my own home. "Get dressed," I said to Danny. "We're going home."

"I'm hungry," he said, looking at the stove, the counter, and then into the refrigerator. If he'd looked in the sink, he'd have seen our breakfast. Five minutes later, dressed, hungry, angry, and disheveled, we started out the door.

"Can I drive?" Danny asked.

Mom stopped her fussing at Dad and said, "No, you're too young to drive."

I handed the keys to my son and slammed the door behind us.

Dad had told me he'd given Danny a few nerve-wracking driving lessons, but they obviously didn't take. The car tried to back out of the driveway, stalled, jerked, and stopped. It started again and lurched backwards into the street without slowing down and without the driver looking to see if any other cars were in the way. I couldn't help it. I closed my eyes and screamed. From somewhere close by, tires screeched, and curse words floated in the air.

Under the guidance of my constant "No! Don't! Stop! Slow down!" and "Dear God, help us!" we made it to the house I'd left last August, but it no longer seemed like home. My parents' house had felt like home; this one was just a memory of a place I'd once lived. For a few minutes I sat in the car, wanting to run home to Mommy and Daddy.

Waves of fluctuating optimism and uncertainty rushed through me as I stepped out of the car. Almost immediately, I slipped and fell on my back with my head in the mud and my body on the driveway, looking up at a cloudless sky. "Why?" I asked no one as optimism dried up and anxiety seeped in.

By the time I got up and into the house, Danny was already there, turning on lights and heat and opening and closing pantry and refrigerator doors. It was all I could do to take those first few steps through the front door into the living room. It was strange to me, the cold, quiet, dark house, with none of the lingering aromas of food left out all night. No lotions, furniture polish, or those fetid smells of a teenage boy's room. No television blasted its commercials; no loud music competed for airwaves. It was sterile. Danny and I were alone.

Danny was already on the phone, evidently telling his girlfriend the news that he was home. Too tired and weary to do anything else, I turned on the television and curled up in a blanket on the couch. I was awakened by the doorbell and Danny searching through my purse.

"Don't worry," he said as he pulled out a twenty and ran to the door. "I got it."

Panic set in. Was it Venom? By the time I'd jumped from the couch and started for the door, Danny was headed my way carrying a box with a heavenly aroma. He'd ordered pizza. He sat the box on the coffee table and brought me a Coke. After eating, he cleaned up the mess. I thought I heard something outside, like someone walking in the yard. He looked out and said it was the wind. I slept on the couch that night. He slept on the floor beside me, wadded up in his red plaid blanket.

28

The next morning, I found out why Danny had been so gracious the night before. After I opened my eyes but before I got off the couch, he sat up and said, "I know you just got home and all, and I love you, Mom, but I need to go spend a few days at Dad's."

It took a few moments for my brain to comprehend what he was saying.

Danny jumped up and headed for the kitchen. "He's gonna take me driving and to look at cars."

I managed to sit up and put my elbows on my knees and rub my hands through my hair. Flecks of dirt landed on my sweats and the floor. I shook my head.

"He's gonna let me drive all the way to Oneonta and back."

"Coffee," I whispered.

"You probably could use a little alone time." He sounded like my mother.

Maybe if I took a shower, something would make sense.

"You okay with me not being here?"

I ignored him and wobbled into the bathroom, where the towels I'd left hanging last August were still on their rods. The shampoo and conditioner still rested on the side of the tub, but the tub was filthy. I stood in it anyway and let shampoo, soap, and warm water wash life into my body and mind. Danny wanted to go to Daniel's? No, absolutely not. How could he leave me alone right now? I needed him. What if Venom came back? *Get a grip, Sam. He's your son. Why would you want him here if Venom came around? Anyway, he's in jail, and everything is back to normal. You've got to let Danny visit his dad.*

I might be scared, but I could do it. There were no pink walls here. No old witch to torment me. No pain pills either, but I would be fine. I could do it.

As I walked into the kitchen where Danny had my coffee ready, I said as cheerfully as I could manage, "Yes, of course, you may go to your dad's." The words came out stiff and rehearsed.

"Thanks," he said as he took limp pizza from the microwave, set it in front of me, and ever so briefly, put his arms around my shoulders. Outside it was cold, dreary, and miserable. Inside it was warm and cozy, the way I'd dreamed it so many times while in that pink prison. While we waited for his dad to pick him up, my son and I were together in the same kitchen at the same time; we ate our pizzas together and talked about his new semester and how he was going to try to make better grades. For a few minutes, we were actually communicating, until he broached the subject I'd been dreading.

"I'm glad you're home, Mom, but I'm still mad at you."

"For what?" Of course I knew what, but it just popped out of my mouth, like one of those dumb questions people ask when they're stalling.

"For keeping Dad and me apart. Why'd you do it?"

I thought about my answer. How could I explain that his father had been a spoiled, selfish man who cared more about money and having a good time than about either of us? No way could I tell him his father had wanted to kill him before he was born. All I could say was, "I'm sorry."

"Yeah, me too." I tried to read his emotions by the expression on his face. Anger? Disappointment? Both? "But did you have to lie about him? Tell me he left for no reason? Did you want to punish him? Or me?" With each word his voice grew louder, and my calm, helpful son turned back into a teenager.

"It wasn't like that," I said.

But he stood up, walked to his room, and shut the door. At least he didn't slam it. I never realized how much he was like me—that would have been my exact reaction.

I'd made the absolute worst mistake of my life and hurt my own son. Now, it was his turn to hurt me. With all my heart I regretted keeping him and his dad apart. When I was pregnant, I thought about calling Daniel but kept procrastinating—for fifteen years. Now, there was no way to fix the past or make up for all the pain I'd caused both of them. During all the time I was in that basement, he'd been there for Danny, had even found a house of his own so he and his son could be together. Maybe Daniel had grown up after all.

That afternoon, Daniel came to get his son and brought Danny's girlfriend, Kylee, with him. She and Danny played video games in the living room while Daniel and I talked in the kitchen. I told him I was ready to discuss arrangements for joint custody.

"Remember that one Christmas and New Year's Eve we had together?" he asked while we sat at the table

"Of course," I said. "I'm surprised you do."

"I really did love you."

He'd had a fine way of showing it. "And that's why you left me, right? With nothing but some money for an abortion I didn't want?"

"I've regretted it ever since, especially now," he said quietly, eyes never leaving mine. Then he pulled a small, wrapped, Christmas present from his coat pocket and handed it to me.

"What's this?"

"Open it."

I was pretty sure he could see my hands quivering when I pulled and tugged at the bow. Instead of coming loose, the ribbon knotted even more. I felt anxiety and humiliation building up inside me, even at such a small thing. I wanted to run away, but I just sat there and kept fumbling with it. Daniel put me out of my misery. Without a word, he opened it for me. It was a small, shiny red ornament. It was from the only Christmas we had spent together. I knew it because it had little globs of soap on it. We had wanted to make our scraggly, Charlie Brown tree look like it had flecks of snow on it, and we had mixed soap flakes with water and flung the mess at the tree. It had to have been the ugliest tree that had ever been decorated, but in my eyes, it was the most beautiful.

I gazed at the ornament, so fragile, so easily crushed, like love. I had loved him back then. For a moment, I was back in Valparaiso, mixing soap and water. He picked a handful from the bowl and threw it at the tree. It landed all over the wall, draperies, and floor. I did the same. He flung some at me. I threw some at him. We giggled like two kids playing in the snow. He rubbed some in my hair, I massaged it into his face, then later we showered together. I thought our bliss would last forever.

Suddenly, reality set in, and I was back in the present and way too close to this man who had broken my heart. My mind commanded me to get up and run. My body didn't obey. My mouth finally opened and said, "I can't believe you kept this. Why?"

"Don't know. I didn't mean to," he said. "Found it when I sold the Mountain Brook house."

Almost imperceptibly, his chair moved close to mine and his arm went around my shoulder. His skin was warm, and he smelled of musky cologne. Awkward. So very dangerous. Pleasure and pain. I had to get away, go somewhere. Talk about something, anything. "Did you find a job yet?"

"I'm selling furniture until I get a better one."

Move. Stand up, bake a cake. Instead, I said, "You're charming. A perfect salesman type. You'll do well."

He smiled. "Charming, huh?"

"You could be more charming," I said, "if your breath didn't smell like onions and garlic." Then, for only the second time in months, I laughed for real. "Why me?"

"Why you what?" he asked.

I pushed his arm back, leaned forward, and turned my head toward him. "Why were you with me back then and not with one of those beautiful girls you liked so well?"

"I always thought you were beautiful. Besides, I liked you better." He said it with that captivating, flirty smile he'd used on so many women.

"Or maybe it was just to spite your parents," I said pointedly. "Tell me the truth. I can take it."

Oh, but he was good. In a graceful, fluid movement, he put his arm back around me, and his hand massaged my neck. His lips were dangerously close to mine when he said, "That, too."

My first instinct at that minute was to slam the box on the table and break the small tribute to our yesteryear. But the longer I sat there, the more that deep-down sentimental part of my brain took over. I wanted to keep that small ornament in there with those other milestone memories, like that Christmas when Danny was five, and I'd caught him looking out the window at midnight, hoping to see Santa. I knew I would keep the small, red ornament and treasure it.

I pulled away from him and said, "Your parents got the last laugh, didn't they?"

"No, it wasn't like that. Remember the first time you met them?"

Of course, I did. His mother was next in line after Rose for the title of Witch of the Year. "They didn't like me."

"But I was proud of you. You didn't let them get to you. You stood your ground and talked to them like you didn't know they were filthy rich."

"So what? You left me, anyway. I didn't care about your money then, and I don't care now."

"Not much left to care about." He paused, as if trying to come up with the proper speech. "We've talked around the most important things: you and Danny. How are you really? And please be honest with me."

I found it hard to believe he actually cared about me or how I was. He wanted something. "I'm fine. Ordeal's over now. How do you like your new house?"

"I like that it's close to Danny and you."

"I appreciate you helping Mom and Dad with him while I was . . . while I was away. They think I should be more cooperative with you and quit saying bad things about you."

"So do I."

"I'll try to be nice if you will."

Without a preamble or even a warning, Daniel said, "Are you serious about Michael? Do you love him?"

It caught me off-guard. I didn't know how to answer. After a few seconds of coughing, clearing my throat, sipping tea, and general hem-hawing, I confessed, "I don't know what you're talking about."

"I know you don't believe me, but I loved you when we lived in Valparaiso, and I love you now."

No, he didn't love me. He just wanted a meal-ticket. I wouldn't believe him. Instead of acknowledging Daniel's statement of love, I said, "Did you know Greg told me the same thing?" And immediately wished I hadn't said it.

His expression was that of little boy who'd lost his turtle. "I guess that's my cue to go."

Without a word, he picked up his jacket, slipped it on, and was out the door, calling for Danny to follow him.

I wanted to run out to him, tell him I hadn't meant it like that. I really didn't mean to hurt his feelings. But he was gone, and we still hadn't talked about custody of Danny.

29

While Danny was gone with Daniel, I retrieved the rest of our clothes and personal things from my parents' home and started getting the house organized and ready for the start of the new semester. I was hyper-alert but not as scared as I thought I'd be all alone. As long as I was busy with a task, I couldn't dwell on the memories I wished would just go away. I cleaned the months-old dirt from the cabinets, counters, door frames, and floors, and washed all the bed and bath linens while listening to Bruce Springsteen, Billy Joel, Whitney Houston, and all my favorite recording artists as loud as possible. It didn't completely drown out the nagging tape in my head that contained all the things I didn't want to think about, but it helped me ignore it for a few hours.

When I finished cleaning, I called Michael and invited him over to talk. I still needed to decide if he had been telling the truth or not. To be honest, I missed his presence in my life, and I wanted to be able to trust him again.

He arrived shortly with KFC in tow, and we sat across from each other in the kitchen. He was wearing a Christmas sweater with a picture of Santa and the word "Believe" stitched on it in a pattern of snowflakes. We were silent as we began eating. Michael either couldn't think of anything to say or was in some faraway place in his head where I couldn't join him. All I could do was stare at that sweatshirt.

After a few awkward minutes, he asked, "Are you okay?"

I nodded, still staring at his torso.

He looked down too and then back up at me with a grin. "I like the message."

Oh, right. He could sense what I was thinking. I couldn't help it. I laughed. "You, uh, you do know Christmas is over, don't you?"

"It's still a good message."

Silence again. Could it get any more awkward? Yes, it could. As we ate, the only sounds were our crunching and munching the chicken. I wanted to talk about Rose and Venom but couldn't make myself start. Images of that ugly pink basement tried to surface in my mind, but I refused to go there. I willed myself to focus on Michael, to notice his eyes and expressions, and to ask him questions and demand a straight answer. Had he really not known?

"I really didn't know," he said, answering my unspoken question.

"How could you not know?"

He set his drink down so hard the ice jumped. "I told you I didn't know."

Was calm, peaceful Michael actually getting angry?

"Want another one?" I asked, and without waiting for his answer, jumped up and opened the refrigerator door.

As I walked back to him and poured more soda in his glass, my hand trembled. He reached out to help me, and I instinctively jerked my hand away from his touch, splattering liquid all over the table and his ugly Christmas sweater. After a second of stunned silence, we both laughed and began to clean up the mess.

"Take your shirt off. I'll stick it in the dryer," I told him as I threw away soiled napkins.

"If you insist," he said with a smile, peeling off the wet fabric to reveal a plain white t-shirt underneath.

"Want another drink?" I asked as I opened the dryer door and threw the shirt in.

"Absolutely not," he said. "This is it. No more shirts."

We went into the living room, sat side by side on the couch, and again lapsed into silence. Last summer, conversation and laughter had been easy for us. Now? How could we talk with a dirty pink prison lurking between us and neither of us knowing how to get around it?

Finally, he reached into his pocket, smiled, and handed me a small jewelry box, beautifully wrapped in shiny silver paper with a red bow. "I wanted to give this to you at Christmas, but not in front of your family and Daniel." Inside was a silver chain with a tiny mustard seed inside a crystal pendant and a card that read *Keep the faith*. "Merry Christmas, Samantha, and a much happier new year."

"It's so beautiful," I said as my arms flung around him and my lips kissed his cheek. "Thank you." I meant it. This man could not possibly have been involved with the evil people that had targeted me and my family.

He fastened the chain around my neck and when I turned to show him how it looked, he hugged me again, and I could feel the energy and joy of the last few minutes drain from his body. As he let go and slid an arm's length away from me, an image of little boy Alan rushing from the pool to find someone to save his sister flashed through my mind.

"His name was actually Michael Alan," he said. "I need to tell you about him."

I'd gotten used to him answering questions I hadn't asked and without thinking, said, "The papers . . ." I stopped and stared into his eyes. The light bulb went off in my head. "You? You were with Georgie when she drowned? Oh, my God." My hands automatically went to my mouth.

He nodded. "The papers got it wrong. Besides getting my name wrong, they also said I was her brother. Georgie was my sister's daughter. I was her uncle, even though she was older than me."

"What happened?" I asked in a whisper.

"It was my fault," he said. "Georgie lived with us, and she was always pushing me around, hitting me, and telling me what I could and couldn't do. She was bigger than me, but I always fought back. That day was just like any other day. We were scuffling at the edge of the deep end. I pushed too hard, and she fell in, hitting her head on the side. She went under and didn't come up. I watched the surface for a couple of minutes before I jumped in after her. I took her hand and tried to pull her. Blood floated around her. I managed to pull her to the shallow end but couldn't get her up the steps. I was so scared, I just left her there. I got out of that pool faster than I'd ever done anything."

As he spoke, he was looking towards a lamp standing in the corner of the room, but his eyes were faraway. His face was ghostly white as tears rolled down his cheeks. His words were flat and quiet. "I left her face out of the water, on the top step. Honestly, I did. But she must have drifted back into the water. She was . . ."

"It was an accident," I interrupted, hoping to make him feel better.

He ignored my sympathy. "I ran as fast as I could to get Mother and Father and tried to tell them what happened, but I was screaming and crying, and my words didn't come out right. They told me to shut up; they were drunk and thought Georgie and I were playing. I was jumping up and down and racing back and forth. They wouldn't listen. I went to Nathan's room and told him, and he was the one who pulled her out and tried CPR. He yelled at me to call 911."

"It wasn't your fault. You were a kid."

"If I'd gotten her out instead of running, she might still be alive and so would Susie. If I hadn't fought with her; if I hadn't pushed her . . ."

I didn't know what to say. No wonder he was a screwball. He needed a shrink more than I did. "Where was Susie?"

"She was messed up. Booze, drugs, some guy she met at a bar and ran off with. I think they were in Las Vegas when it happened." He paused, as if trying to remember and not remember at the same time. "My mother and father didn't even get in trouble. It was ruled an accident." His words were streaked with bitterness. "It was my fault. My mother told me I should've saved her."

Any sympathy I'd ever had for Rose vanished. I wished I had strangled her.

"My father left us. The going got tough, and he left. He never liked Susie, and he didn't like Georgie living with us."

"His own granddaughter?"

"He wasn't Susie's or Nathan's father. Mother had been married before him. Their father disappeared and never came back. She married my father and he left her, too. I stayed with her until I was out of high school, but eventually I couldn't take it anymore either. When I took your class, I was living alone in a rundown, studio apartment, working as an orderly at a hospital and trying to get through nursing training."

"I'm so sorry," I told him.

There was nothing else to say.

30

Before I was ready, it was time to go back to work and begin another in-service day. I'd gone to the last one and didn't get home for four months. Since I'd been home, I'd barely been able to step outside my door into the backyard. How could I manage to park in that concrete trap? The place where cars waited for their owners while malevolent strangers stalked the aisles? Not only that, but it was a cold, rainy day that threatened to sleet and freeze overnight. What if it happened before I left campus and I couldn't get home? What if my car ran off the road again? I messaged with the school president, expressing my reservations about coming to the in-service day. The president responded with adamant encouragement for me to come anyway, suggesting I bring someone with me for support. Mom was very happy to come along and Dad drove us.

Co-workers and friends I hadn't seen since last summer came up to me and welcomed me back. No one mentioned or asked where I'd been. It was like having cancer; everyone sympathized but nobody could say the word. Mom and I sat on the back row and for a while listened intently to the president, but like two teenagers, we soon started texting and stifling giggles. Mom commented on the outfit of a woman sitting three rows ahead of us. She had on what looked like a poodle skirt with sneakers and socks. I texted back that it was better than the young woman with the extremely tight, low-cut sweater opposite her. Then we made plans for a shopping trip soon to buy better, fashionable clothes for both of us.

When we came out, it was already dark, and the parking lot was a sea of cars on almost-frozen asphalt with dozens of educators scurrying through driving sleet to find their automobiles. I didn't see Dad anywhere, so I grabbed Mom's hand and started walking. Familiar fear welled up inside me, and I couldn't wait for him to find us. I had to move, do something, get out of there, out of harm's way. The cold wind blew my hair and stung my eyes. "You see him?" I asked Mom.

"No, but I know your dad. He's here somewhere."

I blinked and rushed, my head tilted down, trying not to slip and fall, but wanting desperately to find him. Suddenly, I bumped into someone and looked up. My heart raced; my stomach churned. I tried to get around him. Get away.

"Samantha?" he said. "I'm sorry about . . ."

I didn't let him finish. "Get out of my way, Venom."

"Do you need help?" he asked, putting his hand on my shoulder and causing me to recoil.

"No." I pushed him away as Mom stepped between us.

"My husband's right there," she said, pointing toward the headlights easing toward us.

Venom looked into my eyes and said in a sincere-sounding voice, "Good to see you're doing okay."

Mom jerked my hand and we marched away. Thankfully, Dad really was driving toward us and stopped to let us in.

"You can't go home," he said when we told him what had happened. "I won't leave you alone in that house with Venom on the loose."

"I thought he was in jail." I sounded like an eleven-year-old pleading for a Barbie swimming pool.

"So did I. Until I saw him at Home Depot a few minutes ago. He came up and talked to me like we were friends or something. Asked how you were."

"I guess he thinks I should be grateful to him," I huffed.

"Seems he made bail sometime before Christmas," Dad informed me. "If I'd known that, I wouldn't have let you go home. You've got to come back and stay with us, at least until his trial."

"You know I can't stay with you and Mom forever. I have to act like a grown-up sometime. For Danny's sake, if not for yours, Mom's, and my own."

"Just this once, Samantha, will you do something for me without all that carrying-on? Just come home with us now." He sounded totally frustrated and almost ready to burst open.

Mom was on his side. "For Pete's sake, Craig, don't ask her; just go home."

I acquiesced. I'd wanted to scream and protest and tell them I could take care of myself and my son. But I couldn't. The rest of my life would be forever defined by "before Jason" and "after Jason" and "before Rose's dirty pink basement and "after Rose's dirty pink basement." I was a walking zombie, going through motions, wanting to be strong and capable, but afraid to be too far from my dad.

"Was Jason at work today?" I asked as we drove to their house.

He nodded. "Yep."

"I want to see him."

He agreed. We dropped Mom at their house, and I called Jason and told him we were coming over. Carrie was there. While we were still in the driveway, she ran up and hugged me like we were old friends.

"You okay?" she asked.

"Fine," I said shortly.

"Good to see you," Jason said, but he didn't sound like he meant it. He didn't try to hug me or even shake hands.

Dad didn't wait to be invited in but pushed his way into the house and sat down in the living room. We followed. The entryway hadn't been changed. Still the same picture on the wall, a non-descript landscape with a little white house by a stream. We'd bought it at a garage sale for a dollar. Same beige color on the walls. Same mahogany table, but the vase and flowers were different. A wilting poinsettia in a red and silver aluminum-foil wrapped vase sat there now.

"All right, Jason, start talking. What do you know about Venom? Did he have anything to do with Samantha's car wreck?"

"Nothing," he said. "I know the sheriff's office questioned him about it—several times. He keeps saying he doesn't know anything about the wreck or . . ." He stopped and looked at me, like the mention of my kidnapping might set me off or something.

"I wouldn't put it past him," Carrie said. "I don't like that guy. Never liked him."

"But what reason would he have to want Sam out of the way?" Dad got up and went into the kitchen as if he lived there and got a Coke from the fridge. His eyes had the glare of a murderer about to ax his victim.

"I don't know," Jason said.

"He doesn't need a reason," Carrie said. "He's mean. Downright mean to the bone."

"He's been trying to change his life around," Jason said. "And he has nothing against her—had no reason to hurt her. I don't think he helped the old lady."

"But she couldn't have done it by herself," I said. "She was strong, but I must've been dead weight."

"Is Venom still selling drugs?" Dad sat stiff and rigid, a Marine instead of friend, and he wasn't questioning Jason as much as interrogating him.

"Yes." Jason's right hand gripped his can of beer like he wanted to squeeze the life out of it. "He's not having an easy time. You fired him, remember?"

"You still buying?" Dad demanded.

"What the hell? It's none of your damn business."

Dad wasn't deterred. "You think Venom's gonna try to hurt Sam again?"

"How would I know?" Jason crushed the beer can and its contents spewed out onto his hand and puddled on the end table. He was getting agitated. I could see the vein in his neck protrude and his face turn red.

Dad persisted. "He better not. You tell him for me that if he tries anything, I'll kill him. And you know I can do it."

"You better leave, Mr. McKenzie," Carrie said as politely as if she'd asked him if he wanted a cookie.

"She's right, Dad. We need to go," I said. "I don't think Jason knows anything. He'd tell me if he did." I stared straight into Jason's eyes when I said it. "I'm sure he doesn't want me to get hurt, do you?"

"Of course not."

Dad calmed a bit but glared into Jason's eyes as he warned him, "Nobody hurts my little girl." Then, as if nothing had happened, he said, "See you tomorrow," as he got up and started toward the door.

"I've got to go home, Dad," I said as we got back in the truck. "My home."

"On one condition," He said, taking his seat belt off again. "We're going to borrow Pepper. Jason won't mind, or at least he better not. I'll go by your place tomorrow and put in an alarm system, then I'll take her back to him."

Jason didn't mind. Danny and Pepper had an animated reunion to say the least. Danny petted and hugged her and she jumped all over him. They loped through the yard, and it was hard to tell who was chasing who. Danny threw balls and sticks until they both collapsed, and dog and boy wrestled on the grass, Danny laughing, Pepper barking and wagging her tail.

The next morning, I had to go to my first class of the semester. I'd worked hard to prepare the syllabus and lessons but was as scared and insecure as a teenager on her first date. Would they like me? Would I like them? Would there be bullies in my class? Could I handle it? As it turned out, I could.

It took every ounce of courage I could pull together to walk from my office to my classroom, and every step was laden with the heavy weight of dread and fear. The door was open, and the room filled with students. Some were talking to each other, some were already sitting at their desks, staring at me, waiting for me to teach them something. As I inched my way to the front of the class, all eyes turned toward me.

"Good morning," I squeaked.

They stared at me. I stared back, waiting for words to pop into my head. A few seconds of anxious anticipation. Then my mouth opened, and I said, "I'll bet you're all wondering why in the world you have to take history and how it could possibly help you in your life."

A couple of them gave me a half-hearted laugh; the others still stared. An older woman, maybe in her fifties, smiled a knowing smile and nodded slightly, so I talked to her. "Well, I'm here to teach you that history is important and it's definitely not boring."

And the rest of my words came to me. I was home. Where I was meant to be.

Finally, my life was almost normal again. Danny went to school. I went to work. I graded papers, prepared lessons, and conferred with students, parents, and other teachers. Time worked its wonders on me. I was too busy to think much about my previous captivity, except at night when I tried to sleep and pink nightmares flooded my brain.

Daniel was doing well selling furniture, which didn't surprise me due to the fact that more women pick out furniture than men. Michael began working at a nursing home. I saw them both at least once or twice a week. Danny spent weekdays with me and weekends with his dad. Routine was wonderful. Busy was good. Yet I couldn't shake the nudging naysayer in the back of my mind.

Most of the time I went through my day trying not to think of anything, either positive or negative. Just neutral, hum-drumming along. However, at times when I least expected it, the tapes would begin playing again. I'd be sitting in my office, trying to grade papers, and an image of Rose would pop into my head. She'd snap her belt at me, grin a hideous, malevolent grin, and point the gun at my head. Or I'd be at home doing laundry, and I would suddenly see Jason, his eyes so hard and cold, telling me he wanted me out of his house. Or I would see him lying in the hospital bed.

And I knew. I knew it wasn't a coincidence. Something was missing. Somehow it must be connected. There was something the sheriff's office had missed. It had to be Venom. He had something to do with it. But what?

31

It was a mild day in late March. Spring Break. I was free. It was one of those days when I got to sleep late, sip coffee slowly, and go back to bed or watch television or whatever I wanted. Danny was with his dad. I had an entire Monday to myself, and of course, I woke up early.

Oh well. It gave me a chance to sit in my backyard and listen to the birds and watch them peck at the birdseed. Except I still got antsy when I was alone. But that was silly. Everything was normal. In a rut, really. Ruts were good, though. Ruts were underrated.

After all, it was almost a year ago when my Jupiter and Mars collided, and I landed on an entirely unknown and unheard-of planet. The planet Mayhem. I couldn't just sit around; I had to get up, go somewhere, do something. The words Turkey Creek jumped into my mind. Should I? I jogged around the yard, trying to erase the chattering in my brain, but it didn't help. I stopped, slipped my phone from my pocket, and hit Michael's name on speed-dial.

We'd become friends again, and I trusted him completely—almost. There were times when I felt close to him, like the Saturday night we'd sat in the living room watching *Arsenic and Old Lace*, one of my favorite 1940s movies. The room had smelled like popcorn as I sat slouched on the sofa in front of the TV, popping the fluffy kernels one at a time into my mouth. Michael sat next to me, not touching. I looked forward to seeing him and talking with him. I depended on him for warmth, comfort, and his assurances that everything was going well.

I stared at the phone for a minute or two and hit send.

"Hi, Samantha," he answered quickly as if he had been waiting for me to call. "I wish you'd wait until I get off work. We can go together."

How did he know?

"I need to go to Turkey Creek. I haven't done anything alone since . . . Well, except driving to work, and the president gave me a parking space right by the door, so I wouldn't have to walk across the parking lot."

"You need to wait for me."

"You having one of your feelings again?"

He didn't answer, like he was trying to think of a good one.

"Maybe it's just normal, natural worry," I said. "Anxiety. You think somebody might kidnap me again?"

"That's what you're feeling, isn't it?"

"Of course. That's why I have to go. Like falling off a horse, you know?"

"You can't, not this time," he said. "Stay home, watch soap operas or doctor shows or old movies, but don't go anywhere until I get there. Please."

"What's going to happen to me?" He knew something, or at least felt like he did, and he was scaring me.

"I don't know, but I see someone with you, someone who wants to hurt you. Venom's still out there. Maybe it's him. I don't know."

"I'll go in broad open daylight and stay on the road, and if he comes near me, I'll scream like a scared chicken," I said. "I'm tired of being afraid to go to the mailbox or grocery store or even sit in the backyard. I'm tired. If I had any guts at all, I'd go to your mother's house and face it and curse and tell it to leave me alone."

"Why don't you wait until I get off and we'll do it together?"

"Fine."

I honestly tried to wait, but I couldn't sit still, watch television, or read. Anxiety rushed through my body, crushing all determination to wait for Michael. I didn't know what possessed me, but my apprehension turned into mindless action. I slipped into my jeans and gray fleece jacket and drove to Turkey Creek. It was closed. Thank goodness. I hadn't failed. I simply couldn't complete my mission. Not my fault. I'd have to wait for Michael after all.

I drove to his mother's house. I didn't want to, but something compelled me. I wasn't going in; I just wanted to look at it again. When I got there, there was an old red Mustang in the driveway. I pulled in behind it. Michael didn't tell me he'd rented the place out. Maybe some drug addict had taken up residence there. But an addict with a vintage red Mustang—in mint condition? I couldn't help it. I got out of the car and walked to the front picture window.

I cupped my eyes with my hands and peered inside. I squinted to be sure. No, it couldn't be. Why would *she* be here? She didn't even know Rose. I ran to the front door, jerked its knob, banged and cursed, and kept my finger constantly on the bell. No sound from inside. I tried turning the knob a dozen times, kicking the door.

"I know you're in there!" I yelled. "Open this door!"

Nothing. Finally, I took out my phone while screaming, "I'm calling the sheriff's office right now, Carrie!"

She opened the door and in one fell swoop had me inside the house and my phone in her hand. For a couple of minutes, we just stood there, staring at each other. Disbelief hung in the air. She looked nothing like the Carrie who had rescued me from Venom in the Target parking lot almost a year ago. She still had blonde hair, but it was dull and limp with frizzy ends and several inches of dark roots showing. Her face was haggard, and she wore a huge shirt that hung to her knees with baggy black leggings. This was not the real Carrie; she was more like Rose. No, surely not. No. My mind screamed. Maybe my mouth did, too.

"What the hell you doing here?" she said, her voice filled with hate and suspicion—just like . . . no . . . this was not Rose . . . it was . . .

She stood there, hands on hips, waiting for an answer. Her eyes had that half-closed, stoned look, and she wobbled a little. "Get outta here, Sam."

"What're you doing here?" I was all rage and curiosity, resentment and confusion.

She thought for a minute. "I'm cleaning it up for Rose." But her tone and expression were menacing, the look of someone who dared you to take one step over an imaginary line.

I looked around. The place still smelled musty, and there was something else. What was it? The stairs and pictures on the hallway walls were still covered in dust. If she was cleaning house, she was absolutely the worst house cleaner in history.

"How do you know her?"

She walked away from the front door, and I followed her into a living room with the picture window, a fireplace, and a Victorian-style red couch and matching chair. She sat down in the chair and motioned for me to sit on the couch. I didn't want to sit down, not with her. I wanted to run and get out of that God-forsaken place.

I took a deep breath and said, "I came to see the house." I felt like I'd been dropped into someone else's nightmare. "So maybe I can forget what happened here and get on with my life."

I slowly wandered toward the nearest door. Before I'd taken three steps, Carrie was in front of me.

"Don't go in there," she said.

"Why?" My knees turned to quivering gelatin, my heart pounded in my chest, and my hands shook. But adrenaline took control of my mouth. "What the hell's going on?" I demanded as I pushed past her and walked through the door to find myself in the kitchen.

Then I saw. On the counter were small packages. One of them open so I could see the white powdery stuff. I stuck my finger into it and lifted it to my lips. Definitely not confectioners' sugar. I recognized what was on the other counter—marijuana. I couldn't believe it.

"Does Jason know?" I asked.

"No, and you're not going to tell him."

"How did you get involved in this? How do you know Rose? Is Michael in on this?"

"I barely know Michael," she said. "I've heard a lot about him from Rose, of course. Does that make you feel better?"

I didn't know whether to believe her or not. What would she gain by lying? "So Venom's your connection to Rose? Or is it Jason?"

She laughed humorlessly. "Me and Jason and Venom, we go way back, you know. Since grade school."

Yes, I did know.

"We've helped each other from time to time," she said cryptically.

"I don't understand." I was almost in tears, but there was no way would I show it. I swallowed hard. "Were you the one that helped Rose bring me here?"

"You really want to know?" she asked. "I'll tell you. Sit down."

I did. In a dingy, white, straw-bottomed chair.

"It's your son's fault, you know." She smiled while she said it.

Fighting words. Fear was replaced with anger.

"It's like this," she said, as if talking to an old friend. "I love Jason, and while he might sometimes take a pill or smoke a joint, he ain't going to sell the stuff. I needed money. So did Venom; he always needs money."

"Me, too," I said. "That's why I work."

She ignored me. "Rose supplied us with stuff, and we sold it. Good arrangement. Until Jason saw Venom selling weed to your son. He got all offended and self-righteous and said he was going to turn Venom in. We couldn't let that happen."

She reached into a drawer of the dirty white metal cabinet next to her and pulled out a gun. "So I told Venom he could stalk you to keep Jason in line, but then you started whining about it, and Jason asked me to help you. So I had to make him stop."

"Why didn't you just tell Jason?"

"You stupid bitch!" she suddenly snapped. "He loved me, but you just wouldn't let go, and that made him think about you all the time. Even after you were gone and I moved in, he talked about you. While he was still in that hospital room, he kept asking how you were. You think when he was coming out of that coma, he asked for me? No. When he opened his eyes, his first word was 'Sam.'"

It was sinking in. Jealousy was the oldest criminal in the world. Why Cain killed Abel. But I was no threat to her. Why did they pick on me? I had a great urge to jump up and run while I could, but instead I yelled, "How did y'all get me here? Were you following me that night? Why?"

"You think you were worth worrying about? That I planned to get rid of you because you were some threat to me? Don't make me laugh. You were nothing to Jason. If you'd only left him alone."

"But I didn't."

"I was on my way to see Rose, get more stuff, and there she was in the middle of all that thunder, wind, and lightning, tugging at something. I didn't know what it was." She stopped to laugh. "You were out of it." She laughed again. "Your mouth was open and rain was falling in and making you choke. Rose screamed at me get my ass over there and help her. She said you were her baby." Her laughter almost drowned out here words. "I figured, what the hell? What did I care if Rose was nutty as a fruitcake and decided you were her long-lost daughter? It got you away from Jason."

Pure, unadulterated terror seized my mind and body. Carrie had wanted to get rid of me, and I'd walked right up to her so she could. Now what? Slowly, quietly, I rose to my feet. She pushed me back down.

"You could've been happy here; you were Rose's daughter. She would've always taken care of you."

Yeah. I knew how Rose took care of her children. I opened my purse and searched for my phone. Carrie waved it at me tauntingly.

"Michael knows I'm here." Despite all my attempts to sound fierce, my voice quivered. "He should be here in a few minutes."

"I don't think so," she said, getting up from her chair and picking up her gun at the same time. "You're not much of a liar, are you?"

I backed away from her. She pointed the gun at me. Sheer terror. Every thought drained from my brain. Every cell in my body screamed at me to run, but my feet didn't move.

Carrie waved the gun toward the basement door. No. No way in this lifetime or the next was I going down there again. I'd rather die right then and there than go one step toward that pink dungeon. That was when my adrenaline went into overdrive and took over every action. Bits and pieces of what happened next are forever sketched into the folds of my brain; some parts are lost forever.

I walked ever so slowly toward that abhorrent door, opened it, and lifted one leg. She was right behind me, the gun held in her right hand, close but not touching my back. I jerked the basement door, slamming it into her, and ran as fast as I'd ever run toward the front door.

She screamed in anger, firing one shot just as I cleared the front porch and ran toward the trees. I dove into the debris behind an evergreen. She came toward me.

"I know where you are!" she yelled. "I'll comfort Jason for you when you're gone!"

I didn't move and barely breathed, lest she hear me. She came closer. The road was only a few yards away, but few people travelled it, and I'd be a clear target. I looked around for a rock; what I found was a big clod of dirt entangled with roots. Oh well, better than nothing. I threw it at her head. It hit just above her right eye and exploded into flying pieces of dirt that splattered all over her hair, face, and clothes. She jumped and bounced around like a kid on a trampoline, wiping at her eyes, yelping, screaming, and cursing—just long enough for me to run deeper into the woods. I jumped behind a scraggly pine. She fired her gun again.

Then nothing. I couldn't hear or see her. For what seemed like an eternity, I could hear the sound of my own breathing, critter sounds, a breeze blowing leaves, and smell the damp earth and new green of spring. Birds chattered loudly, probably warning each other that their worst enemy was close by. My heart beat even louder, and I was sure Carrie could hear it and find me. I longed to be home, in my backyard, safe and bored. And by God, I would. This woman would not get the best of me. She'd robbed me of my peace for months. She wouldn't do it again.

Suddenly, bushes rustled. A faint footstep. She was getting closer. I looked around my feet for a rock. Please let there be a rock. No, of course not. But I did find an old shoe, a flip flop, right smack dab in the middle of a bunch of cigarette butts, beer bottles, and used condoms. I gagged, but I had to do it.

I picked up the shoe with my fingertips and flung it as hard and far as I could, which wasn't very far. She shot at it, and then she started towards me. Closer. I waited as quietly as the squirrel in the next tree. When she got even with me and her head turned in my direction, my mind froze. My body took over. It took a deep breath and leaped. I came down on her back. Her breath gushed out of her and she landed face-down in the dirt and dead leaves. I sat on top of her and beat the top of her head. She tried to reach the gun she'd dropped. I jumped up and stomped on her arm. She tried to push herself up onto all-fours. I grabbed the gun and threw it. She managed to turn over and grabbed for my ankle. I fell on top of her. I didn't learn until later that a neighbor had heard gunshots and called 911. Thank God. I'll never know for sure, but I think I could've killed her.

When Michael and the deputy pulled me off her, I was sitting on her stomach, pounding her in the face with my fists, screaming and sobbing. Michael tried to hold me up. I jerked away, sunk to the earth on my knees, put my face in my hands, and cried. I didn't quit crying for days. Intermittent, of course. I was back where I'd been when I got out of that pink basement. One-minute, utter despair. The next, uncontrollable anger. Still a prisoner. Would I ever be free?

32

Mom and Dad took me to their house. Again. I went to bed in my little girl bed. Again. I never wanted to get up. I couldn't eat. I slept little and was so tired that getting my feet to the floor was a huge effort. I vaguely remember Danny's birthday. Mom baked a cake for him, and we had a small party. His last birthday party had been at Jason's with friends. This one was Mom, Dad, Daniel, Danny, and me. I tried to act normal, but every movement of my body felt like it was pushing against rushing water. My mind had trouble comprehending what they were saying, and no words made it from my brain to my lips. A zombie at a birthday party. The others talked quietly, as if any loud noise might send me off the deep end.

I couldn't go back to work, and I had to give up my house by the creek. I was a child again. A broken one. Dependent on Mommy and Daddy. And Michael. He didn't call or come by as often as he used to, but when he did, he told me I was fine and that my aura was almost glowing again. He hugged me and told me he loved me. I had to believe him; I wanted my aura to glow and my life to be normal again.

The sheriff's department had determined that I acted in self-defense and no charges were filed against me. I did, however, have to keep all my appointments with Dr. Sawyer. No calling to tell her I couldn't make it. No progress, either. I didn't want to go; Mom forced me. But she couldn't make me talk—or listen. At every session, Dr. Sawyer's mouth moved, but I was more interested in the Impressionist paintings in her office. Sometimes Dr. Sawyer called my name and startled me into the present. Why wouldn't she leave me alone, give me some of the good pills, and let me go to sleep? The ones she gave me didn't help.

More than anything, I wanted to be left alone. I knew Mom, Dad, and Danny loved me; they meant well, but they didn't have to come see me every day and talk to me as if I were a small child they had to comfort. But I couldn't find the words to tell them so. I was aware they were there and talking, but their words were meaningless babble.

There was never an "ah ha!" moment, a time when everything abruptly changed and I started to understand what they were saying. Slowly, I became aware of words and sentences, especially when Mom talked about her classes and students, Dad described his latest project, or when Danny extolled the virtues of his newest girlfriend.

One day, Mom was folding my clean t-shirts, shorts, and jeans and putting them in drawers as she talked on and on about her student. "He's smart, but for the life of me, I can't figure out how to motivate him. His mom came to see me and told me it was my fault he made a D and that I'd better do something about it."

My head nodded on its own volition. I knew what she was going through.

She didn't notice and kept on talking. "And it was on a day when I'd been up until two in the morning grading essays, and his hadn't even been turned in."

I laughed, not a real, out-loud one, but more of a spontaneous, quiet chuckle. It just came out along with the words, "Know what you mean. Been there, done that."

At first, she kept on talking as if I'd said nothing, then she stopped mid-sentence and gazed at me as if she'd seen a ghost. An instant later, her face lit up and she ran to the bed and hugged me. For a minute, I thought she might cry. As if nothing had ever been wrong, she stood up and started folding again and talking about our mutual problem: underachieving, smart students who wouldn't do the work but expected good grades anyway. I understood.

For a while, I was still fatigued and unable to focus, but every day I made an effort to sit up in bed and listen and respond when Mom, Dad, or Danny came to see me. I noticed the trees and clouds outside my window. Sometimes, on sunny days, I made hopping shadow bunnies on the wall.

One morning, as if I were a normal person, I went to the kitchen and had coffee with Mom and Dad. Of course I hadn't bothered to shower or brush my hair and still had on my pajamas, but I was sitting up and my mind pulled up real words and was able to listen to theirs. As she did every morning, Mom handed me a capsule and a glass of water, and I slipped it into my mouth and gulped the water. I only now remembered what it was. Dr. Sawyer had said it would take a few weeks for the Prozac to kick in. When she had first suggested it, I'd screamed and carried on and told her I didn't need it. I wasn't crazy, and she could take them herself. Mom never tried to force me to take it; she simply gave me that capsule every morning, and I didn't ask what it was. At the time I guess I didn't care. I smiled at her. She smiled back.

The morning of my next visit with Dr. Sawyer, Mom didn't have to pull me out of bed, push me through the bathroom door, or threaten me with bodily harm if I didn't shower and wash and brush my hair. By the time she came into the bedroom, I was up and ready to go.

The minute Dr. Sawyer saw me, she smiled and said, "Good Morning, Samantha. You look great today."

"Thanks."

I sat in the same aqua chair I always sat in and she sat in the one opposite. Since my release from the pink prison, we'd become friends and though I usually didn't, I felt like I could tell her anything. Whether I sat stiff and bored or screamed at her and told her she didn't know what she was talking about, she never lost patience or raised her voice. She listened and seemed to care, but she didn't criticize me or tell me I shouldn't be thinking like I did.

"How are you feeling today?" she asked as she stirred her coffee and set it on the indestructible table that, no matter how hot the coffee cup or how much I spilled, it wiped right up and never left a mark. I needed a table like that for my . . . No. I didn't have a home anymore.

"I think the Prozac is kicking in."

"Tell me about it."

I knew she was going to say that. It was the way she always started our sessions. "Well, I have energy enough to get out of bed, shower, and dress now."

"But you're still tired?"

"Yes. Sometimes it's all I can do to get to the bathroom or kitchen and back to bed."

"Have you tried getting outside in the sunshine or walking around the yard?"

"I've thought about it. I've imagined myself sitting in a lawn chair, my eyes squinting in the sunlight." My eyes closed, and for an instant, I was in my old backyard by the creek. I could almost feel the warmth on my skin—until a gush of cold air from the overhead vents brought me back to reality. "But when I actually tried to do it, my arms and legs were heavy, and I felt like I was walking through water. I didn't make it."

"How do you feel now?"

"Tired and short of breath."

She smiled at me, that knowing, patient smile when she knew I understood the question but chose not to answer. "You know what I mean," she prodded gently.

"Oh, yeah. Inside. Emotionally, right?" But I didn't stop to let her answer. "Like a failure. A child. It's the story of my life."

"Why do you think you feel that way?"

I tried to think of an answer. Why? I didn't know. My mind searched through my memory banks. I saw Dad and me throwing a football in the backyard. Mom and I shopped for Christmas presents at the mall. I was in a hospital room with Mom telling me to breathe, but I was already breathing as hard as I could.

I'm not sure why or what happened inside me then that made me start blurting out stuff—incoherent babbling that wouldn't stop. One minute I attacked Mom and Dad for their overprotection and the next praised them for always being there for me. I ranted on and on about Jason and how he made me leave and had never really loved me, and it was the same with Daniel. No man had ever loved me, except Dad, of course. What was wrong with me? Why had Greg turned on me? He had been my friend. And what the hell was wrong with Michael? I was sure I loved him, but sometimes he was batty as a bedbug. Danny? He was the one bright spot in my life, but he was growing up and wanted to spend more time with his dad than me, and how dare that good-for-nothing joke of a man come back into my life and take my son from me? When I raged about Rose, I yelled at Dr. Sawyer as if she were Rose, and I told her exactly what I thought about her.

Dr. Sawyer didn't yell back at me like Dad would have or walk off in a huff like Mom. She listened and appeared to be absolutely fascinated by my tirade. I don't know why, but that made me mad too. Finally exhausted, my thoughts and my speech slowed down. I quit shaking, my hands quit trembling, and I was so very tired.

She waited a few seconds and said, "Talk to them, Samantha. Tell them how you feel and listen to them."

"I can't." My heart knew if I confronted my parents, it would hurt their feelings and they'd treat me like a little girl.

I could never again talk to Jason about anything, and Michael would tell me about my aura and make predications for the future as if he were some prophet. Greg? Maybe someday I could talk to him again.

"Why not start with Daniel? Tell him how you feel and listen, really listen to how he feels. Do it for your son's sake. That seems to be your main concern."

She pulled in the one thing that made me stop all my ranting and blaming and self-pity. Danny. My son. I had to get myself together for him. Yes, I could start with Daniel. Make peace with him. We had already begun to during Christmas, when he had given me a peace offering in the form of one of our old ornaments. I had accepted it, but my heart had still been so closed off from him. I needed to finish healing that part of myself. For Danny and for me. I only had a few years left before my son left me for a life of his own, and if they were to be peaceful years, his dad and I had to be at least cordial. I had to do this.

"I don't know. I'm afraid," I whispered.

"Do it anyway. You're a capable, competent person, but you're hiding from the rest of your life. I can't tell you he won't hurt you, but whatever happens, you can handle it. You know you can. We'll keep you on Prozac for six months to help you through this, but you won't need it after that."

She was right, of course, and the more I thought about it, the more I knew I had to pull my life back together. The nightmare year of my life was over, and like Dr. Sawyer said, I was a capable, competent person. It was time to move on.

33

I went to Rose's house for the final time. This time, Dr. Sawyer went with me. As we walked through the rooms, she said nothing but let me wander and think. When we got to the basement stairs, she pointed and said, "Let's go down there."

I shook my head and said as emphatically as I could, "No."

We went anyway. The place was in total disarray, as if the deputies who searched it had failed Housekeeping 101. She told me to run my hand over the pink wall. My fingers poked it and withdrew as if they'd touched a hot stove.

She bent over and picked up a pair of the sweatpants and shirt I'd worn so often and opened the wardrobe to pull out a nightgown, one that had been too small for me. "Hold these. They're just cloth. Nothing malevolent about them."

I held them in my hands, and a vision of me wearing the sweats and lying in the small bed raced through my mind.

"Now, sit on the bed."

"No."

"It's just a comforter, entirely incapable of doing anyone any harm."

"No." The walls closed in on me. I was in a tiny pink room, filled with Rose's large form. She laughed and shook her gun and belt at me. Fear and anger waged war in my head. Neither Dr. Sawyer nor I said anything while I ambled like a tottering old woman through the room and touched the bed, kitchen counter, television set, coffee table, the floor, and walls. I kept looking back at the door at the top of the stairs to be sure it was still open.

"You do understand, don't you? This house can't hurt you unless you let it. It can forever live in your mind, or you can dismiss it right now. It's just a house. No thoughts. No feelings. Same with your visions of Rose and Carrie. Picture them in your mind, see them standing in front of you, and tell them to get lost, to leave you alone forever."

I sat on the bed; it didn't hurt. I stood up and bounced on it like a kid, then jumped down and picked up the coffee maker and flung it at the wardrobe. It thudded and crash landed. Its top popped open and the little pod shot across the floor and water dripped from its insides. I screamed as loud and as hard as I could as I kicked chairs, the table, the legs of the bed. I pulled Susie's clothes from the wardrobe, pretending they were Carrie and Rose, and stomped on them and yelled and screamed and told them to leave me alone.

Finally, I said to Dr. Sawyer, "I'm ready to go now."

I wish I could say that was the end of my torment and depression, but I was still tired, and melancholy seemed to reside so deep inside me I couldn't get rid of it. The overwhelming depressive spells, however, did get shorter and the time between them lengthened. Writing it all down in my new notebook helped me sort out my thoughts and feelings.

Sometime in early June, thanks to my doctor, medication, and journal, I woke up one morning and felt almost human. I showered and dressed and walked, no, sprinted outside into the sunshine and fresh air. Dad was at work, but Mom was watering her begonias and irises.

"Good morning," she said in that bright, happy voice she usually reserved for children. "I haven't seen you look this well in a long time."

I hugged her. "Good morning."

"Want to help water and weed?" she asked.

"No, I'm going to call Dr. Sawyer this morning and see when I can get back to work."

"Yes, I think it's time." She turned off the water and pulled the gloves from her hands. "How about some coffee?"

Absolutely. It was, after all, the first day of the rest of my life. "Let's get dressed and go out for lunch," I said.

The steak and baked potato were the best I'd tasted in a long time, and the chocolate pie was fabulous. At first, Mom and I struggled to find things to talk about. She asked if I was feeling okay. I said yes. She asked if there was anywhere else I wanted to go.

"Shopping," I said between bites of pie.

"You could use some new clothes and so could Danny. He's getting so tall now."

"Just like his dad," I said.

With no warning that she was going to get mushy, she took my hand in hers and said, "I'm sorry. You've been through something awful, and your dad and I weren't able to protect you. We don't even know how to help you."

I was dumbfounded. An admission like that from Mom? She must've practiced it for weeks. All at once I sensed sincere sympathy and felt a closeness and understanding I hadn't felt in a long time. I squeezed her hand. "You've always been there for me. Both of you. You don't know how much I appreciate it."

So much for the mushy stuff. It was all either of us could take, and we rarely talked about it again.

While we were waiting for the waitress to bring our check, I noticed Michael coming in with a woman I'd never seen. She was younger than me with smooth, clear skin and dark, shiny hair that fell in large curls around her face and down her back. She looked like a model. As they followed the server to their table, he smiled at her and held her hand. He didn't see me.

Mom was offended. "Will you look at that? He sure didn't waste any time, did he? And he could've had the decency to at least say hello to us. After all, we did invite him to Christmas when he had no one else."

"Maybe he just didn't see us," I said, trying to soothe her and myself.

"Maybe he didn't want to see us."

I stood up and threw my napkin on the table. "I'm going to find out."

He didn't notice me until I touched his shoulder and said as casually as possible, "Hi, Michael. Haven't talked to you in a while."

He stood up and hugged me as if we'd talked yesterday. Then he looked around and waved at Mom, who waved back.

I looked at his friend, and he said. "This is Jen. She and I work together."

"Call me," I said as I walked away. "We need to talk."

He did, later that afternoon. We went for a walk at Turkey Creek in the late-day sun. It was hot and humid, my hair frizzed, and perspiration beaded on my face. "Have you gotten tired of me or something?" I asked, dreading the answer.

He led the way, pushing limbs back and stepping over rocks and fallen limbs. "What do you mean?"

"You said you loved me, but I haven't seen you much at all lately."

"I do love you, Samantha." He stopped and turned to face me. "Remember when I first called you last spring and told you that by next year you and Danny would be fine?"

"Of course I remember."

"This is next year," he said as he pushed a stray clump of damp hair from my face.

I wiped sweat from my forehead and pushed my bangs back. "So? I'm fine now, and you don't want to be in my life anymore?"

He hugged me. "Your aura's stronger now; your life is where it should be. Jen's, though, isn't. She's in trouble. Serious trouble. She needs me. Like you did last year. You understand, don't you?"

I shook my head. "No."

"I think you do," he said as we continued down the path.

We sat on a rock at the edge of the creek and dangled our bare feet. "I thought you really loved me, but now I feel like I was just a project to you."

"No, never a project," he interrupted. "I will always love you. It's time to move on. You're fine now. Your spirit is better."

We sat there for a while, not speaking, each of us in our own thoughts. I gazed at the water rushing downstream, watched how it flowed over the small rocks and curved around the large ones but never stopped, and I noticed how small fish swam with it. The sounds of the rushing water, the breeze rustling through leaves, and other people, dogs, and small animals making their way through the bushes and trees were like the music of God. The sweet scent of honeysuckle and deep smell of forest and water had to be God's perfume. It was the most spiritual feeling I had ever had, as if Michael, God, and I were one.

Finally, without saying anything, he slowly stood, took my hand, and helped me up, and I followed him down the path toward our cars. It was like walking across the stage on graduation day. The joy of accomplishment, sadness of completion, and apprehension about the future all filled my heart.

Michael whispered in my ear as he hugged me tightly, "I love you, Samantha. Remember my words, and please remember me, always. I know I'll remember you." For a few minutes we held each other in that other-worldly, spiritual sort of way. I wanted to hold onto him forever. "I hope you'll talk to Daniel soon," he said as he let go of me. Then he got into his car, waved, and drove away.

Whatever it was we'd shared, the spell was broken. Remember him? Of course. How could I forget? I loved him, and he was leaving me, just like all the men I'd ever loved. For a long time, I stood in that one spot with a sad emptiness inside. Who could I confide in now? Who would listen and care and tell me everything would be better? Now he had other demons to conquer. Was that it? I didn't need him, so he didn't need me? He did have something about helping damsels in distress. It probably had a lot to do with the fact that he hadn't been able to save Georgie or Susie. But I loved him. I knew that, finally.

I sat in my car but couldn't make myself drive back home to Mom and Dad. Not yet. I had a sudden urge to see Danny, and he was at his dad's place for the weekend. I hadn't been to Daniel's new house yet, but I had the address. I turned the keys in the ignition and began making my way to go see my son. Unlike Michael, Danny was a part of my life forever. I had to see him. Hug him. Touch him. Right that minute. Even if it was his time with his dad.

During the drive, those old overwrought and overused resentments tried to resurface, but even I could hear in my head how tired they were. By the time I got to Daniel's house, I'd quashed them and talked myself into being civil. I pressed the doorbell. It didn't make a sound. I knocked. And waited. And fidgeted.

Finally, Daniel opened the door, turned, and ran toward the kitchen, yelling, "Don't shut it!"

The odor of burned meat and smoke clouds drifted toward the living room. I ran to the back door and opened it. He grabbed at a skillet but immediately drew his hand back and yelled out in pain. I jerked the dish towel from around his neck, grasped the skillet handle, ran outside, and dropped it on the back porch.

"What're you doing?" Daniel shouted. "That's our dinner!"

We stared in unison at the black hamburger patties. "Grease burgers?" I asked.

He glared at me then walked into the kitchen. He was barefoot and wearing shorts with faded palm leaves on them; his hair was tousled and his face was red and sweaty with traces of flour. But he had on a forest green polo that wasn't faded and it wasn't ugly. It did, however, have grease stains on it. The kitchen was a wreck, dishes stacked in the sink, sticky tile that made a noise when I walked across it, and on the table was a large bowl filled with a lump of dough surrounded by scattered piles of flour. I couldn't help it. A badly disguised snort of laughter escaped my mouth as I surveyed the room.

"Did you come just to laugh at me?" he asked. But the side of his lips twitched, and then we were both laughing out loud.

"I came to see Danny. But you've certainly made it entertaining."

He set some chips and dip on the table. "Want to stay for dinner?"

"Where's Danny?"

"At his girlfriend's house. He'll be back in about an hour."

"I'll wait. I need to talk to him."

We sat down at the table together, and I noticed Daniel looked tired and frazzled. He sighed wearily. "How did you do this all those years?"

"Do what?"

"Working, cooking, cleaning, keeping up with a boy with no 'stop' button?"

I knew the feeling. "Not very well," I admitted. "I couldn't have done it without Mom and Dad."

"Sure, you could've."

He was wrong, but he was trying to comfort me. The familiar dark cloud that hovered around me settled in my body, made it feel heavy, sad, and fatigued, and took over my thoughts. "No, he grew up without a father, and it's my fault. I wish I'd given you a chance. I was selfish. A terrible mother."

"Not true." Daniel placed his hand over mine. "You thought you were doing the right thing. You were afraid his no-good, selfish, immature father would hurt your son like he hurt you."

I shook my head. "I tried to raise him on my own, but I kept failing. Back to Mom and Dad. Try again. Fail again. He needed you."

"You talk like he's an old man. He's still a teenager and needs his parents—both of us. We can start now by cooperating and not arguing about every little thing."

He was right, of course. If he could make the turnaround from a selfish, childish, young man into a caring adult, I could let go of my resentment, anger, and, yes, self-pity. We could communicate peacefully and raise our son, united, and figure out what was best for him. "Yes, I'd like that."

When Danny came home, we had our chips and dip for dinner, talked and laughed, and I hugged both of them as I left. I was surprised to find myself not particularly sad to leave Danny at his dad's. And even more surprised to find myself enjoying the feeling of being alone for the first time in a really long time. Maybe I was going to survive it all after all. Maybe . . . maybe I was even going to thrive.

Like Michael had said, it was this time next year.

34

I drove home and marched into the kitchen where Mom was cooking spaghetti for dinner and Dad was helping by sampling the brownies. "I'm going to find a house, and this time I'm going to buy it. It'll be mine, and no one will be able to take it from me. And I'm going back to work, and nobody can stop me."

Mom and Dad turned and gazed at me as if I'd lost my mind.

"What brought this on?" Mom carefully placed her spaghetti sauce-covered plastic spoon on the spoon rest that sat on the counter. "Of course, when it's time, you certainly should get a place of your own and go back to work."

"It's time," I said.

"You're right," Dad said.

He was agreeing with me? He, who always wanted me home?

"We love you, Sam," he said. "You know that, but we won't be around forever, and you've got to be able to stand on your own."

Mom glared at him. Obviously, they hadn't rehearsed their response.

He frowned at her and said as emphatically as he'd ever said anything to her, "It's time. We talked about this."

"Why? So she can shack up with Daniel again? Or maybe Michael?"

Okay, so she wanted us to be Mom and teenager again. Though I had no intention of living with anybody except my son, I blurted out, "If that's what I want, yes."

She gave me her famous evil-eye stare. I stared back. She broke first as she reached for the colander filled with hot spaghetti, and I thought for a minute she was going to throw it at me.

Bless Dad, the Marine. He finally stood up to her. He stepped between us and turned toward Mom. "Leave her alone, Ellie. Right now."

Her whole body froze. That's when the argument turned; it was no longer about me.

"How dare you speak—"

He didn't let her finish. "When will you get it through your thick skull that she's grown up? She has a right to make her own mistakes and live her own life."

When had he started thinking like that? What was happening here?

"When she starts acting like one!" Mom shouted.

"Like you're so perfect."

"More perfect than you!"

I thought she was going to absolutely explode. Her face turned red, her body shook with anger, and her hand was perilously close to the colander.

Dad didn't give her time to come up with an answer. "Can you not remember how you were when we met? Have you forgotten what it's like to be young and make mistakes? To be human?"

"How dare you?" She took several deep breaths as if contemplating her next move and started to stomp away.

He grabbed her arm. "Not this time."

"Let go of me!"

"Why not tell her the truth?" He calmed a little and let go of her arm. "I liked you better when you had faults and admitted when you needed help, when you had emotions. I don't know you anymore."

Her body sagged; her facial expression changed from defiance to defeat. "You tell her whatever you want. Just go away and leave me alone."

"No."

He pushed her into one of the kitchen chairs and sat down beside her. "Sorry. I shouldn't have said that."

"Why not? You've been thinking it for years."

"Dammit, Ellie, can you come down from your perch on high for one minute?"

He got up, marched to the garage, and slammed the door.

Guilt, absolute, deep-inside, southern-girl guilt overtook me. I didn't mean to cause a fight. All I wanted was a life of my own. Now I knew there was something Mom should've told me but didn't. It was one more thing to worry and wonder about, along with how to live the rest of my life and do what was best for my son. Now I had to deal with the fact that I'd caused a rift between my parents. How would I live with myself if this led to them splitting? I was still standing in the exact spot I'd been when they'd started to argue, and I wanted nothing more than to do something to make things better. But what? I was afraid to move or make a sound or do anything that would make things worse.

Then, a miracle happened. Mom, in slow motion, put her hands on the table and pushed herself up. She walked to the garage door, opened it, and said, "Craig, come in here and act like a man."

His face was hard-set, his eyes half-squinted, the vein in his neck throbbing, and his fists were clenched, but he came back. "I only want what's best for her."

"So do I," Mom said, walking towards their bedroom.

He followed her, yelling, "You don't know what's best for her!"

She slammed the bedroom door. He opened it and slammed it again. I'd seen them do that before. Lots of times. No way could I hang around their house for the rest of their fight and making up. I had to get away.

That's how I happened to be alone in Parkville on a summer night with no place to go. I ended up driving to the public library and just sitting on the hood of my car in the empty parking lot. I dwelled on my conversations with Michael and Daniel. I didn't need Michael anymore, but I was grateful he'd been there for me when I did. He had helped me see what simple, unconditional love was like, and how healing it was to have forgiveness and to trust that everything would work out. But I would not again—ever—let a man define my life or make me feel less than I am.

A horn blew behind me. Adrenaline flooded my body. Before I could think, I was running toward the road. Hands grabbed my shoulders from behind.

I screamed, turned, kicked, and hit whoever it was with my fist.

"Whoa," the voice said. "It's me. It's Jason."

I stopped and looked into his face. It really was Jason. "What the hell? You scared me!"

"I'm sorry," he said. "I saw your car and wanted to be sure you were okay."

I couldn't help it. Despite my previous resolve about for-giveness, I tried to kick him in the shin, but he pushed me back and held me at arms' length. Finally, my heart slowed, my head cleared a little, and I went limp like a rag doll. He pulled me close and held me tightly, the way he had before last year, and the scent of him, that sawdust and adhesive smell, was familiar and comforting. Thoughts of murder and mayhem deserted my brain. When at last I could talk, I said, "I'm sorry about Carrie."

"I didn't know," he said, still holding onto me.

I believed him. He had never been a good liar. "I know," I said.

"I saw Danny not too long ago. I told him under no circum-stances was he ever to buy drugs again, and that if anyone tried to get him to, he could come to me and I would help him."

"Good." I nodded as I pulled away and stepped back a couple of steps. "Has he?" I asked. "That you know about?"

"No. If he does, I promise I'll let you know. By the way, his old man keeps a tight rein on him, doesn't he?"

I didn't know what he was talking about, and my expression must have told him as much.

"I saw them arguing one night in town. Danny appeared to have been drinking. His dad wasn't happy about it, but he didn't yell at him. He handled it very calmly, but he was firm. Your son actually apologized and got in the car. Strangest thing I ever saw."

I didn't know what to say for a moment. I let it absorb how much Danny truly needed Daniel, and that Daniel was continuing to prove himself a good father. "Thanks for caring about Danny," I said finally. "I wasn't sure you still did."

"How could you think that?"

"How could I not think that?"

"Do you want to come over to the house? We could talk some more there."

"No," I answered abruptly. "I don't think that's a good idea."

Jason looked at me with a mixture of pity and regret. "No one's going to hurt you anymore. Carrie's in jail. She confessed to everything. Venom's still waiting to go to trial, but he'd never hurt you. He's told me a dozen times how sorry he is. He's still selling, but he quit selling to kids."

"How noble of him." I rolled my eyes.

"I'm off the pain pills," he said, sounding sincere. "For good."

I gave him a small smile. "That's good. I am too."

I struggled for more words. We'd lived together for five years and had discussed every topic imaginable, and now I had run out of things to say to him. All the questions I'd wanted to ask no longer resided inside me.

He reached over and took my hand. "I never quit loving you. I want you to know that."

I let him hold it for a moment before gently pulling away.

"I really am sorry about what happened to you," he said. "I was hoping someday we could be friends again, or . . ."

"No. No 'or.' Not again," I said. "Friends? Maybe. But we can't go back."

I walked away. Feeling some regret but even more resolve. A small part of me had wanted to see his house again. Had even wanted it to be my home again. It would've been easy. One word from me, and Jason would've said yes, and we could've started over. He was lonely. He'd chosen the wrong woman and was full of guilt, but I couldn't help him. Not anymore.

I got in my car and drove away. Another bridge crossed and burned. What now? For a while I drove the back roads, and eventually I ended up at Turkey Creek for the second time that day. The path, forest smell, the rock Michael and I had sat on, and the rushing water were comfort and serenity to me. My body and mind calmed and my thoughts drifted. I pulled off my sneakers and dangled my feet in the cool water.

The sun was beginning to set, cooling the air, and I was one with all of nature. An ethereal Michael sat beside me, put his arm around my shoulder, and whispered, "Remember my words, Samantha."

"Which ones?"

Words like "competent," "Danny," and "love" spilled into visions of my son and me in our backyard. Our own backyard. And me, being the mom he could rely on, the mom he deserved. For a while I couldn't move, lest I lose the vision and the feeling, but eventually something inside me compelled me to take action. I returned to my car and drove to my old house, the one by the creek. There was a "For Rent" sign in the yard. I wondered if the owner would be willing to sell it to me.

I knocked on his door and asked him, and he said he'd think about it. In the meantime, I could rent it if I'd like. Yes, I'd like.

By the Fourth of July, Danny and I were in our own home again. Daniel, Mom, and Dad helped us move in and then stayed for a barbeque. It was small but just right. Maybe next year I'd have a large party.

Daniel grilled some hamburgers for us, standing by the grill while I sat nearby in lawn chair and Danny talked on the phone to his girlfriend. Mom set out plates on the table while Dad oversaw Daniel's work. The conversation was light and easy, but knowing my family, it could switch to a heated argument at the drop of a hat. However, I knew that if it did, it would end with apologies and "I love you."

I sighed in peaceful contentment as I fiddled with the mustard seed necklace around my neck. Once again, I had returned to my beautiful creek house after recovering from hitting rock-bottom, but this time it felt different. It had little to do with Daniel's presence and much more to do with my faith in my own newly-formed competence. Dr. Sawyer had helped me see that my fears only had power if I gave it to them. The dirty pink walls of my dungeon were now no stronger than sheets of paper. It was only the beginning. I might fall again—might have to pick myself up again, but I knew that I would. My love for my family, my freedom, my life, kept me going.

Later that night, when it got dark enough, Danny walked with his father and grandfather to the small field next to my house. Daniel had purchased some fireworks, and it was the perfect place to set them off. I stayed on the porch to watch, and Mom retreated into the house, complaining about the noise rattling her nerves. The loud pops and bangs did make me jump, and I had to force back memories of Carrie firing her gun at me, but I wouldn't miss it for anything. They were only noises. They couldn't hurt me. I had never before felt the significance of my freedom like I did on that particular Independence Day. I knew I would never take it for granted again.

To my surprise, Daniel joined me on the porch, taking the seat next to mine.

"Done already?" I asked, even though there were still fireworks exploding over my head.

"They still have a few more to go," he said, looking at me with a strange expression. "I just thought you might want some company."

We didn't say anything more for a few moments, just listened to the screeches and pops of fireworks and the sounds of my father's and son's whoops. I prayed they were being careful and that Danny wouldn't blow his hand off.

"I was thinking of having a bigger barbeque next year," I told Daniel offhandedly. "Danny could invite his friends, and we could do an even bigger firework show—this is a good place for it. I could invite Michael too." I lowered my gaze from the sky to look at him. "If Greg is in town, he might—"

"I don't think Greg will be coming back," Daniel said, cutting me off.

I hesitated before saying, "You might be wrong about that. Although . . . we haven't talked in a while. He's probably busy."

"Or he knows what's good for him," Daniel said resolutely. When I stared at him like he'd just sprouted wings, he explained, "I told him to back off. To quit calling you. That I love you and intend to marry you one day." Before I could say anything, he reached for my hand and held it tenderly in his. "If you want to be with him, I won't try to get in your way. I just want you to know where I stand."

Then he turned his face upward as another spray of sparks lit up the sky. I was too stunned to make a reply. Had he made this declaration weeks before, my doubt in the sincerity of his words would have taken over my mind. But now I allowed that doubt to dissolve the same way my fears did, and I focused instead on the warmth spreading on my skin from where his fingers touched mine. And instead of wondering at the truth of Daniel's heart, I wondered at the hope and possibilities stirring in mine.

"Well?" he finally said, clearly expecting some type of response.

I smiled, not at him, but at the stars and planets above me. "We'll see."

CPSIA information can be obtained
at www.ICGtesting.com
Printed in the USA
LVHW091511191220
674607LV00005B/179